THE CIRCLE OF THE GODS

Arturo's dream, like that of his father, Baradoc, is to unite Britain against the marauding Saxons. Always a wild and arrogant youth, he grows up and leads a rebellion against Count Ambrosius. He raises a small force of men which attacks Saxon settlements. Then, with Durstan and Lancelo to lead the troops, Arturo's great campaign begins . . .

Books by Victor Canning
Published by The House of Ulverscroft:

BIRDS OF A FEATHER
THE BOY ON PLATFORM ONE

The Arthurian Trilogy:
THE CRIMSON CHALICE
THE CIRCLE OF THE GODS
THE IMMORTAL WOUND

VICTOR CANNING

◆

THE CIRCLE OF THE GODS

Book Two

Complete and Unabridged

ULVERSCROFT
Leicester

First published in Great Britain in 1977

This Large Print Edition
published 2012

The moral right of the author has been asserted

British Library CIP Data

Canning, Victor.
  The circle of the gods.
  1. Historical fiction.
  2. Large type books.
  I. Title
  823.9′12–dc23

  ISBN 978–1–4448–1208–4

Published by
F. A. Thorpe (Publishing)
Anstey, Leicestershire

Set by Words & Graphics Ltd.
Anstey, Leicestershire
Printed and bound in Great Britain by
T. J. International Ltd., Padstow, Cornwall

This book is printed on acid-free paper

Affectionately for
Diana Charnock Smith

Contents

CONTENTS

The Brooch of Epona

Aritag sat in the sun looking down over the village, its huts stone-walled, the roofs, turf-and-heather thatched, weighted with boulders against the winter gales. The river running down from the distant moorlands was low with late summer drought. Where the river met the sands of the small cove it fanned out in a shifting web of shallow channels. Some of the younger children, naked, their brown bodies gleaming like polished oak wood, played in the water, watched by a small group of women who sat in the shaded lee of the tall rocks which ribbed through the white sands at the foot of the cliffs. Now and again he caught the sound of their laughter as they worked at their spindles, teasing the wool of the moor sheep into yarn. At the edge of the sea, docile under summer zephyrs, older boys and their fathers were working on two of the fishing curraghs. From time to time, despite the summer's heat, he coughed and shivered under the striped cloak drawn close about his shoulders and, with each cough, felt the chest pain stab him, a pain which had grown fiercer with the passing of each year.

Among the women he marked the fair, gorse-bloom hair of the one named Tia who had come to them with her babe claiming it to be the child of Baradoc — the son of his long dead brother; Baradoc who — if he lived still — was chief of the people of the Enduring Crow. With her had come Merlin whose word no man doubted, Merlin who with one eye looked into the past and with the other into the future; Merlin who had said that one day Baradoc would return and speak the truth of the villainy which the woman Tia had laid against Inbar, his own son. But, since he, Aritag, now stood in Baradoc's place, he had refused any judgement until Baradoc should come himself and, amongst them all in the boulder-flagged village circle, should speak the evil to Inbar's face. *Aie . . .* but in his heart he, Aritag, knew the truth already for he knew his own son.

A shadow stretching over his shoulder from behind darkened the close-cropped grass and the scent of crushed marjoram and thyme rose briefly in the air as Merlin sat down cross-legged. Merlin ran a hand over the jet black hair which fell long to his shoulders and then scratched at the tangle of his thick beard. Short and strongly built, he had the look of a man of forty, but it was said, Aritag knew well, that he had more years than any

2

other human man would ever have since Nodens of the Silver Hand, in return for some great service, had given him the gift of endurance.

Merlin said, 'The corn is ripe for gathering, the fleeces are stacked and the heather ready to cut for winter. All that lacks now is the silver shoaling to fill the great jars with salted fish against the winter.'

Aritag was silent for a while. Then, stifling a cough as pain wracked his chest, he said, 'If the gods are good I shall live to see it.'

'You will see it, Aritag.'

Aritag smiled. 'How many times?'

'Only the gods know that. That a man will die in bed or battle they sometimes proclaim, but they set no day in the foretelling for they often alter the pattern of men's destinies to meet the changing times.'

Aritag nodded and said, 'I would live long enough to see Baradoc return. Do the gods tell you about that, my friend?'

'He will return. That I know.'

'Then let it be before I die. Without me here, when Inbar is chief he will take the woman, Tia. There is a heat in him like a peat fire for her. He longs for my death to give him that freedom.'

Merlin picked up a ladybird from the grass and watched it crawl across his palm. 'No man has the freedom to take a woman against her will, or if she is another man's wife. Strength and arrogance he may have, but not freedom. Because of this woman it is written that he will come to his death.' He blew gently at the ladybird and it took clumsily to the air.

'Say more.'

'I cannot.'

'Will not?'

Merlin laughed. 'You think I live in the belt pouch of the gods? Good Aritag, when in my dreams I play cupbearer at their feasts, there is too much laughter and noise to catch more than scraps of their talk. Anyway, I came not to talk of the future. I came to say that my time here is ended and I go this day.' He stood up and briefly brushed dried grass and dust from his loose trews and long tunic.

Aritag smiled. 'For a man who can hear the beat of a moth's wings above the roar of the wind and the waves in gale time it is strange that in dreams the laughter and noise of the gods' feasting makes you so deaf. But I press you no more. Go to Bada and he will give you all the stores you need and a moor pony to carry you.'

Merlin shook his head. 'I need none of these.'

'You will be back one day?'

'One day.'

'But I shall not be here to greet you?'

'If not — ' Merlin nodded his head westwards to the great run of the sea that met the horizon in a silver haze, ' — there will be a greeting one day in the Blessed Isles.'

He raised a hand in parting and turned down the grass slope, following the narrow path to the cove. He walked through the shallow river channels and across the white sands to the rocks where the women sat working. Before he reached them Tia saw him coming and left her companions.

Merlin halted and waited for her to come to him. In the years since he had brought her with her babe to the people of the Enduring Crow she had grown a little taller and her body had lost some of the slender suppleness of a young girl and found the beginning of the dignity and maturity of a woman. Her hair, short like a boy's when he had first seen her on Caer Sibli, was long now, worked into gold braids that hung loose over her shoulders. Watching the movement of her body under the belted working smock of dyed coarse linen he knew how Inbar must feel when he saw her. The gods, he thought, gave men their desires and had created women to inflame them. The gods, he felt, sometimes expected too much of mortals. *Aie* . . . but then, who was he to question the gods who now and then amused themselves with him by tossing him his occasional scraps of foresight, even directing him to Caer Sibli, the island, lost now in the northern sea haze beyond the Point of Hercule, where Tia had given birth to Baradoc's son. Arturo; a son never yet seen by Baradoc who had been swept away by the currents from the island in his small boat.

Tia came up to him and he briefly set his hands on her shoulders in greeting.

Tia said, 'You are going.'

He smiled. 'How could you know?'

She nodded at his feet. 'The whole village walks bare-foot, but Merlin wears his sandals. You travel light?'

'Yes. And far.'

'And leave the boy and myself — and no man to stand by my side?'

'While Aritag lives you need have no fear. And he will live long enough. You will come to no harm.'

'How can you know that?'

'It is written.'

Tia gave an impatient shrug of her shoulders. 'No, do not comfort me with such words. You are like Baradoc. Something calls you and you must follow it. To excuse yourself you say that the gods have decreed it. But that is not true. You use the gods for your own ends. You put words in their mouths.'

Merlin laughed. 'Or they in mine. I have done enough for you. Now you must do everything for yourself.'

'And Inbar?'

Merlin nodded at the leather belt that girdled her smock. 'You carry a knife.'

'And would use it.'

'Then, if needs be, use it — with no more thought than in gutting a sea-bream.'

For a moment or two Tia was silent. Then she said in a softer tone, the hint of a plea in her voice, 'I am strong and can look after myself and Arturo so long as Aritag lives. And without him I have friends who would stand by me. But friends may not be enough. If you can . . . then, before you go, give me some word of comfort.'

Merlin shook his head. 'When the seafolk murdered your people you ran into the forest like a hunted deer without thought of comfort. When you cut Baradoc down from the tree where Inbar had hanged him in the great forest of Anderida you cut him down and gave comfort. When he took you to your uncle at Aquae Sulis you could have stayed in comfort, but you left all the pleasures of a Roman villa to follow him westwards and be his wife. For you comfort lies in the giving, not the receiving.'

Tia laughed suddenly. 'Oh, Merlin, whose tongue is as twisted as a unicorn's horn, sometimes I think that from the moment the gods made you their occasional cupbearer you have mourned the comfort of being as other men.' She gestured to the far group of working women in the shadow of the rocks and went on, 'Look — there are single women there who would join their lives to yours and give you comfort. I have seen you eye them with the eye of a man. Stay here and wait for Baradoc's return.'

Merlin, grinning, shook his head. 'Not for me, my Tia. My feet grow restless, my ears grow tired of talk of crop and catch and my eyes weary of faces grown familiar. I must move as the seasons and the stars move.' He gestured with one hand down the beach to where the five-year-old Arturo, naked and brown, was rolling in mock fight with old Lerg the great hound, splashing in shallow water and scuffling up the white sand, and said, 'There is another who will never be content at any hearthside for long, nor ever be full held by any woman and will rouse wrath in men before he gains their love. Take the withy switch to his brown hide when he offends for there is an arrogance in him which ill fits the young but will serve him well when the gods open his eyes to his destiny.'

Tia shook her head, her eyes narrowing with mockery. 'You talk like a man who has been at the mead too long. One word begets another and you spawn fine phrases careless of whether they die or live in the memory — or even make sense. Now be on your way, for I see your feet shuffle the sand with impatience. But take with you my gratitude for all you have done for me.'

Without a word, laughter in his eyes, Merlin half-bowed his head, touched his forehead in salute, and turned away. Tia watched him go across the sands and up the narrow path that climbed the cliffs to the north while above him the seabirds wheeled and called in the bright air, among them the black choughs, red billed and red legged, the tribal birds of the people of the Enduring Crow. She watched him until he reached the cliff top and his figure dwindled and finally disappeared over the headland.

When she turned it was to find Inbar standing behind her with Arturo squatting on the sand beside him, digging into it with his hands to build a barrier across a small rivulet of the spreading river.

He was taller than his cousin, Baradoc her husband, and darker of hair and colouring. His bearded face was long, strong, and pleasant so that it was hard to believe any villainy of him. Yet Lerg, the old hound, and the other two dogs Aesc and Cuna never followed him as Arturo did. Maybe, she thought, because they had seen the moments of villainy when Inbar and his companion had strung Baradoc to the oak tree to die so that Aritag, his father, should become chief and he, Inbar, chief after him of the Enduring Crow. He stood looking at her, smiling, showing the edges of his white teeth, his lean, hard body, sea and sun-tanned, bare except for the rolled up trews, held by a leather belt which carried a short sword in a whaleskin scabbard.

Inbar said easily, 'So Merlin goes. What mad dream does he follow now?'

'Only the gods know.'

'He makes too much of the gods, and fills people's heads with nonsense.'

'You don't believe in the gods?'

He laughed and putting out a leg rolled Arturo over into the rivulet with a flick of his foot. Arturo laughed and threshed the water with his hands and feet like a stranded fish. Inbar said, 'I live in this world. The gods in theirs.' Then nodding at Arturo, he went on, 'Baradoc will not return. Merlin cossets you with that dream because he is against me. But one day soon you will be my woman, my wife, and I will give you sons as strong as this one.'

Tia said evenly, 'There are plenty of unmarried women over there.' She nodded at the group in the rock shade. 'None would deny you.'

Inbar smiled. 'Show me one with hair like the turning wheat, with eyes like the blue flash on a jay's wings, with the body of a goddess and the pride of Rome in her blood and I might be tempted. There is none, and no need for you to tight-draw your red lips into a bow of contempt. I am a patient man. The tribal law sets you free by summer of next year if Baradoc does not return. By then I shall be chief for my father has little time left in him, and the tribal law says that no woman may turn away from the honour of being the chief's woman.'

'To marry her husband's would-be murderer?'

'It is a lie.'

'If Lerg, Aesc and Cuna could speak you would be proved the liar. But more, I have Baradoc's word for it, and there is no standing against that.'

Inbar shrugged his shoulders and smiled. 'Baradoc has no true love for this tribe. His eyes have always been fogged by his own dreams of greatness. He would have come back here to gather what young fighting men he could. He would have turned back to the east, impatient for battle against the Saxons, impatient for his own glory . . . *Aie*, maybe for a kingship which lies for the taking beyond our Dumnonia and Isca. He needs no hearth fire or woman for warmth, only the heat of battle and the red embers of power to cloak him against the bite of winter frosts and ice. He made you his woman, his wife, because he wanted sons to carry his name and glory after him.'

'And you?'

Inbar scraped a rough line in the soft sand with one foot, his head lowered momentarily, his eyes hidden from her briefly. Then raising his face to her, a wooden, expressionless face, he said quietly, 'I want no more than to be chief of the people of the Enduring Crow with a woman of my own choosing to bear me sons, a woman whose love for me and mine for her will forever be lodged in my heart like a wren in its moss-bowered nest.'

'A woman you would take by force?'

'*Aie* . . . but not the force which you picture.' He stared at her boldly for a moment or two and then a slow smile bloomed faintly around his lips. He turned abruptly and began to walk away across the sands, following the river channel upwards to the long hanging valley between the cliffs towards the huddle of huts and village buildings from which rose the blue haze of hearth fires.

Tia turned and went back to the women working on the rocks and Arturo followed her, clutching at the hem of her belted smock. Following them came the three dogs, Lerg the big grey wolfhound, ageing now, his muzzle whitening, Aesc, the water dog with the long-furred red ears, grown stout and limping on one fore-leg a little from an old bite from a sea otter, and Cuna, small, short-legged and wire-haired, now in his prime.

Joining the other women, taking up her hand spindle, Tia watched the dogs settle close to Arturo as he curled up on the sands and dropped into the quick sleep of childhood. For a moment Tia glanced up to the sky as though, circling heavily up there, she might see the black, diamond-tailed shape of Bran, the raven. But Bran had gone on the day that Merlin had brought her here with Arturo from Caer Sibli, now lost in the summer haze far out to sea. The dogs had held to her as once they had held to Baradoc. But Bran had gone. And Baradoc had gone. Maybe when Baradoc returned then Bran would come winging back.

A shadow fell across the sands at the rock foot and Tia turned to see Mawga settle herself in the lee of the limpet-covered rocks.

Mawga was her own age, dark-haired, red-lipped, her summer shift leaving one sun-browned shoulder bare, her long body large-breasted, her eyes dark and shining like closed sea anemones. From a rush basket at her side she took cheese and a flat wheat cake, broke them and passed portions to Tia. When they worked on the beach or at the tilling or cattle watching on the slopes above the village they always ate together and they shared the same hut where Mawga lived with her mother. Her father and only brother had put to sea four summers ago to follow the mackerel run and had never returned.

Mawga said, 'I have an uncle, Ricat, who is horse-keeper to the Prince of Dumnonia in Isca. He is a good man and would welcome a woman to manage his house.' She smiled. 'No more. He has but one love and that his horses. When he next comes here you could go back with him.'

Tia smiled. 'You think of me — or yourself?'

Mawga laughed. 'Both. Before you came Inbar was always at my heels, and there was an understanding. Now . . . ' She shrugged her shoulders.

Tia put out a hand and touched Mawga's bare shoulder. 'I stay here until Baradoc comes.'

Mawga sighed. 'When Aritag dies, you will see a different Inbar. Ever since he was a boy there has been a madness in him which breaks like a summer storm without warning. If he did what you say to Baradoc, hanging him high and leaving him to die, it was in such a quick rage that it overcame the friendship between them. You would be safe in Isca until Baradoc comes back. Think about it. Think also — Baradoc may never come back.'

Tia shook her head. 'He will come. Merlin has said so. But more than that — ' she touched her breast, ' — in there I know so.'

Mawga shrugged her shoulders. 'Then the gods grant that it is before Aritag dies.'

At that moment from the high cliffs behind them came the slow wailing of a horn, three long drawn-out blasts that echoed back from the crags and sea-lapped rocky heights.

Mawga leaped to her feet, spilling cheese and wheat cake, and cried, 'The shoaling! The silver shoaling!'

From the cliff top the horn rang out again, but this time calling and echoing in fast, quick notes that set the seabirds clouding into the air from their roosts and perches and turned, the long run of sandy beach into a scene of frenzied activity. Men and boys abandoned their boats at the water's edge and ran for the village, and the working women left their spinning and joined them, and as they ran the cries of 'The shoaling! The shoaling!' rose and mingled with the now sharp imperative blasting on the bull's horn.

High on the cliff edge above the village Aritag stood by the horn blower and watched the scene below. Men, women and children were all running from the sea, boat work and net-mending abandoned, running fast up to the tribal huts, and from the huts came the old women and the old men leading or carrying the very young babes. For a while he watched them as the trumpeter filled the sunbright day with fierce horn blasts. Then Aritag's eyes turned to the sea. A bow shot off-shore he could see the movement of the fish, countless sprats swinging in great silver swathes as they twisted and curved through the water. Shoal after shoal came crowding into the shore until the sea began to hiss with spume and froth like a great cauldron boiling. The bright bloom of the fish hung in an eye-dazzling mist over the sea as they flung themselves into the air to escape the marauding mackerel and herring that followed them in. From above the gulls and seabirds, the diving gannets, guillemots and razor-bills, the black shags and the blacker shearwaters cried and wailed so that at times they drowned the noise of the insistent bull's horn, as they dived and flung themselves into the feast of the waters.

Aritag raised an arm and the trumpeter lowered his horn and wiped his aching lips with the back of his hand. Aritag turned and went down the path to the great stone-flagged circle around which the huts were grouped.

Inbar came to him, the tribespeople crowded behind him, carrying rush baskets and panniers, old cloaks and earthenware pots and bowls, throwing nets, anything and everything which could be used to scoop and take the harvest of fish which now boiled along the surf edges and thrashed to creamy spume all the waters fringing the shore. This was a harvest which none could gather until Aritag should walk into the sea waist-deep and scoop the first cropping in the bowl of the hide-faced, bronze-bossed ceremonial tribal shield of the people of the Enduring Crow. For any to take the smallest sprat, the puniest fry, of the great shoaling before the tribe leader would be an offence to the gods and bring ill-luck to them all.

Inbar handed his father the shield and Aritag, slipping his left hand through the thonged arm-crotch and gripping the short cross-bar, began to walk to the sea, following the fall of the shallow river, splashing across

17

its sandy shallows, while the tribe followed him in silence, watching the leaping waters ahead. Behind them came some of the youths, pulling the great wooden sleds into which the shoaling fish would be loaded to be drawn up to the drying and salting grounds about the village. Two good shoalings in the worst of poor corn cropping years could hold off starvation, while more meant salt fish for bartering inland as far afield as the markets of Isca.

Aritag walked into the sea, the spray and splashing of the shoal rising about him like a mist. Merlin, he thought, had said that he would see the shoaling again, but not how many. Merlin, he thought wryly, would probably say anything that came into his head that he fancied might feed his reputation and then rely on chance to prove him right — yet, whatever men might say, there was something in Merlin that tied him to the gods. Some even said that he was the son of the great horned stag god, Cernunnos, born to a mortal maid in the far past. The edge of a smile touched his thin lips. More than likely Merlin might have spread the story himself.

Waist deep, he turned in the sea and faced his tribespeople who lined the strand. All about him was the clamour of the feeding seabirds and the hissing and seething of the sea as the shoals silvered it into a mad turbulence. Slipping his left arm free of the shield he held it like a great bowl in both hands above the water. He dipped it into the water and raised it up full of the living, leaping, writhing fish. A great shout went up from the tribespeople.

'The shoaling! The shoaling!'

Then, as Aritag began to wade slowly to the beach, his back bowing beneath the weight of the shield and its living load, all the men, women and children rushed into the water and began to scoop up the catch, filling baskets, cauldrons, looped kirtles, tunic skirts, nets, and lengths of cloth. Between sea and shore they rushed, shouting and laughing, to fill the great wooden sledges. Aritag handed his shield to Inbar to empty and then walked up the beach towards the village without looking back, followed by the horn blower.

As they breasted the steep path a spasm of coughing took Aritag. The attack was so severe that it made his head swim with a giddiness he could not control. Bada, the horn blower, caught him as he swayed.

'Sit and rest,' said Bada.

Aritag breathed deeply and fought the giddiness in his head, slowly forcing it from him. 'No.' he said, 'it passes.'

He walked on, feeling the spell move slowly from him. His time was not yet, he sensed that. But it was not far away. This year there would be other shoalings. He would see them through. But the first shoaling of the year was the most important. Maybe the good god Nodens of the Silver Hand would give him time to see another. He had no fear of death, but he had a love of life, and he would wish to see Baradoc back. From all that came from Isca it was clear that there were even worse times ahead. Inbar would shut his eyes to trouble for he loved pleasure too much. But Britain now needed men who knew how to meet trouble and make danger work for them; and Baradoc, his brother's only surviving son, and rightful head of the tribe, was such a man.

* * *

There were two more shoalings that year before summer passed and Aritag lived to see both of them, and the winter that followed was mild and there was no hunger among the people of the Enduring Crow. It was during this winter that there sprung up between Aritag and Arturo an affection which Tia found pleasing. Generally the children of the tribe were in awe of Aritag and came to him only when bidden. But Arturo, in his sixth year, had a boldness which in other children would have been greeted with a quelling look. Even when Aritag sat in a circle talking with the other men Arturo would work his way to his side and squat or stand by the old man, listening to the talk without fidgeting or drawing attention to himself. And when Aritag walked the cliffs with Bada, Arturo would join them or, if the weather were too bad, slide into Aritag's hut and squat across the fire from him, so that the time came when Aritag, growing used to his company, favouring him above all the other children because he was the son of Baradoc, would talk to him and tell him the tales of the people of the Enduring Crow and of the other peoples of Dumnonia, tales that went back over the years into the mists of past times.

There were hundreds of these tales and Arturo began to learn them by heart, a frown or a disdainful spitting into the red heart of the turf fire by Aritag marking any deviation from the strict form of their wording. The boy had a quick mind and memory and learnt easily. He had, too, a quick temper. If any of the other boys teased him about being Aritag's favourite, calling him nose-wiper, toe-licker, he would waste no words but take to fists and feet no matter the odds against him. Seeing his bruises, and scratched arms and face, Aritag would smile to himself and say nothing.

But in Mawga's hut Tia would scold him sharply for his quick temper, though her anger never lasted long. She was privately proud of his ready learning and quick mind and tongue. During the long winter evenings she began to teach him her own language; not only to speak it but to write it, filling a shallow osier basket with fine beach sand and tracing the letters with a stick. As Aritag gave him the history of his father's people, so she gave him what she knew of the history of her people. Always, too, before he slept he had to be told — though he knew it all by heart — some part of the story of the way she had met Baradoc in the far eastern forest of Anderida in the land of the Regni and had journeyed with him to Aquae Sulis to the villa of her only surviving relative, the aged, long retired Chief Centurion Truvius of the Second Legion; and how she had finally married Baradoc and journeyed westward with him.

'Tell me the bit about the bear and how Cuna helped to kill it. How big was it really? As tall as a rearing moor stallion? Like this?' Excitement building in him, Arturo would leap to his feet, arms stretched high above his head, brown fingers curved into raking claws, and prance around the hut like a pain-maddened bear, growling and roaring so that Cuna, sleeping by the fire with the other dogs, would leap to his feet and, barking furiously, would circle around him.

There was, however, one part of the story of her travels to the people of the Enduring Crow which Tia had not told Arturo yet, knowing that he was too young to understand it fully. This was the story of the silver chalice which she kept, wrapped in an old piece of doeskin, in the ash-wood chest which stood at the end of her bed platform. One day she would tell him of the good Christian hermit Asimus who had given it to her and of the prophecy he had made about it . . . but it would be many years yet she knew before Arturo would be ready for the tale. Sometimes, looking down at the boy as he slept, her longing for Baradoc would rise to a high peak, a longing now which was often — despite Merlin's word — shadowed with a growing doubt about his return. He had built a boat to take them from Caer Sibli to the mainland, had put to sea to test it and had never been seen again, and the boat had drifted back to the shore empty. He could have been drowned, but Merlin said no, and she held firmly to her faith in Merlin's word. Arturo showed only a little interest in Baradoc. His world was too full of the people and things around him to leave room for concern over a figure as remote as an unknown father.

On a night of wind and rain towards the end of the year Inbar, heavily cloaked against the storm, came into the hut where she sat by the fire thonging a small hide jerkin for Arturo who slept in his bed. His entry set the flames of the oil lamps in their wall niches briefly wavering and guttering. Mawga and her mother were away for the night, death-watching round the body of one of their relatives in another hut. Inbar, she knew, was well aware of this. He stood for a moment smiling at her, his cloak rain-beaded, his dark hair rain-plastered to his head like a moleskin helmet.

He said, 'I come from the beach watch. There is a cold in me which fire and a beaker of mead will warm.'

'Both of which you could find in your father's house a spearthrow from here.'

'True . . . but he holds a council there, haggling with Ricat, the Prince's horse-master, and the elders over the tribute of young stallions from the moor.' He slipped the throat clasp open at his neck and dropped the wet cloak across the rough beechwood table. The flame from the wicks of the lamps steadied and the light lay across his bare brown arms, gleaming like polished bronze.

Tia rose and went to fetch the mead jar from the store room at the far end of the hut. She passed close to him but he made no move to touch her. Coming back she set the mead and a slab of goat cheese before him. He cut himself some cheese with his dagger, ate, and washed down the food with a draught of mead. When his mouth was free, he said, 'Ricat and his men go tomorrow. It is known that he has asked you to join him, to keep his house in Isca. You go with him?'

Tia shook her head. 'No. My place is here.'

Inbar shrugged his shoulders and grimaced. 'Any woman of this tribe in your place would have gone.'

'This is my tribe. But my blood is my own.'

'And good blood, too. Proud blood. But Isca is a fine place even these days, and Ricat is an honourable man who has given all his love to his horses. So why do you stay? Baradoc will never come back and next year is the seventh of his going, and you know that the need in me for you grows stronger every day.'

'Baradoc will return. I shall never be bed-warmer, wife or bearer of your children.'

He finished his mead and then, shaking his head, laughed and said, 'No other woman would ever dare say that to me.' He stood up and, reaching out suddenly, took her by the right wrist. With his other hand he pulled free from its sheath the small dagger she wore in the belt about her working shift. Still holding her wrist he held the dagger in the flat of his palm. 'You would kill me with this on the night I took you?'

'If not you — then myself.' Tia looked down at the hand that held her wrist, and said quietly, 'Free me.'

For a moment Inbar hesitated. Then he released her wrist. In a quiet, almost puzzled voice, he said, 'Why should you not like me? When the seven-year term is spent I would come to you in honour to take you to wife. You would have silver and bronze dishes in your house, the finest furs for the sleeping couch, and silks and linens of the best from the sea-traders . . . *Aie*, and gold torques and enamelled clasps for your robes, and a table that would never lack for food. My father is a rich man and hoards his riches to no point. After him I shall have his riches and would shower them on you like the wind-fall of hawthorn blossom in Spring.'

'You would be kind, no doubt. But there is no gift you could give me great enough to make me forget that once you hanged Baradoc high and left him to die slowly.'

A smile suddenly flashing across his lean, handsome face, Inbar said lightly, 'Then let it be understood that when the time comes I shall take you and tame you to my ways and my love.' He flicked Tia's small dagger downwards suddenly and it lodged, quivering a little, in the rough wood of the table. 'And you will find that you have no heart for dagger work.'

He picked up his cloak, flung it about his shoulders and left the house.

Tia picked up the mead jar and the remains of the cheese and took them back to the store room. When she came back Arturo was awake, though still fogged with early sleep.

He said, 'I thought I heard Inbar talking.'

'You did. He came for mead and cheese.' Tia paused and then, following a prompting suddenly alive in her, went on, 'Do you like Inbar?'

Arturo rolled over, stomach downwards on the soft fleeces of the bed, and resting his chin on his hands said, 'Only for some things. The things he makes me like spear and bow, and the things he shows me how to do . . . like . . . well using a stone sling and how the wind takes off line spear or arrow in flight.' He yawned. 'Oh, yes . . . he's good to me. But I would drop a boulder on his head from the clifftop if you told me.'

Tia frowned. 'Why do you say that?'

'You know why. All the boys know he wants you to wife if father comes not back and — ' He broke off, turned directly to her, and grinned broadly.

'And?'

Arturo scratched at his tousled fair hair. 'And that you do not want him.'

'The boys know too much and talk too much.'

'So do the girls.' He rolled over on his back and yawning rubbed his eyes. 'So when you want a boulder dropped tell me. To kill your first man in your mother's honour would be a great killing.'

Suddenly out of sympathy with his precocity, Tia snapped, 'Arturo — talk not like that!'

Arturo made no reply. Eyes closed, limbs loose in returning sleep, he snored gently, yet although Tia knew that he could fall into sudden sleep she was far from sure this time that his sleep was genuine. But she was sure that, despite Aritag and Inbar's care, he needed the harder hand of a father. He was growing fast and over-knowingly.

Before Ricat left he came to see Tia. She

was in the great cave in the hillside above the village where the rush panniers and earthen crocks of wheat and barley were housed and with three other women was labouring at the two large milling querns grinding into flour the oven-dried ears. When he called to her she came to him at the cave entrance, her working shift looped up at one corner into her belt, her face flushed, her hands and bare arms powdered with flour.

A short, stocky man with the wrinkled face of an over-wintered apple, his belted tunic and gartered trews of the finest wool, the short red cloak of a chief servant of the Prince of Dumnonia open over his shoulders, Ricat laughed, and said, 'If your uncle Truvius were alive to see you now he would not believe it.'

'You knew Truvius?'

'I did. He often when he first retired to Aquae Sulis came to Isca to buy horses and would have none of the moorland breed, only those still bred of the true Cavalry strain, though few of those are with us now. Give a moorland stallion freedom and he will mount any mare he can find. You knew Truvius was dead?'

'No. But I long since guessed it. The gods have gained good company.'

Ricat nodded. 'He once did me a favour

that put me in good standing with my Prince. *Aie*, at a moment when I needed it. I would return that favour through his kin. I say again that there is now or at any time a place for you and your son in my house at Isca — and a safe passage there though you should travel alone if you show this token.'

He reached to the scarlet fall of his cloak flap and unpinned from it a brooch which he handed to Tia.

'What is it?'

'It is the badge of the Prince's master and keeper of horse. Once you are over the river Tamarus and out of the lands of the people of the Enduring Crow not even Inbar would touch you — and,' he smiled, ' — the headwaters are a day or a night's march to the east from here. Show the brooch — there is none other like it — and safe passage will be given.'

Looking down at the brooch, Tia, who over the years had learned much of the beliefs and customs of her husband's people, said, 'It is the goddess Epona.'

Ricat nodded. 'Truvius would have known that, too, as would any legionary cavalry commander in the old days.'

On the bronze brooch, inlaid in silver gilt, was the figure of the goddess holding in her arms a wide bowl full of ears of corn. Behind her stood an arch-necked horse. Around the rim of the brooch were set garnets backed by thin gold-leaf foil to give added lustre to the stones. It was a beautiful piece of work, worth many head of cattle. Tia's eyes misted momentarily at the thought of the man's kindness and concern for her. To part with the brooch, his sign of office, would mean a lot to him.

She held it out to him. 'No. I cannot take it.'

Ricat reached out and closed her fingers over the brooch. 'Keep it. I need no such sign to mark my rank. Every man in Dumnonia knows my standing. An honourable welcome awaits you in my house whenever you find the need for it. And remember this of Inbar. There is good and bad in him and the two are always at war. If Aritag should die soon Inbar's impatience will lead him to break any tribal law to gain his desire. I say this for I think you should come with me now. Put aside the pride which comes to you from your Roman blood.'

Tia shook her head. Ricat eyed her for a moment or two and then, giving a little shrug of his shoulders, touched his forehead in salute and turned away.

Late in the afternoon Tia carried up to Aritag's hall a shallow, straw-plaited basket full of flat bread rounds. Pulling the leather draw-cord thong to lift the heavy inner door bar, she went in to find the living quarters occupied only by Inbar who sat sprawling by the turf fire from which a lazy spiral of smoke curled away to the roof opening. From one of the sleeping booths at the far end of the hall came the sound of heavy snoring. Beside the booth Bada, the horn blower, sat on a small stool keeping watch over his master.

As Tia set the basket down on the long table Inbar slewed towards her and, smiling, said, 'Ricat has gone.'

'Yes. He is a man of great kindness — and honour.' Tia made no attempt to mute the edge in her voice.

Inbar laughed. 'I agree. I rode with him a while to see him off the tribal grounds. He wore in his cloak a plain bronze brooch.'

'So?'

'So — you have the goddess Epona to give you safe riding to Isca should you ever need it.'

'If I ever need it, yes.'

Inbar shook his head gently. 'Your eyes are the mirror of your temper. Now they are the bleak blue of ice under a clear winter's sky. But then, who would want a woman whose eyes never betrayed her feelings. You will have no need of the brooch.' He nodded towards the far booth where his father snored in sleep. 'When my good father dies you will come to me willingly.' He eyed her for a moment or two and, when she made no reply, turned slowly to the fire, resting his elbows on his knees, cupping his chin in his hands, and stared into the red heart of the slow-burning turves.

Tia, as she left the hall and walked towards Mawga's hut, felt for the first time the chill beginning of fear. This country and the world outside it, she knew from her own experience, and the tales which came with the travellers and merchants from Gaul, were in a turmoil where none now knew the security which had marked the days of her father and even her own early days. For the first time, no matter what Merlin might have said, she faced the numbing fact that Baradoc could be dead, that the life ahead of her might have to be paced out without him. She could admit to herself now that she should have forsaken her pride and ridden to Isca with Ricat.

The Moorland Meeting

The following Spring came reluctantly. Cold winds and gale-raised seas lashed the northern coasts of Dumnonia. Leaf buds were salt-blighted by the fierce drift of spray on the high winds, the young corn blades were yellow tipped and the inland pasture grounds were slow to growth so that there was no good early grazing for the over-wintered cattle and sheep. The peregrine falcons returned late from their southern migration and mewed about their eyries showing no sign of courtship displays. Although the high nets of tallowed, fine wool thread were set on the cliffs to trap the migrating flocks of small birds moving up the coast there was little need of them because after each gale the boys of the tribe could gather panniers of exhausted or dead birds of passage. The tribal huts were redolent with the spit-roasting of warblers, finches, waders and pipits whose flesh now eked out the dwindling stores of dried fish and salted meat. Of fresh fish there was little for the sea was too fierce on most days for the small boats to risk a passage to even the nearest fishing grounds.

But the weather did not stop the Spring

raiding of the Scotti bands from Erin for they came in their large boats, indifferent to the rage of the sea, making their camps on the wild coast of Demetae across the Sabrina sea, and also on Caer Sibli, and raided near and far for loot, slaves and food. Three times before the seas began to grow calm, the sun to find cloudless skies to pour warmth on the cold earth, and the first of the choughs to begin to brood a full clutch of eggs, the Scotti came to the settlement of the Enduring Crow and Bada's horn wakened the settlement to arms. The men and older youths sprang to their weapons and swept down to the beach and formed a barrier across the narrow valley mouth leading to their homes and cattle.

The first time, although they were beaten back, they took with them two youths as slaves. The second time the valley mouth defenders broke against their pressure and, before they could reform, the Scotti looted and then burned three huts and bore away the wife and young girl-child of Garmon the chief cattleman who was away with his beasts on the inland pastures. The third time they came unwisely on a night of full moon and the cliff watchers saw them long before they landed. An ambush was set for them and a third of their force was slaughtered and one of their long boats captured. It happened that on this night Tia was one of the two women whose turn it was to sit at the couch side of old Aritag who had fallen ill and could no longer look after himself. Inbar had left the long hall on the first alarm for he was commander of the tribe's fighting men and lacked no courage in facing the Scotti.

Not long after the sound of Bada's horn had filled the valley with the sharp calls that signalled the retreat of the attackers, Inbar returned to the hall. His short cloak was thrown back and blood ran from a deep cut in his sword arm. He sat himself at the long table and called for water and cloths and the woman with Tia rose and went to look after him. As she began to clean his wound he turned to Tia and said, 'This time the Erin dogs were mastered. Those who live will tell the tale and leave us free next year. Twenty now lie dead on the sands that are black with their own black blood. And we have a fine boat, planked and masterly built, which they must have plundered from some sea raider for there is none in their parts who could make such a craft.' He smiled at Tia. 'When the summer comes you shall ride in her on a down-stuffed siken seat and — '

At this moment a small figure slipped through the partly closed hall doorway and Arturo, clad only in a coarse short shift, rushed towards Tia. He stood before her, his eyes shining, his arms and legs bespattered with blood and sand, and holding up his right hand which held a bloodied single-edged knife, cried, 'Look! With my own hand I have killed a man. *Aie! Aie!* I've killed a man!' He began to dance around, shouting and waving his knife in excitement.

Tia jumped to her feet, seized his wrist and shook the knife from his grasp. With her free hand she hit Arturo across the cheek, abruptly quietening him, and as Arturo froze, his face clouded with sullenness, she said sternly, 'Back to the hut, clean yourself and go to bed!'

Arturo made no move, his lips tightening stubbornly. Before Tia could make any move or speak, Inbar said firmly, 'When your mother gives an order, obey it.'

For a moment Arturo still made no move. Then with a slight shrug of his shoulders he turned and walked slowly from the hall.

Tia turned to Inbar and asked coldly, 'Was this your doing?'

Reaching for a beaker of mead that the other woman had set at his side, Inbar drank and then said slowly, 'That he was on the sands? No. There were other boys his age. There always are when the fight goes with us. How else do they get their first sight of battle and their first smell of blood?'

'And the killing of the man?'

'A kindness the gods would approve. He was already dying of a spear thrust. I told Arturo to cut his throat to hasten his passage to the Shades.'

'And you gave him the knife?'

Inbar laughed. 'Now your eyes have the blue flame of burning seawrack wood. No, I gave him no knife. It was already in his hand. Where he got it it would be idle to question. Theft, barter? What boy of his age in this tribe has not a knife hidden somewhere and longs for his first killing?'

That night when Tia, her spell of vigil over Aritag finished, returned to Mawga's hut she stretched herself out on the bed platform alongside Arturo. From the single night light of the wall lamp she could see that he had washed himself. He slept with the even breath of the young. Looking down at him, his face smooth and unmarked, it was hard for her to believe that his hand had helped a man to death and that already there was in him a growing impatience to reach manhood. Lying back, she drew him gently to her, holding him in her arms. In his sleep Arturo made a few puppy grunts of protest and then turned and snuggled against her.

The first silver shoaling of the following year
was still to come when Aritag died. Spring
was fast giving way to summer. There were
new-feathered young in the seabirds' nests,
the sea samphire and patches of thrift along
the cliff edges were moving into bloom, the
cattle and swine were fattening, and the early
lambs of the now scanty sheep flock were well
grown and long past all urge to frolic and
sport about their elders. There was little news
of the rest of the country for there were few
travellers, and no trading ships came creeping
along the now storm-free seaboard. From the
few passing travellers there was no more to be
gained than rumours that King Vortigern who
had married a Saxon princess and become
the pawn of the men of the long keels now
faced the threat of a rival, another Ambrosius
whom some said was the son of the old
Ambrosius, the Western king who had once
held the long line of the Sabrina river and the
lands and hills about it. Only one thing held
with certainty and that was that the young
Prince of Dumnonia still held Isca firmly and
that while no man could claim that peace
reigned in the east along the Saxon Shores or
through the long, looping valley of the river
Tamesis, the old Roman road that ran

north-east from Isca, through Lindinis to Aquae Sulis and on to Corinium was once more safe to travel in well-armed company.

Aritag died as dawn broke with Tia sitting beside him, and while Inbar with the night patrol kept the cliff watch. He died quietly and peacefully as the tide began to ebb. Bada came in, looked at him and then, blank-faced, turned and left. A few moments later all through the still air of the early summer dawn came the notes of his horn, wailing the passing of the leader of the people of the Enduring Crow. Tia held the still hand of the old man and prayed to the gods of the Blessed Isles far out in the Western Sea to welcome him with the honour he deserved and to give him good life in the Shades and fair greeting from his friends and fighting companions who had made the passage before him.

Two days later Aritag was carried in procession on a bier of three shields supported on long shoulder poles up the valley to the first slopes of the near moors to the tribal burial ground. They laid him in a shallow grave and piled it with rocks and boulders to stay the burrowing of foxes and wolves. No grave goods were buried with him for he had already gone to another life and needed nothing there. The earth held only the husk of his manhood in this world. The Druid priest, Galpan, who lived a hermit on the moor, placed a fresh-cut oak branch on the pile of stones and spoke aloud for him to the gods, naming them in turn and linking them with the different virtues of the departed Aritag; Taranis the sky-thunderer, lord of heaven and prince of light, the course-setter of all human lives and the giver of signs, Esus, son of Taranis, the god of skills and crafts and trading and the protector of all single travellers, Coventina, the guardian of springs and wells and rivers and all waters which were the life blood of man, and ended with an invocation to the great Dis, the father of all the gods and the ruler of all the stars and planets that spun their courses through the heavens. When he had finished the priest placed a sprig of mistletoe with the oak branch and turned and moved away up to the moor top. Inbar, without arms, followed him while the rest of the tribe turned away and walked back down the valley to the settlement.

Mawga, alongside Tia, said, 'In seven days Inbar will return. Seven years have gone now since Baradoc went from you. You are free to be wife to any man who pleases you, but Inbar will not wait upon the trifle of your pleasure. Bada will find you a good mount.

You have but to pin the Epona brooch to your cloak and ride away.'

For a moment or two Tia was silent. She knew that Mawga spoke nothing but good sense, but there was a stubbornness in her which hardened her against flight. Baradoc lived and would return. Merlin had said so. Her place was here with Baradoc's people and Arturo's people. Inbar had stolen Baradoc's birthright. Although she could claim no common-sense for her stubbornness, to leave would be a betrayal. Inbar would use no force with her for he knew that she would kill him no matter how long she had to wait for the moment to do it. Death in battle would do him honour with the gods, but death at the hands of a wronged woman, forced to his bed, would condemn him to the dark wandering of endless time.

She said, 'I am a freewoman by tribal law. I stay because my heart says stay although there are times when my mind urges the comfort of cowardly flight.'

Mawga shook her head. 'You are wrong. You are a young wife who has been seven years without her man. Your heart and body have become strangers to your mind. They seek comforts and means which they hide from you. But when the time is ripe they could betray you.'

'You talk in riddles and I have no time for them.'

'Then I talk no more of this, except to say only that Bada will always find you a good mount.'

They walked in silence from then on back to the settlement. As they crossed the rock-paved circle before the long hall where Inbar would now rule as chief, the three dogs Lerg, Aesc, and Cuna came to welcome Tia followed by Arturo, naked except for a loin cloth. Lerg thrust his grey muzzle briefly against Tia's hand, but Cuna barked and leapt around her and then made mock savage attacks at first Arturo and then Aesc. Arturo, shouting with laughter, grappled with Cuna and rolled in a fighting heap with him on the ground. Watching them Tia thought of the time, eight years since, when she had walked into the Anderida forest glade and seen Baradoc strung by his wrists to a tree, left there to die by Inbar, and the dogs silent and watchful below him. Her lips tightened in scorn at the thought of Inbar's treachery, her whole body suddenly strung with anger and her heart full of contempt for the man. *Aie*, she knew well enough what Mawga had meant by her heart and body now being strangers to her mind. What woman with seven years of barren love-ache would not?

43

But for her, let it be seven times seven, it would be an ache of which she was always mistress.

At the end of seven days Inbar came down from the moor and in the long hall there was a great feast for all the men to celebrate his chieftainship. At the end of the feast all the men rose one by one and swore faith to him. Tia, who had been helping in the serving and cooking for the feast, watching them knew that had the womenfolk been called upon to swear the same oath, no power on earth could have made her step forward.

Two days later when Tia carried the weekly store of fresh-baked bread to the long hall Inbar, his beard freshly cut, his long hair trimmed to his ears and wearing a white linen tunic over soft doe-skin trews, was sitting at the table. Before him was a jug of mead and two beakers. He gave her no greeting as she came in, but when she returned from the store carrying the empty rush pannier, he nodded to the bench on the far side of the table and said, 'Sit.'

Because he was the Chief and to be obeyed Tia sat down. The slowness and reluctance in her movements made him smile.

He said, 'So far you obey me. You force your body to pay respect, but in your heart there is the stiffness of denial.' He filled the two beakers and handed one to her. 'No matter. A woman's pride can come to unexpected flowering. Drink.'

He raised his beaker and drank and slowly Tia did the same. Baking was hot work and she was glad of the drink. For that alone, she told herself, she took it. As she put the beaker down she said, 'I thank you for that.'

Inbar nodded and then half-speaking to her, half-musing aloud, he said, 'Before I come to what is topmost in my heart, there is a matter I would speak about first. Baradoc and myself were taken as slaves from the long beach over the headland. We were cousins and friends. We were sold into slavery together and we came in the end to serve the same master.'

'This I know.'

'But much you do not know. We had a good master, a retired soldier, a Roman, a man of learning, of good grace and many parts. Before I left him with my freedom I learnt many things . . . your tongue, your people's ways. I came back here because I would bring the knowledge of the things I knew to my tribe . . . the knowledge of a way of life, of skills and arts which, if they would accept and learn them, would make their lives fuller and less crude. Now that my father has gone I can begin that work. If it indeed were true, do you know why I would have strung Baradoc to a tree to die?'

'String him there you did.'

Inbar shrugged his shoulders. 'I am tired of denying the fact — and you slip my question. But I give you the answer. From our master Baradoc loved only the knowledge he gained of warfare, of arms, of fortifications and of handling troops and horses, the care of men and the provisioning of baggage trains and the way to look at a valley or fertile plain, not for its beauty or the crops it grew, but for the way it could be held or seized in battle or night attack. Baradoc would have brought back a dream of conquest and strife, of raising all men into troops and battle parties to turn eastwards and fight the Saxons — '

'And what is wrong with that?'

'Alone nothing — except that in his heart there is less hatred of the Saxons than there is lust for military glory and power. Baradoc would be a *dux bellorum* — nay, more than that. Baradoc — another Caesar. He would have left you here while he went east again. Or dragged you hither and thither in the end with less thought of you than his baggage train or the well-ordering of his men.' He paused for a moment, his eyes steady on her. Then quietly he went on. 'You saw none of that in him? Nay, your brain is too sharp not to have guessed at it.'

Tia stood up slowly, her mind host to two truths; one, that the truth of Baradoc was much as he had drawn it, though she had known it and accepted it when she had married him, and, two, that for the first time this man had made plain to her a truth in him which she had never expected to find.

She said evenly, 'There is nothing you can tell me of Baradoc. I am his wife of choice and whatever way of life he brings me I accept out of my love for him.'

Inbar stood up and slowly shrugged his shoulders.

'No. The laws of this tribe make you a free woman. Each week when you bring the new bread — and I have given orders that it shall always be you — then, as now, I shall ask you to become my wife and work with me for something my people need more than the arts of ambush and the naught-gaining perils of distant campaigning. They fight best who have most to lose. When in the long years ahead the first Saxon warbands reach the borders of Dumnonia there shall be no lack of sword hands to rally to the Prince — just as there is no man tardy to the beach now when the Scotti come raiding. Be my wife. Help me to bring to the people of the Enduring Crow a way of life which when the time comes will be worth death in battle to pre-serve. This I ask out of true love.'

'No. I am married to Baradoc, and he will return.'

For a moment or two Inbar eyed her. Then he laughed and, picking up the half-filled beaker before him, drained it. He walked to the doorway and said, 'I could pull the latch thong of the door in and none could enter. I could use force and school you to love and scorn the danger of a hidden knife, but I want no golden-crowned dove to keep in a wattle cage.'

He opened the door and stood aside for Tia to go out. Standing in the doorway he watched her move down the path slope. With her went the three dogs, Lerg, Aesc and Cuna, who had been waiting outside for her. The sight of the dogs took him back to the day in the forest when with a companion he had strung Baradoc up to the oak. The dogs had been away hunting for their own food or they could not have laid their hands on his cousin. That day he had acted on impulse, sudden, unthinking and swift. But now he knew the real truth which had been in him, forcing him to unpremeditated violence.

That night as Tia lay abed with Arturo and Mawga snoring gently on her couch on the far side of the hut, she found Inbar strong in

48

her thoughts. So far she had only thought of him as a treacherous man who had tried to kill her husband in order to ensure that he, as now, eventually became chief of the tribe. That his treachery held any more motive than a desire for power and self-gratification had never occurred to her. Yet now, though she could never condone his act, she could acknowledge that behind it lay a worthy motive. The tribespeople, roughly housed, and beyond a few badly organized efforts to make store of one season's crops, cattle and catches against the want and barrenness of another, lived simply from day to day. Bred to hardship and lean times they were almost unaware of these. Each house had its midden heap outside of bones, the empty shells of mussels, and other cast-away refuse amongst which the dogs and swine rooted and the flies bred in summer. The narrow river ran pure and clear down from the moor, but through the settlement it was polluted by seepage from the middens, by the women who washed the family clothes along its length and by the cattle and horses who drank and wallowed in it. There were no privies. Men, women and children disappeared behind the shelter of rock, bush or reed patch to ease themselves. The pottery they made was crude and coarse. The clothes they wore were of roughly cured skins and badly woven wool. The grain milled on the big quern stones in the cave was seldom properly oven-dried and its flour quickly grew a blue mould in the wet winter gales. Thinking this . . . remembering the well-ordered, civilized life and economies of her father's and uncle's villas, the baths and piped water, the fine table ware and the clatter of pots and pans in the spotless cooking quarters, the store rooms well-aired and damp free and, in winter, the gentle heat that flooded each room through the wall and under-floor ducts from the furnace, she suddenly realized that in her few short years here she had not only passed from one world to another, but had accepted this crude, insanitary life as though she had never known other. But this had not happened to Inbar. As a boy and on into young manhood he had, no matter if as a slave with a good master, lived the life she had once known, and conceived the passion to bring some part of it at least back to his people. No man, she felt, who nursed such a desire could be wholly bad.

At this moment Arturo stirred in his sleep. Then, not even half-awake, rolled over her and slipped to the floor. By the light of the single wall sconce light she saw him pad in his short shift to the door, fumble with the latch-bar and go out. He stood framed against the pale night sky in the doorway and, yawning, piddled over the threshold. He stumbled back into bed and was fast asleep in a few moments, held in the crook of Tia's arm, the hut door left wide open. From up the valley came the long churring call of a night jar, a pendant of pale stars was framed in the doorway against the summer light sky and the flame of the wall light wavering in the faint night zephyrs set strange shadows dancing around the hut. And in her heart Tia found, too, a strangeness of movement which she had never known before and there arose in her, unbridled, a passionate, body-trembling longing for the return of Baradoc.

★   ★   ★

In the following weeks Tia took the bread batch regularly to the long hall, and always Inbar awaited her there and they sat and drank their beaker each of mead and talked — and talked with growing easiness for there now was a slow dying of open hostility towards him in Tia. And because there was, almost unconsciously, a growing nostalgia in Tia for her old life, she was always glad when he spoke of his days in service with his old Romano-British master. He made no move-ment to court or woo her, though he always went through the ritual of asking her to marry him and she without feeling always refused him. When she left he would always open the door for her and, unfailing, before she passed out would pay her some compliment that arose from his desire, phrases that reminded her of the way Baradoc, too, had found a poetry to match his love . . . *My heart is a bird without song because there is always winter in your smile . . . I walk the moor through the blaze of gorse bloom and know that, like yours, it is a beauty masking a snare of thorns . . . What man needs a summer house of laced ash boughs and a seal skin couch if the calm of the night knows not the love sigh of his beloved?*

Apart from these brief meetings he took no notice of her when he saw or passed her in the business of daily life. But slowly more and more he kept Arturo close to his company as he worked with the other men, and openly favoured him above any of the other boys as though he would say 'One day this will be my step-son and more to be favoured than any son of my own loins.' And once he said to her over their mead, 'Be my wife and have my children, but know that I will swear before the tribal priest in open company that he shall follow me as Chief of the Enduring Crow people.'

Yet, for all he favoured Arturo, he had no hesitation in punishing him, for Arturo in his eighth year was already growing in thought and deed beyond his age. There was a small cove, not far from the main settlement beach, which was the place where twice a week the women and young girls bathed naked and washed themselves and sported with one another. One day Arturo, who could now swim like a fish and dive like a cormorant, covered his head with sea-weed and drifting offshore let the tide take him down to the cove so that he could watch the naked girls and women and was discovered by Mawga's sharp-eyed mother. He was taken before Inbar and Inbar beat him with a hazel switch and raised weals across his rump. Watched by everyone Arturo made no cry. When the beating was done he drew up his ragged trews and pulled down his tattered shirt and walked from the open space before the long hall and up the river towards the moor without word or look at anyone.

As he lay at Tia's side that night, Arturo out of the darkness said quietly, 'One day I shall kill Inbar.'

Tia smiled and turned to him where he lay face downwards to avoid the smart of his weals against the bed boards: 'Why? Because he beat you for a deserved reason?'

53

'No. I think nothing of that.'

'Then why?'

'For the same reason that you will not marry him. Because — be my father dead or alive — I should one day be Chief of this tribe. If my father does not return to kill him, then when I am grown the duty becomes mine.'

For a moment Tia was silent and then she asked, 'If your father never returns and I should marry Inbar as he wishes — what then?'

'I would still kill him — and find you a worthier man.'

Tia laughed quietly, but as she did so it came to her that this was the first time she had ever put in words to anyone the thought that Baradoc might never return and that she might marry Inbar. To cover the confusion in her she said sharply, 'Sleep and put such thoughts from your mind.'

But from that day on Tia noticed that although Arturo behaved as usual with Inbar he spent less time with the other boys and was always ready to go up to the moor and take provisions to the hermit Druid priest, Galpan, who lived alone in a turf shelter, and that there were nights when she woke to find him gone from the bed alongside her and to answer for his absence would only say, teasingly, 'I could not sleep so I sat on the clifftop and watched the rock foxes dance.' Or, 'I lay by the Big Bend pool and the king salmon who waits there for spawning time put his great kype from the water and taught me a song the mermaids sing.'

'Then sing it for me.'

'Nay — it is not fit for the ears of my gentle mother.'

Galpan, the priest, meeting Tia on one of his rare visits to the settlement, stopped and said to her, 'Your Arturo has the gift of memory and the fault of imagination. When he comes to me with bread and meat I teach him all the stories of this tribe and the other tribes of Dumnonia and of our country and he learns them word perfect, for so only should they be remembered less time and man's memory abuse them. He learns fast and accurately but sometimes, to anger me so he thinks, he will tell them in his own fashion. Would you know what that fashion is?'

'You would have me know or you would not be speaking to me.'

'True. He retells the stories and always the great priest, the great warrior or prince he calls Arturo. And always the feats of bravery or acts of piety are more wonderful than they were in life, and always — which is why to my shame I allow him the licence — his words are, even for such a child, golden with the gift of the true bards and his phrases so beautifully wrought for one so young that I forget to be angry.'

'Yet still, you do not tell me why you say all this to me. All children embroider a story in the telling.'

'As children, yes. As men only the truth must be spoken. But as a man, unless my years and wisdom already fail me, your Arturo though he act with valour and skill will make of his acts and the feats of others a false wonder.'

'Then he should be curbed or beaten free of the failing now.'

Galpan shrugged his shoulders and rubbed one bare foot against the dusty ground. 'No. The cock crows to the rising sun. The lark cannot soar from the bare heath without song. There is no altering them. Your Arturo will become what he will, but few men will ever learn from his own lips the full truth of what he is, or does, or dreams. For my own peace — and despite my liking him well — I have told him to come no more to me for I would not have my calm and meditation corrupted by his bright fancy and golden tongue.'

'He has shown none of this to me or others here.'

'Why should he? Until its wings are flighted the young plover is a stone among stones.'

So, Arturo stopped going to the priest and instead attached himself to Garmon, the chief cattleman, and became herd boy spending his days and many nights on the high moor slopes, and since Garmon rode his distant rounds on a spirited mealy-mouthed pony it was not long before Arturo was riding some of the rounds for him and for this Garmon was well content. He grieved still for the loss of his wife and daughter to the Scotti raiders and often his grief found comfort in a goatskin of mead or barley beer. He was content to lie fuddled in the sun and let Arturo do his rounds and always with Arturo went Cuna, alone, for the other dogs, Lerg and Aesc, were now too old for long days and hard going. There were times even when Arturo had to lift Cuna to the pony's back and ride with him uneasily couched against his crutch.

But although Arturo had joined Garmon mainly for the chance to learn to ride and for freedom from the small but constant dull tasks which the settlement boys were set to, his natural inquisitiveness, sharp eye and brain could not stay idle. He fast became a good herdsman and long before high summer saw the yellow flowering of bog asphodel and the sloughed skins of adder and grass snake on the granite rock slabs, he could pick out from three bow shots away the sick animal in a flock or, running his eye over a herd of cattle, know at once which one was missing since to him they all had personalities as well known as the settlement boys for whom he now had little time. In the evening when he came back and had fed and watered and hobbled the pony, he would sit with Garmon over a meal and then, enjoying his ration of two beakers of mead if any remained, would regale the man with highly coloured stories of his day's doings — mostly to the accompaniment of Garmon's drunken snoring.

There were other times when, doing the rounds alone, if Arturo should find the herd harboured close to Garmon's hut he would use the spare time on his hands by riding southwards across the heathland and moor to a lonely tor from whose summit he could look down on to the dusty, rough road which ran from Isca in the east through the old Roman outpost of Nemetostatio and so westwards to link hamlet and settlement all the way down to Antivestaeum and the great land-ending promontory of Belerium where, so old Galpan had told him, a man could stand on a clear day and see the dancing mirage of the Blessed Isles, beyond which the seas ran away into the endless mystery of time and space. But Arturo's young eyes turned mostly to the east for that way lay the world of which his mother had told him so much, the world of fighting men, of great woods full of wolf and bear, and the high mountains beyond the Sabrina river and the rich lands of the Catuvellauni and the Coritani where great chiefs ruled and fought, and where a man who could handle spear, sword and bow could gather others to him and find adventure.

Sitting astride the dun pony he would watch the road and the small bands of travellers raising a trail of dust as they moved on foot, mounted or by cart. Sometimes they would see him perched on the tor and often would give him greeting by the long clear call of a horn to show that they passed in peace.

One day Arturo watched a small party coming along the road, travelling eastwards. A man walked at the head of a horse which was pulling an open cart in which sat two cloaked figures pressed close together against the bluster of wind and rain squalls which were sweeping the moorland. Tethered to the rear of the cart was a milch cow and a spare horse. When the party was directly below Arturo, no more than half a mile away, the cart lurched in one of the deep road ruts and the sudden movement alarmed the tethered horse.

It reared on its hind legs, tossed up its head and broke the halter rope. The animal galloped off the road and took to the moor ground in alarm. Faintly on the wind Arturo caught the sound of the shouts and cries of the party and for a moment or two he sat his pony, grinning at their plight. Before they could unhitch the cart horse to go in chase of the escaping animal it would be well away into the moor and — the thought was suddenly strong in him — an easy prize for him to capture.

Impulsively he kicked his heels into the flanks of his pony and began to ride fast down the tor slope on a line to bring him to the escaping animal. Behind him, barking and losing ground, came Cuna. Excited now at the easy prize which lay before him Arturo, as a squall of wind and rain beat into his face, cried, '*Aie! Aie!* The gods give and Arturo takes!'

Thighs and legs gripping tight on the pony's sides, Arturo swung the animal around rocks and heather and gorse clumps and fast overhauled the horse which had now dropped to a slow canter, flinging up its head once and neighing as though celebrating its escape. On the far ridge of the tor Arturo drew level with the horse and pulling the pony back to match its gait he rode alongside, talking and calling to it until, either from his cajoling or the presence of the pony, it dropped to a slow amble. Arturo leaned over and caught the free-flying halter rope and drew horse and moor pony to a halt.

Flushed with his prize, he sat back and looked down at the road party. The man was making no effort to unhitch the horse from the cart to follow him. But one of the two people in the cart had jumped to the ground and was running quickly up the long slope towards him. Arturo grinned as he watched. He had but to turn and canter away with his prize and none could stop him. Mischief rising in him, he waited, planning to hold his ground tantalizingly until the figure neared him before riding away. The runner was a bowshot away when the passing of the fierce rain squall allowed him to see clearly. He saw that the pursuer had thrown off his cloak and now came towards him wearing only a rain damp red tunic, and carried no arms. Then, as the gap between them narrowed, he saw more — that the pursuer was no man or youth, but a girl with long black hair and that she ran faster than he had seen anyone run before and with the sure-footedness of a deer. He was on the point of turning away with his prize in escape when the impulse to kick his pony into action died in him. He sat and waited for the girl to come up to him.

She drew up before him and stood, squaring her shoulders as she took deep breaths before speaking. She was, Arturo guessed, little older than himself and more beautiful than any of the settlement girls. Her hair was as black as a raven's wing and lay now plastered to her head and neck with wet like a sleek helmet, and the same rain had drenched her tunic so that it clung to her body like a skin, firming into bold prominence her apple-small young breasts. Her legs were bare except for light leather sandals, the thongs between big and second toes cross-gartered high up her bare legs. But more than the boldness of her young body which Arturo covered unbashfully with his eyes, was the beauty of her face. Her skin had the soft, dull polish of a hoarded hazel nut, her eyes were a bright, clear, piercing blue and her lips were red as the wild rose-hips which grew on the banks of the lower combes of the moor. Arturo had never seen a girl so beautiful and the sight made him clear his throat with a grunt as though his gullet were dry with sudden thirst.

Her breath recovered, the girl stepped forward and laid her hand on the halter of the escaped horse. In an accent which told him that she had never been born or bred in Dumnonia she said, 'I thank you stranger for catching our horse.'

Tempted by some demon of mischief, Arturo answered, 'And I say no thanks are needed since I do not mean to give him up!'

The girl laughed and tugged gently at the loop of the rope that curved between horse and Arturo's hand. 'Then you must get down and fight for him — but watch as your feet touch the ground lest I fairly slit your gullet with this.' As she spoke she pulled up the long hem of her tunic and drew from a sheath held by the top-gartering of her sandals against her thigh a long single-edged knife. Seeing the look of surprise on Arturo's face as he still sat his pony, she laughed and said, 'I see you have no stomach for knife work!' With the last word she jerked the free end of the halter from Arturo's unresisting grasp.

Arturo, confused and suddenly no master of himself, said, 'You are not of these parts?'

'No, nor wish to be if it is peopled with horse thieves.' She spoke harshly and then as though from her mastery she had decided to be magnanimous, went on, 'We come from Gaul and landed two days since in the bay which is named after the island of Ictis and we make our way to Lindum.'

'Where is that?'

The girl smiled. 'To hear my father tell it — where every other spring flows wine instead of water, where the birds on the trees have golden wings, and the cattle grass grows knee-high and lush through winter. You want to leave your bog hut or beach shelter and come? You would be welcome, less for the company of yourself than the gain of your pony and the friendship of your dog.' She stooped and fondled the ears of Cuna who sat at her feet.

Arturo slowly mastering the unusual confusion which had spread quickly through him said with a return of spirit, 'One day I will come to Lindum and seek you out. You shall see — when I am grown I shall come and woo you and we shall lie in the long grass, listen to the golden birds sing, and drink the new wine. This I promise you.'

The girl laughed, shaking her head so that the rain drops sprayed from her long black hair, and said, 'You have a boy's build but a bard's tongue. How will you ask for me since you know not my name?'

Enjoying himself now, excited by her presence and the day's adventure, Arturo grinned then spat like a man over his pony's neck and said, 'I need no name for I shall ask for one who has eyes like the blue bellflower, lips redder than the thorn berry and hair like polished black serpentine.'

The girl rubbed the back of her hand across her nose as the rain, which had begun again, ran down it and said, 'There could be many such.'

'*Aie* . . . so. But not any who can lift a tunic skirt to take knife and show a red birthmark like a swallow's gorge on her thigh.'

The girl was silent for a moment then shook her head and asked, 'How many years have you got, boy?'

'Ten,' lied Arturo.

She shook her head, and said, 'I doubt the truth of that — but one thing is true, your tongue outruns your years.'

As she finished speaking there came through the wind and the rain from the road below the high, winding sound of a horn.

'Your father calls,' said Arturo.

'Then I go. But — ' she grinned impishly, ' — to save you trouble in the years to come I give you my name for I would not have you wandering the streets of Lindum lifting the skirts of every dark-haired girl looking for a swallow's gorge birthmark. Tis Daria, daughter of Ansold, the swordsmith.'

She turned from him, as the horn blew again, leapt to her horse's back, kicked him with her heels and set him at a canter down the slope.

'And mine — ' shouted Arturo after her, though the rain and wind drowned his words, ' — is Arturo, son of Baradoc, chief of the people of the Enduring Crow and . . . and . . . and . . . ' He spluttered into silence as a sharp squall burst into his face.

He sat then, still on his pony, watching Daria rejoin her father, seeing the escaped horse re-tethered to the cart, and unmoving still sat on, watching, until the slow-moving party disappeared over a far crest of the moor.

★ ★ ★

Two days later Tia walked the river path from the cave up to the long hall. She was smiling to herself because Arturo had returned from the moor that morning with Garmon and had come straight to her in the cave where she worked, stuffed himself with two of the fresh-baked wheat cakes, and had insisted that she draw a map in the sand of the cave's floor to show him where Lindum lay. But when she had asked him why he wanted to know he had been evasive and she had not pressed him. In the last few months, since he had spent less time with boys of his own age, and had frequented first the priest and then the herdsman she had sensed a growing impatience in him, a restlessness of spirit and body, and a precocity which far from pleased her. When he slept at home now it was no longer to share her bed platform but to lie in the long empty bed of Mawga's father. The children of the tribe grew faster and matured earlier than the Roman and Romano-British boys and girls of her own childhood. Since most of the youths and maidens of the tribe moved about in the good weather half-naked it was a development to be expected — but it was an early ripening which, she felt, needed the control more of a father than a mother so far as Arturo was concerned. Had she a daughter she could have dealt with her, but Arturo was fast slipping beyond her grasp. He needed the firm hand and sharp tongue of a father to guide and school him. For a moment or two her heart was full of fierce longing for the return of Baradoc. By all the gods she needed him for Arturo's sake and for her own . . .

When she entered the long hall Inbar was sitting alone at the table lashing the three-tined head of a fish spear into the socket of a new ash pole with waxed leather thongs. To one end of the table was set the customary mead jug and by its side two beakers. He rose as she came in, holding the door wide to let her pass with the great rush basket of new bread, and stood watching her as she carried it through to the store room. When she came back, without any word or greeting, he motioned her to sit at the table. He went to the door, glanced around as she sat with her back to him, then closed the door and with a flick of his fingers drew the leather latch thong inwards through its hole so that none could open the door from outside. He came back round the table and sat facing her. He lifted the jug and filled the two beakers and Tia saw at once that instead of pouring mead he was pouring wine. Seeing that she had noticed this Inbar smiled.

'There is a reason,' he said.

'And for these, too?' Tia touched her beaker with a finger. Like the other it was not the usual earthenware beaker but two fine glass drinking cups each engraved with the snake-wreathed head of the gorgon Medusa. Such glass work, she guessed, could never have been made in this country.

'For those too,' said Inbar. 'In his time my father traded for and hoarded much treasure. But he seldom used such things as these — unless someone as important as the Prince of Dumnonia or his high steward came this way.'

'Then who is honoured today?'

'You.'

'Why?'

'Because this is the day of my birth.' He smiled. 'That is if Galpan, the priest, in his keeping of the calendar is to be believed. So I make you my birth day guest, and for this meeting plague you not about marriage, but ask in its stead that you pledge my health.'

Tia smiled. When he was in this mood, despite all he had done to Baradoc, she could find herself easier with him. She took the glass and breathed in the bouquet. How many years had it been since she had last drunk a fine Falernian? Besides his treasures old Aritag had hoarded wine, too; wine bartered for in the peaceful days when the trading ships came coast creeping all the way from the Mediterranean.

Tia said, 'In return for a truce to marriage talk, I drink willingly.'

'You do me honour. Tis but a small glass, so drink deep.'

Tia nodded, raised the glass higher in salute to him, and then drank. As the sweet wine caressed her palate she remembered vividly the last time she had tasted it. It had been with old Truvius in his Aquae Sulis villa on the first night that she and Baradoc had arrived there. The memory was sharp, but curiously without poignancy and the sudden conviction flowed through her that there might soon come a day when, for her sake and Arturo's and from the slow-dying of hope of Baradoc's return, she might forgive this man the sin she held against him, forget the past since it was blighting her future, and marry him. She drank deep and as she put the glass back on the table Inbar raised his own glass.

He said, 'From this day I ask no more that you should be my wife, but wait only for the time when you shall look into my eyes and I shall know that the thirst I have for you lives also in the woman who for me is the woman above all women.'

He drank, emptying his glass, and as he set it back on the table he touched its rim against the rim of Tia's glass and a small, silvery note rang high and then died through the silence of the long hall. Then he stood up and moved slowly round the table to come to Tia's side. As he did so Tia's head began to swim and, smiling at the conceit, she fancied that suddenly there was not one but three Inbars who approached her, three that swam first apart and then merged into one and then broke again into three, and then, as almost uncaringly she began dimly to know what had happened, the middle Inbar came to her and lifted her from her seat. As he drew her to him, knowing now that the wine had been

70

drugged, she tried to push him from her. His arms encircled her and his lips came down to hers and took them, and he held her until there was no resistance left in her.

He lifted her from her feet and carried her, kissing her face and neck as he walked, to his sleeping booth at the end of the hall. He laid her down on the great white spread of bearskin, the pelt of one of the northern monsters which dwelt among the icebergs and frozen seas which only the Viking sea raiders knew, and rested her head on the red of the damask cushion stuffed with the nesting down of eider ducks. She lay there, breathing gently, with her eyes shut and her fair beauty fogged his eyes with tears of joy.

Yet to himself, as his hands began to unlatch the buckle of his deerskin surcoat, he said, the edge of regret in his voice, 'A little more of patience and gentleness, good Inbar, and she would have come to you freely, tamed by her own desire. Now loving itself must be the shy mare's gentler.'

His belt dropped to the floor, but as he moved to slip free of his surcoat there came from outside the distant sound of people running and calling, the noise growing louder with each second.

Then clearly through the still summer air came the fierce, insistent clarion calling of

Bada's horn, beating and searing and wailing, as he heralded the first shoaling of the year.

As the sound of shouts and racing footsteps came nearer and the horn's clamour grew fiercer and fiercer, Inbar looked to the indrawn latch thong of the door and then down to Tia. Slowly a wry smile spread over his face. A man could plan, he thought, but there was no escaping the intrusion of the gods. As Chief of the people of the Enduring Crow there was no escape from honouring the great gift from the sea.

He picked up his belt, rebuckled it, and then went to the wall and took down the great shield. He opened the door as Bada and a gathering of tribespeople swarmed across the forecourt. Seeing him they rushed forward and eager hands began to pull him away, across the court and down the valley while the horn blower paraded before him, waking the cliffs to wild echoes and setting the seabirds awing and awailing.

Only one of the tribe loitered and turned back to the long hall. Mawga, before the opening of the door, had seen that the latch thong had been pulled inside. She went in and saw the wine glasses and jug on the table, and Tia lying clothed and untouched on the bed.

A Chaplet of Purple Vetch

Inbar guessed that Mawga had helped Tia to escape. Two nights later he took her to the long hall, dismissed the old woman from the cooking quarters and the other house servant. Then he flung her on the bed and beat her until she confessed (which she did soon enough) that she had brought a moor pony to the long hall, set the partly recovering Tia on it and had led her until long after nightfall across the dark upland until they had reached the Isca road. Here, recovering fast, Tia could manage the pony herself. Wearing the Epona brooch of Ricat, she had ridden off eastwards.

Four days later Inbar had married her, and Mawga, despite her weals, was well content. To Arturo he said nothing for long since there had been no lack of boys and gossips to tell him the story. But he took Arturo into his household and treated him as his ward. Arturo, behaving himself and docile, took advantage of being lodged in the hall and the ward of the Chief to avoid any task which displeased him. Within himself he nursed the promise that he would leave the settlement as soon as he had grown to self-sufficiency and, if chance could be wrought, would kill Inbar before he left for attempting the dishonour of his mother.

In Isca Tia was met by Ricat, the horse-master, as she rode down in the pearl-haze of a summer morning to the shallow ford across the river. Beyond the river rose the great Mount of Isca topped with the long-abandoned Roman fortress. It had been beyond the memory of most men since any cohort commander had made the night rounds of legionary sentinels, and the fortress now was slowly lapsing into ruin as the townspeople robbed it for its quarried stone, its well-wrought woodwork and the great red tiles which had roofed stables, barracks and officers' quarters. Beyond the Mount at the foot of its slope was spread out the British town, a huddle of squalid reed and straw-thatched dwellings. A haze of cooking smoke rose in the still morning air, cattle grazed in the water meadows, and pigs rooted and foraged through the middens that spread around the skirts of the lower town. Above all, flying from the topmost rampart of the old fortress, the scarlet standard of the Prince of Dumnonia hung from a stout pine flagpole like a lazy flame as the idle wind now and then unfurled it to show the Dumnonia symbol of a great oak tree.

Ricat greeted Tia warmly and then, without asking her for any explanation of her coming, he said, 'One of my horse handlers saw you wearing the Epona brooch as you came down from the moor at first light, and the signal was passed from watch post to watch post.' He took her right hand and pressed it to his forehead briefly. 'You are welcome, Lady Tia.'

He took her to his house which was stone built and tile roofed and stood at the side of the old Forum. Its entry was through a small courtyard where roses grew in red earthenware urns, and across its front struggled an ancient vine which held now small clusters of green grapes. He led her into the house and showed her around and told her that the top room, which was approached by an outside flight of stone steps, was hers. He handed her the key bolt to its great wooden lock, and said, 'You shall do such work as you wish, but each day there comes Berna, an old woman from the lower town, who will help you. I am often away on the Prince's business, but when I am a night watch will keep the courtyard.'

Tia, her spirits still in slow turmoil from her escape from Inbar, took his hand and kissed it. As he stirred with embarrassment, she said, 'You are good to me, Master Ricat. The day will come when you shall be rewarded for your goodness.' Then unpinning the Epona brooch she held it out to him, saying, 'I thank you for the loan of this.'

Ricat shook his head, smiling. 'Keep it as a gift, Lady Tia. A gift to welcome you in my house.' Before Tia could protest he had gone.

Touched deeply by his kindness she went up to her room and, putting the cloth-wrapped bundle of her few belongings which Mawga had hastily packed for her on the low table which stood in the centre of the room, she sat at the window and looked out over the untidy sprawl of the town beyond which the slow curves of the river shone like a silver ribbon. In a niche at the side of the window stood a bronze bowl which held fresh sprays of large white ox daisies and meadowsweet. Though he could have had but little time to order their gathering she knew that they came from Ricat. The thought of the goodness which was in the man laid the beginning of a slow balm over the misery of her own feelings. Arturo stayed with Inbar, but she had no fears for his safety. Some strange god, she fancied, watched over Arturo. From the moment that his small baby hands had clasped the silver chalice and the water in it had been suffused with the red flush which would come for no other she had known that he was marked for greatness. He would live to be and do whatever her own gods, or the

Christian god of the old hermit Asimus, had already foreseen for him. For herself, stronger now since she had known how close she had come to abandoning it, lived only one faith, one conviction — that someday Baradoc would return to her. Never again would her woman's body or weak woman's mind ever waver from that belief.

* * *

Ten months after her marriage Mawga gave birth to a girl-child which was given the name Sabele. By this time Arturo was well into his ninth year and grown taller and thinner as though his strength and bulking were hard-pressed to keep pace with him. Inbar showed no impatience that the child had not been a boy. There was time and plenty for that. Eleven months later, when Arturo was into his tenth year, Mawga gave birth again and this time to a man-child who was called Talid.

Inbar gave a feast in the long hall to celebrate the birth and long before he and the other men were too drunken to talk or understand sense he called for silence and then told the men of the tribe the changes he was going to make in the running of the settlement. He had now, he said, a son to follow him and a man of wisdom and goodness had a duty to lay up, not only treasure for the son's future, but a future which should be peaceful, industrious and well-ordered. This was the duty of all men. He then told them the changes which were to be made in the settlement life. All the middens were to be cleared away and one main midden set up on the beach verge where the high spring tides would scour it away periodically. The river would be rock-dammed at the foot of the valley beyond the last of the huts and there and only there should the women do the washing. There would be cattle and pig pens well-fenced for the winter-folding. Crops and cattle were to be held in common and each family to draw meat, fish and flour according to their size and their standing. Every youth would be trained to arms for defence against raiders, but no man or youth was free to take leave of the settlement without his permission. If any did so his family would be punished in his stead. When traders came whether by sea or land then a council of elders from the settlement would negotiate the bartering and there would be a fair division of all the goods purchased. There was talk, he said, of war and raiding and the rise and fall of new war lords throughout the land beyond Isca and as far as the shores of all the Saxon seas, but such trouble was no concern of the people of the Enduring Crow. If such trouble did eventually come then the Prince of Dumnonia would call the levies from each settlement and lots would be drawn among those of fighting age to determine who should go.

There was more he said, but in truth few of the men paid much attention for not only had they heard most of it before, but they knew in their hearts that many of the things would not be done and that life would go on much as before. It was idle to speak against him and delay the moment of feasting and full drinking.

Some time after this Inbar's manner to Arturo began to change. When Arturo approached Inbar one morning after the Chief had spent most of the night drinking to ask permission to go out with one of the fishing boats Inbar refused him. Arturo began to argue and in the midst of his protest Inbar struck him and knocked him to the floor. Arturo, tight-lipped, picked himself up and left the long hall. He went down to the beach and sat on a rock staring at the sullen grey sea of late autumn. He was no fool and knew that Inbar's changing manner towards him came from good reason. He was held now in the settlement always under the eye of one of the tribe, be it man or older boy. He was allowed no more to the cattle and horse grounds on the moor, nor even permitted a visit to old Galpan, the priest. Although no one had ever said so, he was a prisoner in the settlement.

As he sat there, brooding, and watching a handful of black-headed terns diving for fry in the shallow water, Mawga came across the sands with two other women and, seeing him, left them and came to him. In the crook of one arm, wrapped in the loose folds of her gown she carried her babe, Talid. The gown was of good stout linen, dyed blue and sewn with black beads around the hem and throat. Mawga now wore such clothes as she had never known in her life before. She gave him greeting and sat beside him.

After some idle talk she said to him, 'Arturo, you are grown now enough to know better how to approach Inbar. When he drinks and after drinking is no time to ask him for favours.'

Arturo was silent for a while and then he answered, 'There is no proper moment for me to ask anything of Inbar. Every time he sees me he thinks of the shame he would have done my mother. *Aie* . . . and more than that. He sees that I am the son of Baradoc and the rightful one to be Chief of this tribe when I reach full years.'

80

'Nay. There is goodness in Inbar. Speak him fair and hold yourself proper to him and one day he will name you to be Chief after him.'

Arturo looked at her, his eyes widening a little and the line of his lips slanted wryly. Mawga was good, but she was simple. He said with a nod to the babe in her arms, 'You know not Inbar. He waits but to see that Talid grows into sturdiness and health. *Aie* . . . maybe he waits for more than that. For the time when you bear him another healthy boy-child. Then will come the thing he wishes for me.'

Mawga's face clouded with anger. 'Speak not so. You are his ward. The gods would mark him if he harmed you.'

'Tis a small point. He will not kill me himself — any more than he could boldly kill my father. But I can be killed by the chance fall of a rock from the cliffs. Or the mischance of a badly aimed hunting arrow. *Aie* . . . or from the sudden movement of a boat as I help haul the nets while fishing.' He leaned forward and placed the tip of his forefinger on the soft nose of Talid, and went on, 'He is pink and soft and helpless like a new-born harvest mouse in a straw nest. And so, for the moment, am I.'

Mawga shook her head. 'Your mind is full of black images. Inbar is a good man.'

'That you must say — for he is to you. But if he is so good, then ask him for permission for me to go and join my mother in Isca.'

'That I cannot do for it is not my place to meddle in Inbar's affairs.' Then seeing Arturo grin broadly, she went on, 'Why do you smile so?'

'Because — and I do not blame you — you did not draw back from meddling the day you helped my mother. Tether me a pony in the thorn scrub at the valley bend and one night be careless with the lock of the great hall. Inbar would never suspect you, though he might beat you for carelessness with the key.'

'You ask too much — and without reason. But for love of your mother what I have heard I have not heard.'

Mawga rose and walked away, and Arturo watched her without emotion. He had not expected her to help. Nobody would help him for none was rash enough to meddle in the affairs of Inbar. Raising his eyes from watching Mawga, he saw that on the high cliff behind him one of the older youths was sitting on an outjutting crag looking down at him. So they watched, he thought, day by day, and the night saw him safe within the long hall. Well, then he must use the cunning of the cliff fox, the patience of the fishing heron, and find his own way out, for to Isca he would go. He picked up a piece of dried bladderwrack and began to pop the black blisters in its strands. As he did so it seemed to him that suddenly the gods were speaking to him and giving him the sign which would show him the way to escape. He lay back on the rock, watching the grey scud of clouds sweeping eastwards up the coast and began to chuckle to himself. Yes, the gods had spoken and given their sign. Yes, he would go to Isca, but not to stay for long since even the Prince might for his own reasons send him back. What matter that he had so few years? The years would come, and there were always travelling parties that would take him as horse or mule boy. He would find his own way, make his mark and when manhood was with him he would come back. *Aie! Aie!* . . . the whole world lay to the east and a man should see it before he came back to his own people to settle down.

That evening in the long hall Inbar was good to him, sat him at his right hand to eat and allowed him an extra beaker of mead and Arturo showed a due gratitude and cheerfulness which he did not feel. He knew quite well that Mawga must have spoken to Inbar on his behalf and urged him to show more kindness to him.

The next morning Arturo set about

gathering the things he wanted to make good his escape and since he did not stray from the settlement area little notice was taken of him. Not that he would have cared if he were watched closely for none could have drawn suspicion from his movements. Not once did he go down to the beach or beyond the settlement bounds for the next week. He loafed about the cave, watching and talking to the women baking bread and grinding corn. He spent time each day to sit and talk to Bada who, apart from being the horn blower, was a skilled bowmaker. Arturo took delight in the man's adroitness in shaping and fashioning the layers of wood to make bows, and learning from him how to tell by look, feel and hand-tensing the best lengths of gut and sinew for use in finely plaiting drawstrings. Since autumn would soon pass into winter, and selected cattle and swine were now being taken to the slaughter pen for killing and curing against the hard days to come when fresh fish would be scarce and corn and flour would only by tight rationing last through to the next year's crop, he would sit atop the fence of the killing pen and watch and talk with the tribesmen working at the skinning and quartering of beasts. He was polite, ever cheerful with everyone and willing always to humour Inbar and to serve him.

But though this, he knew, pleased Inbar, he noticed that always someone, man or boy, and different every day, watched him.

Only at night lying on his bed did his face show his real thoughts, stubborn thoughts that matched the stubborn lines of his face and which made him clench his teeth and grind them slowly. But when everyone else in the hall was asleep, he would sit up quietly and, by the dim light of the red glow of the turf and peat fire, he would draw from inside the straw-stuffed palliasse of his bed the things he had quietly filched during his loafing days. He needed little light to work by for his preparations were simple.

By the near end of October when the new moon was passing to its first quarter and the bright evening star Venus showed only briefly in the south-western sky after the setting of the sun, Arturo had everything ready, and waited now only for the right conjunction of time, and tide and chance. For chance, he needed Inbar to sit after Mawga, himself and the servants had retired to bed, as he did sometimes, warming himself at the night-piled fire and drinking a last beaker of mead or wine before retiring. For time he had to have the tide on the turn, and setting on an easterly course up the coast.

When the right moment came he was

favoured by the weather. As though he thought, as he lay abed, fully dressed and with his needs for escape concealed under his tunic, the gods were on his side and wished to harass all pursuit until he should reach the safety of the cliffs, and even there, confuse the sight and hearing of the cliff and beach patrols.

Through his partly open bed curtains he watched Inbar sitting on a stool by the peat fire, leaning forward with his elbows on his knees and a great beaker of mead cradled in his hands as he warmed it. The thought had been in his mind during his planning that he could kill the man, but he had decided against it. Inbar could engineer some accident to kill him and there would have been no trouble. But if he killed Inbar without honour like some assassin, then the blood-mark would have been put on his name by the Prince of Dumnonia and no man in the west would have given him aid or shelter. No matter, he thought, as he watched Inbar raise the beaker and drink, the time for an honourable killing of Inbar would come. This was no moment to use the knife which he carried bound to his right leg under his long trews.

Inbar coughed and hiccoughed as he swallowed his drink and his body swayed a little as he was lulled between part sleep and part intoxication. Arturo slipped from his bed platform and with no attempt to quieten his movements walked towards the fire.

Inbar heard him and half turned. In a good mood from warmth and drink, he smiled and said, 'What, not abed and fully dressed, my Arturo?'

'I was cold and couldn't sleep, my lord.'

Inbar said nothing for a moment or two, but the smile stayed on his lips. He held out the beaker and Arturo took it and drank a little of the mead and then handed the beaker back.

'It puts warmth in the gut,' said Inbar.

'And dreams in the head,' said Arturo, thinking that if the opportunity he needed did not come then he would try again some other night and there would, because of this night, be no suspicion in Inbar.

Inbar belched gently and said, 'And what dreams does my Arturo dream?'

Humouring him, Arturo answered, 'That the days between me and manhood were gone.'

'And if they were?'

'Then my lord I would ask your leave to take my arms and go east to fight against the Saxons now that the troubles have started again.'

'How do you know that?'

'From every pedlar and packman who passes. Ambrosius and Vortigern are in arms again.'

'More likely against one another than against the long-keel men.' Eyeing him for a moment in silence, Inbar gave a sudden laugh. 'And which would you serve? Vortigern, who to save his life once married the harlot daughter of Hengist? Or Ambrosius, who, like his father once, dreams of wearing an Emperor's purple?'

'Ambrosius is of our race. I would serve him and, by serving well, do honour to the people of the Enduring Crow.'

Mellowed by the mead, Inbar handed him the beaker and said, 'Here, cool your hot blood with this and wish not your young years away so readily.'

'Nay, my lord. I have had enough.'

Inbar nodded his head and withdrew the beaker. 'And so have I. Enough so that my bladder calls for relief.' He rose slowly and putting his hand on Arturo's shoulder said, 'Go to bed, and dream not of fighting.'

'Ay, my lord.' As Arturo began to turn away Inbar stopped him.

He said, 'You are a good youth, Arturo, and I would not have you think I bear you any ill. Firm I am with you for your own good as with any other youth in the tribe. But more, I would have you know that never in my life have I . . . ' — he swayed a little and cleared his throat noisily — ' . . . offered your mother any disrespect for all that malicious gossips may say. We drank wine together to honour my birthday and she from overtiredness and the wine grew faint so that she lay on the bed to recover . . . Yes, no more. So harbour no bad thoughts. Now get to your bed.'

Arturo nodded and showed nothing on his face of the swift upsurge of contempt in him for the man, knowing that the mead was speaking in him strongly and fogging his thinking. Had he forgotten that his mother had taken flight to Isca to escape him?

As Arturo began to walk to his bed Inbar moved to the main door and drew from his belt pouch the long key of the heavy wooden lock. He unlocked the door and went out. The night air swept in and sent the grey fire ashes swirling. The door swung almost closed behind him. As it did so Arturo turned quickly and went to the fire. He picked up the stout length of oak plant which lay there for prodding the turves and ran to stand against the wall so that the inswinging door would hide him.

Outside he heard the sound of Inbar relieving himself, and from the far end of the hall came the light sound of Mawga snoring. Without harming Inbar he could have slipped out and run for liberty, but Inbar would have raised the alarm and every man, boy and dog in the settlement would have been soon hunting after him. Such a shift would have served him nothing. He needed time. And too, although he could not use his dagger on Inbar, there was pleasure in the use he could make of the oak post.

Holding it two-handed Arturo waited. He heard Inbar belch outside and then the shuffle of his feet as he turned to enter. As the door swung open slowly Arturo raised the oak plant, stepped forward to clear the swinging door and crashed the long post down on to the man's skull.

Inbar collapsed to the ground and lay still, and the door swung back to be held by his prone body which sprawled across the threshold. Arturo, moving now without excitement or clumsy haste, bent over Inbar and pulled him free from the threshold and then took the key from the lock. He went out and locked the door from the outside and began to run towards the scrub and bracken growths that grew up the side of the valley. When he reached the first of the bracken he sent the key flying deep into the now dying growths.

Reaching the crest of the valley side, keeping well below the skyline to avoid being seen by any of the settlement patrols, he dropped his pace to a steady trot heading always east and on a parallel line to the cliffs. Although he had long discarded the temptation of striking inland and making a bid overland for Isca, he was momentarily tempted to try it for the escape he had planned was not one he relished. Commonsense told him, however, that he had no alternative. Inbar would soon recover and when he did the pursuit would begin on foot and on horse and the chances of his reaching the river Tamarus and making the crossing were remote. His best chance of escape was by a route which none would dream that he would risk.

He moved steadily along the line of a wide gully that ran parallel with the sea on his left. There was light from the stars and the thin slip of the new crescent moon. After a time the gully sloped upwards and was lost in a maze of rocks and broken ground not far from the cliffs' edges and here Arturo followed a narrow path which took him out along a headland which he knew well. When he reached its point he climbed down its face, disturbing the roosting seabirds, until he finally stood on a flat rock at its foot. Some way below him the rock foot disappeared into deep water, the sea heaving and swinging as the tide which some time before had been at full ebb was now setting in flood eastwards along the coast. Under the light of the stars and the moon Arturo could see the dark line of current streaming away from the headland out to sea. It was a current which the men of the settlement used in their fishing for one could work the tides to go west or east on the ebb and return on the flood. Arturo knew that many, many miles away to the east the current swung inshore again and would carry a man with it if he humoured it. To fight it was to ask for an early drowning, and to ride with it for the long swing out and back called for the strength and endurance of more than most men since the body weakened fast with just the effort of keeping afloat.

But, as Arturo had realized when his bursting of the bladders of sea-wrack had set him thinking of escape, that which a man could not achieve by strength he might well, with some risk, bring to fruit by artifice.

He sat down and began to work fast. From beneath his tunic he pulled out three pigs' bladders stolen from the slaughtering pens and, blowing them up, trapped the gut ends with thin but strong lengths of old Bada's bowstring sinews, leaving small loops in the thonging through which he ran a long length of thickly braided gut to fasten the three bladders together so that he could slip them over his head and secure them under his armpits to keep him afloat without any effort on his part. Inside his tunic he had, wrapped in a large piece of pig bladder, two flat rounds of hard bread and a slice of smoked neat's flesh. The tidal current would eventually bear him safely to shore but, although the sea lacked yet its biting winter cold, it could sap strength and the body's warmth. Against this the blood's fire must be stoked with food. As for thirst . . . well, that must be endured if there were not juice enough in a handful of small crab apples which he carried with the other food in the blouse of his belted tunic.

His preparations complete, the bladders securely about him, he went to the rock edge, waited a while to judge the surge of the slowly heaving seas, and then jumped as a great swell rose below him, keeping his arms stiff at his sides to hold the braided thonging that joined the bladders from slipping. He landed backside first and as he went under felt the fierce tug of the thonging cut into his armpits as the bladders dragged above him. Then he surfaced, riding high and comfortably, and the current took him and bore him away from the cliff point seawards, swinging him gently up and down in its long-paced swell.

* * *

In Isca, living in the house of Ricat, Tia had found, if not happiness, at least a form of contentment which bolstered the patient faith she had in Baradoc's return. Although the old woman servant kept the small house clean and did the marketing and cooking, there was plenty for Tia to do in making Ricat's bachelor quarters more homelike for him. She made new cushions for the benches, repaired his sheets or renewed them, kept his clothes in good order and, against his protests, restuffed the old palliasse on which he slept. She polished the silver and bronze ware and, as time went on, took over some of the accounting for the Prince's buying of fodder for the horses against the winter and brought up to date the parchment pedigree rolls of the bloodstock mares and stallions.

But there were two things she loved most of all to do. One was when, through sickness or absence, there was a lack of hands to exercise the horses and she, wrapped warmly in loose tunic and baggy, cross-gartered trews, would ride through the water mead-ows, the autumn air sharpening to near winter's bite blowing in her face and setting her long golden hair streaming behind. She loved horses and, though Ricat was not one

94

to fashion fine compliments to a woman, he praised her for her riding and for the silent communion she seemed at once to establish with even the most difficult beasts for there was much mixed blood in some of the mounts and they could be as wayward and unexpected as sudden April showers. The other thing Tia enjoyed was the entertaining of his frequent guests when they came to eat with him.

Most of them were horse dealers and traders, some rough, some polished, who came to buy or sell, men of all tribes and some of mixed nationality who, despite the unsettled state of the country, travelled the old Roman roads north of Glevum to Eburacum, west as far as Moridunum in Demetae and over the wild Cymrian mountains to far Segontium facing the shores of the island of Mona. None, though, went so far east as the Saxon lands, for the men of the long keels had no way with or need for horses. Thus, it was from their talk at table — where she always sat as hostess for Ricat, leaving only for her own quarters when she sensed that wine and mead were loosening their tongues to unguarded frankness of speech — that she began to learn for the first time of some of the things (though many of them meant little to her) that had happened in the days which had passed since she had taken the babe, Arturo, to the people of the Enduring Crow.

Ambrosius the Elder was long dead and his son, Ambrosius Aurelianus, reigned now through all the northern lands west of the Sabrina river and had refused to give any aid to the despised Vortigern in the past years when the Saxon folk had broken out of their holdings in the east. There were many mixed opinions about Ambrosius; a braggart and a poltroon, said some, who sat safe in the marches of his own land while the rest of the country slowly tore itself to pieces; a dreamer and a man of courage, said others, who, now that Valentinian, the last legitimate Roman Emperor of the West was dead, bided his time before coming down on the Saxons and, through victory, would claim right to wear the purple. Men, young and thirsting for battle, flocked to him, but many soon wearied of waiting for action and turned away either to freeboot for themselves or to join smaller captains who took joy in deep raiding down the valley of the river Tamesis or making swift forays as far east as the margins of the Saxon Shore lands once proudly held by the Iceni and the Trinovantes.

There was, too, speculation among the guests of the mind of Gerontius, the Prince of Dumnonia, who sat patiently here in the far

West, holding men and horses enough and slowly enriching himself with a growing trade to Gaul, where many now of his fellow Britons had emigrated to serve under Aegidius. Emissaries had come to woo the Prince, but none so far had been given more than a soft answer, to which criticism Ricat gave reply that he could not speak for the Prince's true thoughts since he was only keeper of his horse and not his mind or heart. But he always said it with a sucking in of one cheek as though he were enjoying some private joke.

Back in her own room while the men talked and drank late below, Tia would lie on her bed and watch the slow movement of the stars through the rough window glass and wonder where at this moment her Baradoc lay, Baradoc who carried so much hatred of the Saxons in his breast and so much pride in his own people that he would not have long sat brooding and enigmatic like Gerontius, or have watered down by inaction the fire in the bellies of fighting men so that they turned from him. Thinking of him she would sometimes raise a hand to her face and find that without her knowing a tear had wetted her cheek; and there was no escaping then a spasm of self-pity for her sadness at being bereft so long of Baradoc and parted now from Arturo.

It was on such a night, long after Ricat's guests had departed, that Arturo came to her. She had dozed off to light sleep when she awoke to hear voices in the courtyard. One of the voices was Ricat's but — dulled with sleep still — the other meant nothing to her. Then came the sound of footsteps on the outside stairs, a knock on her door, and Ricat's voice called: 'Mistress Tia, you have a visitor.'

Throwing a cloak over her shoulders Tia went to the door and opened it. Silhouetted against the star-stippled sky stood Ricat and Arturo.

'Arturo!'

Tia reached out her hands for him and Ricat with a chuckle pushed the boy forward and said, 'When you have finished with him — send him down. There is food and drink enough on the table board still.' He turned away and clattered down the steps.

Tia drew Arturo into the room and embraced him. Even in her joy she smiled briefly to herself, for he stood within the embrace patiently like a well-schooled pony and his lips only briefly and shyly touched her cheek.

Their greeting over she stood back from him, fetched a pine wood taper spill and from her bed light set the wall sconce lamps to flame. Turning back to him she asked. 'You are well?'

'Yes, my mother.'

'Thank the gods for that.'

'*Aie* . . . they helped somewhat. But we must not forget the pigs.' He said it solemnly, but the lamp lights marked a familiar and brief ironic smile.

'Pigs?'

'Forget them, mother. I am safe and sound and have been well fed these last five days since I came ashore.' Then, with a touch of maturity and command, he reached forward, took her arm and led her to the bed. 'Sit down, my mother, and I will tell you all.'

Tia sat down on the bed and Arturo straddled himself across a stool and began to tell his story. As she listened Tia had it borne into her that despite his lack of years, not yet in his twelfth year, he was fast outstripping boyhood. Close about him hung the shadow of the man to be, fairly setup, holding himself with quiet pride and sureness. Ay, she thought, maybe too sure, too proudful. His rough tunic and loose trews were torn and dirty and about his waist he carried a tightly buckled leather belt in which, without benefit of scabbard, he wore a short double-edged sword, its cutting edges keenly honed.

Without hurry he told her the story of his escape and again, despite her joy in his presence, she hid a smile now and then as he fell victim to garnishing truth with fancy.

' . . . so I was cradled by the tide and carried safely far up the coast beyond the Point of Hercule. As I went I ate crab apples and neat's meat and the mermaids sang to me to while the night away and with the rising of the sun the pearl-bellied dolphins made a ring about me and amused me by their sports.'

Coming ashore on the estuary sands close to the mouth of the Two Rivers he had gone inland, walking the high divide between the rivers southwards towards Isca and had found no lack of food or friendship.

' . . . Most gave me food gladly for I told them that I had been taken for slave in a Scotti raid and seized my chance to jump overboard to escape in bad weather. At other times, if I could not eat by charity, I filled my belly by theft, mostly by taking eggs from the hen roosts and sometimes a hen for roasting over the embers of a friendly charcoal burner's fire. And one night, as I sat by a river pool, a dog otter came up from the dark waters carrying a salmon. It killed the fish with a bite across the neck, feasted but briefly and left the rest for me. The taste of raw salmon curd and its red-berried spawning seed is in my mouth still.'

'And the sword you carry — which here

you must not wear for none of your age may openly bear arms?'

Enjoying himself and genuinely glad to have arrived for, in truth, his travels had been far less than comfortable, Arturo grinned and was momentarily all boy, the shadow of manhood gone from him. He asked, 'Would you have the truth or some comforting fable, my gentle mother?'

Delighted with his coming Tia said, 'No matter which I ask you will give me the table of your own choosing.'

'Then hear the truth. Two forenoons gone I sat in the sun by the river and, lo, this same dog otter came from the water and laid the sword at my feet and for gift fee accepted one of my stolen eggs. And if you doubt there is enchantment about the sword see the finely sharpened, bright cutting edges. In a day and a night of rain they took no rust to mar their keenness. It is a sword of magic and shall ever be with me awaiting the day when I shall cut the dog's throat of Inbar with it and send him to the Shades.'

'Arturo! Enough! Either tell me the truth or say nothing.'

'I have told you the truth, but now I would eat and then sleep.' He stood up, reached for her hand and kissed it, and went on, 'I will go down to Master Ricat.' Then for a moment or two he paused, his face slowly clouding and, in an uncertain voice asked, 'When the Prince knows I am here, will he take Inbar's part and send me back to the settlement?'

'The Prince is a man of honour. Through Master Ricat he has given me sanctuary, and the same will be done for you — but you will get sharp punishment if you walk Isca carrying that sword. Give it to me.' As Arturo hesitated, she repeated sharply, 'Give it to me. I will guard it until you are of age even though I shall never know the truth of your gaining it.'

Arturo shrugged his shoulders and then, drawing the sword from the hanging loop on his belt, handed it to her hilt first. Tia sat with it on her lap as Arturo clattered down the outside steps whistling gently to himself. He needed, she knew, a man's hand on him and a father's authority to curb him for he grew too fast and fanciful despite his courage and mounting strength. Ricat would give him some curb and direction, but she had an uneasiness in her that soon no man would be able to hold or control Arturo for long. He was built of dreams and fancies . . . liar she could not call him for she knew that a boy's imagination was shaped of finer stuff than common deceit. The flushing of the clear water in the silver chalice to the soft pink of a swallow's gorge, the pale stain of blood, had marked his destiny. Maybe to achieve it, for it must needs be great if Asimus were to be believed, then the coming years would put him beyond any man's control, the manipulated puppet of the gods. For a while her mother's heart grieved for him. Then she put the thought from her for there was no human standing against the gods if they in their wisdom took one from so many to be their chosen instrument in this world.

She gently touched the keen edges of the sword and then rose and put it away in the ash wood chest under her window.

★ ★ ★

Though Inbar of the people of the Enduring Crow sued for the return of Arturo, Gerontius, the Prince of Dumnonia, refused to send the boy back and made Ricat — who had spoken strongly in his favour — his ward and responsible for his sober behaviour.

But first Arturo was taken before the Prince and left with him in solitary audience. Arturo stood straight and manly before him and listened to his words with a serious face, though in truth he paid little heed to them. They held mostly only a due formality, and he guessed that had Gerontius a real friendship for or need of Inbar he would have been sent back under escort. More interesting to him were the man and the room in which he stood.

Once the audience room of the Roman Commander of the Isca garrison, its floor was clean and cool with black and red tiling. A long window flanked by tall wall niches which had once held statues looked out from the castle heights over the town and river. The wooden shutters were wide open now and the fine kidskin curtains were drawn back to let in the light of the westering sun that slowly marked the dying of a mild late autumn day. A long table held bowls of fruit and a silver tray on which rested a blue glass flagon of wine and silver drinking cups. A fresco ran round the walls in a running design of stiffly prancing and galloping horses. A silk-covered couch held some papyrus reading rolls and a sleeping black-and-white tom cat. At the foot of the couch stood a great marble vase which was full of tall spikes of reed mace, some of the heads already aburst to show the pale spume of breaking seed.

Gerontius sat in a high-backed throne chair. He was a man in his late forties, dark-haired and with dark eyebrows that merged with one another over the high bridge of his hawklike nose. His eyes were half-hooded as though burgeoning sleep sat waiting full capture of him. He wore a long tunic of fine white wool and over it an open toga of green linen under the hem of which showed a pair of soft red sandals fastened with gold cord laces. He looked, Arturo thought, as though he had no interest in the world except to fall gently into sleep, a look which Arturo knew must be deceptive, otherwise in these times he would never be sitting where he was.

The Prince, after Ricat had retired from presenting Arturo, stared at him for a while from half-hooded eyes and then taking a slow, deep idle breath said, 'You are?'

Arturo said, for in truth Ricat had warned him of some of the Prince's manner, 'I am, my Prince, Arturo, son of Baradoc, chief of the people of the Enduring Crow.' He touched his left shoulder and went on, 'And bear their tattoo mark here.'

'Your father could be dead.'

'Then, my Prince, I am rightful chief of my tribe and not my uncle Inbar.'

Without any change of expression Gerontius said flatly, 'Then why not thrust a knife in his gut and settle the matter?'

For a moment or two Arturo was confused by the man's sudden bluntness. As his face showed it the Prince chuckled slowly to

105

himself. He rose from his chair and walked across to the table and poured himself a cup of wine. Behind Arturo's back, he went on, 'Don't tell me that one who had the courage to escape as you did — though I gather the sea maids and the dolphins helped you and even the otters of the river provided you with fresh salmon and a fine sword — lacks the wit to use a knife in the dark?'

As the Prince came back to the chair Arturo said, 'It could easily have been done, my lord — but it would not have been fairly done, face to face. And more, my lord, if my father lives and returns it is for him to do. When there is no more hope of that and I am youth no longer then I shall do it.'

The Prince nodded and asked, 'You believe that your father still lives?'

'It's enough for me, my lord, that my mother believes it and has the word of the wanderer Merlin for it.'

'Ah, the words of Merlin are well known for being so cunningly shaped that whatever he prophesies comes true, though it is not always the truth that one has expected.'

'Maybe so, my lord. But for my mother's sake I pray that the words of Merlin about my father bear only one shape and one truth.'

The Prince nodded, sipped at his wine and then said, 'Well spoken. Now go to Master

Ricat who will set work for you. But for two hours each day before sunset you will come here and be tutored by the good priest Leric.' He waved a hand in dismissal and Arturo touched his forehead in homage and left the chamber.

So began for Arturo a period of hard work and happiness that was to last until he was almost fourteen, and his eyes were lifted skywards each morning to seek the first sign of the returning swallows — the birds of his birth month — and, as he worked at the schooling of horses in the river meadows, his ears were cocked for the first notes of the cuckoo.

Ricat and his overseers worked him hard and after a few months had grudgingly to admit that he had the true gift of the Epona-marked. When he sat a horse they were no longer man and beast, but one entity. Iron-thighed, gentle or masterly handed, he could bring the most wayward steed to obedience, and there were many horses which were so for their blood lines were long mixed from the days when the first Roman cavalry units had come to the country. The old priest Leric (who worshipped horses a little less than his country's gods, and seldom lost a wager on a horse match on fair days) explained to him (strictly in his history lessons) that the blood of the mounts of the cavalry wings of such units as the *Ala Hispanorum Vettonum civium Romanorum* stationed as far back as the time of Trajan in Cymru at Brecon Gaer and the *Cohors I Nerviorum*, mounted by Gallic auxiliaries, had often escaped or badly guarded mares had been covered by the wild hill pony stallions. Wild blood, pedigree blood, pack horse to war horse, hill pony to the high-blooded eastern mounts which many a young *tribunus* or *praefectus* had brought to Britain on his first cavalry command, the blood lines were a maze which no man's memory could now thread. But in Isca, with Prince Gerontius and Ricat and men like them who acknowledged the special divinity of the horse, a new breed was slowly being evolved. The itinerant traders and the Iscan townsfolk who laid their wagers on fair days and lay in the sun on the grass banks above the river watching the horses turned out to pasture, closely guarded and contained, thought that Prince Gerontius followed but a fancy and a princely whim, having no more than a lust in his dark, beetle-browed eyes for horses where other men carried the glint for gold or women. But there were some who thought differently yet kept their counsel, and there were a few who knew the truth and schooled themselves to patience.

Of all this Arturo had no knowledge. He

was content with his work and his station. He was content, too, for the first time with the comradeship he found with the youths of his own age who also worked for the Prince. Like himself they had been hand-picked for one quality or another, though there was one trait — apart from their skill with horses — which they all shared and which often brought them a flogging or a week's stay in a cell on bread and water. They knew no fear so could not resist a challenge which might put their courage or ribald sense of humour in question.

For Leric — a lapsed Druid priest with tentative leanings towards Christianity who had escaped from Gaul and been given sanctuary within the bounds of Isca by the Prince for reasons known only to the two of them — Arturo had an odd mixture of high regard, occasional contempt and, rare for him, pity. Leric was far more learned than Galpan in the Druidical mysteries, far wider travelled and educated in the Roman and Greek tongues, but he was plagued by doubts still over the religion he had abandoned and, too, over the one he lacked the courage yet to embrace fully. To escape this dilemma he often sought comfort in drink, and then became so pitifully besotted and pathetic that orders had been given by the Prince that once he took to the mead he was to be shut in his room and guarded until he was sober. This was a duty that neither Arturo nor any of his friends relished. Nevertheless from him Arturo learned more fully his mother's tongue and enough Greek to cope with the exercises that Leric set him. But of far more interest to Arturo were the lessons in the history of his own country which Leric gave him; a history going back far beyond King Cunobelinus and the great Queen Boudicca, and the days when the Emperor Claudius invaded Britain or the first Saxon Shore fort was built on the island of Tanatus. He taught him, too, some of the songs and stories handed down from the days wrapped now forever in myth when Rome herself had yet to exist.

As for Tia, she was well content with Arturo's progress and paid not over-much attention to his occasional lapses into bad behaviour because on the whole he worked hard and his company was a joy to her. He was attentive to her and she was proud when she walked the streets with him, or watched his mastery of horses in the meadows. On the day he was fourteen and the swallows and house martins had returned she gave him a hound puppy which had many of the markings and much of the build and stance of old Lerg.

To her surprise, although he thanked her and showed pleasure as he stood in her room cradling the puppy to his chest, she could tell from the brightness of his eyes and a restlessness in him that his mind was far from presents. It was evening and still light and he had just come from his lessons with Leric.

He said, 'Put on your cloak, my mother, and come with me. *Aie* . . . I know well 'tis my birth day, but it is also a day of other importance. And ask no questions, for I give no answers.'

They left the house and walked down the hill to the river and then took the road southwards. A little outside the town the land rose. At the top of the rise stood an old oak, its branches blasted long ago by lightning. Arturo stopped at the foot of the hill, and said, 'Go to the tree. There is one there who would speak to you.' His face which he was holding solemn broke suddenly into an impish grin. Then, without another word, he turned and left her, making his way back to the town.

It was then that Tia knew the truth as surely as though it had been announced with a fanfare of trumpets and a proclamation by the Prince himself. She hurried forward through the growing twilight, her heart beating rapidly, her lips and mouth drying with excitement.

A wiry pack pony was tethered to a bole

sapling of the oak and a man stood by it. He was tall, with a lean, strong body, wearing a short-trimmed tawny-red beard, his clothes dusty from travel, his belt carrying a scabbarded short sword and a dagger. For a moment or two he watched her coming. Then, the impatience in him matching Tia's, he moved forward swiftly down the slope and, without word on either side in that first ecstasy of reunion, took her in his arms and kissed her.

From a distance, Arturo watched them, his heart pounding with excitement and his mind active with speculation about this man, Baradoc, chief of the people of the Enduring Crow . . . his father, who, mindful of his own safety and the courtesies due to his Prince, had halted outside the town and sent message asking for a yea or nay to a free and unmolested entry to Isca. While Arturo had been at his lessons with Leric the Prince had come into the room, told him the news and said, 'Go now to your mother and lead her to your father, and when their greetings are made tell him there is welcome here for him.'

That night as Tia and Baradoc lay abed, the pale sky showing through the window cut with the erratic movement of hawking bats and distantly the occasional screech of hunting owls breaking the silence, Tia said,

'Oh, my love, the moment you landed you should have sent a messenger ahead of you and I would have made a feast and a great preparation for you.'

Baradoc, holding her in his arms, kissed her eyelids gently and said, 'I came as swiftly as any messenger and for feasting what needed I more than to glut my eyes on your beauty and to feel beneath my hand the joy throb of your heart.'

When she woke the next morning to find herself alone, but hearing his voice and that of Arturo as they spoke in the courtyard below, she found beside her on the old wax stylus pad she used for making household notes the same lines which Baradoc had written for her in the hut on Caer Sibli when he had been taken from her:

The gods raise the door-latch of night
To let the silver morning in
Sleep veils the brook-lime blue of your eyes
The gay bird of love in my heart begins
   to sing
Returning, I will lay a chaplet of purple
vetch about your hair
And, kneeling, call you queen.

At that moment the voices in the yard ceased. She heard his footsteps on the stairs and the door opened to show him, framed in sunlight, smiling, and holding in his hands a circlet of purple vetch which he had gathered from the river meadows.

Between Sword and Sea

For nearly two months Baradoc and his family stayed in Isca. Each day for the first week Baradoc was closeted for hours with the Prince, who had a hunger for the tales of his long years of wandering and slavery; and when the telling was done a friendship had sprung up between the two men and their talk passed to other matters, though of these Baradoc said nothing to Tia or Arturo.

But at night as they all sat around Ricat's table eating, Baradoc gave them the story of his wanderings, which not only held Arturo spellbound but slowly excited his envy and longing for such adventures. Lying in bed at night he would fancy himself in the place of his father . . . captured at sea by the Northern long boat men, those who had no hunger for land like the coast-creeping Saxon keelmen, but sought only quick plunder or slaves for marketing and knew the world's oceans far beyond the bounds of shipborne traders and merchants.

Passing into the Mediterranean through the Pillars of Hercules, Baradoc had been sold as a slave on the African shore to a band

115

of desert traders and had passed through the hands of many masters, escaped and been recaptured often, but in the end had become a mercenary soldier in the service of the Eastern Empire under Marcian. Later, since he was always seeking to return home (though Arturo and certainly Ricat guessed, if Tia did not, that as there was so much to see and hear there had been times when the call of hearth and family had given way to his passion for learning and lust for experience) he had made his way to Rome and fought with the forces of Ricimer, captain of the German federates who had overthrown the Emperor Avitus. Eventually he had found his way into Gaul and finally back to Britain.

Listening to him talk Tia waited at times for some sign of his youthful flaming hatred of the Saxons, for some show of his old ambition to raise men and take arms against the barbarian keelmen. That he gave no sign of these passions, however, did not deceive her and she guessed that his long sessions with Prince Gerontius must have held more than an account of his adventures. Time, she guessed, and maturity had taught him not to wear his ambitions openly. When he learned of the treachery of Inbar, his face showed nothing except a thin tightening of the lips and he said, 'Soon the Prince will give me leave to return and then Inbar shall be made to answer. Arturo did well to run from him for as soon as his own sons had grown to health and years he would have killed him.'

'And now that you have had time to learn something of your own son — how like you him?' asked Tia.

Baradoc smiled, his dark brown eyes lit with a teasing light. 'He is a brave and kind youth, and the Prince reports well on his learning, his skill with horses and his training at arms. But there is a wilfulness at times in him which needs schooling. For that I am to blame by my absence. But it shall be remedied. There are times too when almost unknowingly he speaks fable for truth. That, too, must go for it will serve him ill when his full manhood comes. Men follow faithfully a leader who talks plain of hardship, danger and chances. The marsh of destiny cannot be crossed safely by the flame of a dancing bog light.'

Tia smiled to herself. Baradoc had changed but there was much about him that remained the same. Fine phrases he kept for his love and his heart stirrings, but for the harsh business of life and the cold press of his ambitions and love of his country only the crystal hard words of truth would serve.

She said, 'What you say is true. But treat

him gently at first for through your absence he comes late to the breaking pens.'

And so, in the first of the two months they spent at Isca before returning to the settlement, Baradoc after his own manner was forbearing with Arturo, but the past years of his own slavery and then the iron disciplines of soldiering had made him readier to punish than to forgive.

Three times in that month was Arturo flogged by Baradoc (though if his father had not been there the flogging would have been carried out by one of the Prince's men). Once it was for taking horse and spear on his free day without permission and riding with three of his working companions, who had been given permission, to hunt boar in the low hills to the north of Isca; and another time for spending an evening in a drinking house in the poorer part of Isca and being too fuddled to do his work properly the next morning, and a last time for brawling with the son of a trader from Lindum in the castle yard in broad daylight. When asked, after the guards had separated them, to explain the reason for the fight, in which Arturo had suffered most, Arturo refused. When explanation was demanded from the trader's son, he had shrugged his shoulders and good-naturedly said, 'If this young cock is silent — then so I am. But — ' and here he had turned to Arturo and said, ' — to him I say this truly. I spoke but in ill-mannered jest and without truth.' Nevertheless Arturo was beaten for breaking the peace within the precincts of the Prince's household. Even so, Tia could see no sign of resentment in Arturo for his punishment by Baradoc. The beatings done, he forgot them, though to his working companions he boasted, 'In a dream long ago the god of healing, Nodens of the Silver Hand, revealed to me a magic word which, chanted to oneself during a flogging, makes the hardest swipes but feather strokes and all wounds to heal without pain.' Offered payment for revealing the word, he had explained, 'Nay. To do so at once kills its magic.' Though most laughed at this, there were some who wondered, for whenever Arturo was beaten his face betrayed never a wince or grimace of pain. Neither was there any resentment in him against Baradoc. His father was right to beat him. It was a simple matter of weighing the punishment against the pleasure of forbidden actions. Within an hour he would be sitting at his father's feet, eagerly pressing him on to further and more exact descriptions of his adventures and hardships, and Baradoc, though he was careful not to show it, took now a rare delight in the company of his son. There was time and enough he knew for the young tiercel to be weathered and manned as he had seen the desert hawks brought to true hunting skills and obedience by the handlers who served in the courts of the Vandal chiefs of his African captivity. Since his long talks with Prince Gerontius, he knew now that the time would come when he would need a skilled and disciplined Arturo at his side to help him with the labour and fighting which should bring his country back to greatness again as it was in the days before Vortigern in his cravenness and the now dead first Ambrosius in his stiff pride gave land grants and privileges to the Saxon mercenaries and so fed their greed for more and more territory and power. Arturo would serve him well, but first he must grow and there was time enough for that since the plans of the Prince needed time too. The Saxon chiefs and commanders for some years now had pressed no farther forward, since they were busy fighting and quarrelling amongst themselves. Time at the moment was on their side, and time was needed for the calling together of men, to train and arm them, and also for the raising and schooling of horses.

* * *

They rode back to the settlement of the people of the Enduring Crow in high summer weather. There were four of them; Baradoc, Tia and Arturo, and Ricat who went as the Prince's surrogate. The Prince would have sent more men, but Baradoc disclaimed need of them. From reports which had already come from his people Baradoc knew that they waited his appearance with loyalty and that Inbar stood his ground from pride and the knowledge that his one hope of escaping being an outcast from his people was to stand and contest by arms Baradoc's right to the chieftainship.

Except for Tia, they all rode armed and Arturo was proud of his right, now that he was free of Isca, to wear on his belt the keen-bladed short sword which Tia had held in keeping for him. The larks sang high in the warm air currents over the moors and the tall grasses, ripening to seeding, swayed like a restless sea in the westerly wind. At the heels of his mount Anga, Arturo's hound puppy, now growing fast to legginess and strength, loped until tired when he was lifted to couch between Arturo's thighs.

They passed one night on the road, taking lodgings at a homestead by a ford across the river Tamarus. Although they could have reached the settlement by the following nightfall they stopped on the high moor above the settlement valley and passed the night in the open camped near the hermit refuge of the priest Galpan.

As they rested here Bada the horn blower came up to Baradoc with a message from Inbar. Baradoc and Bada walked apart from the camp and sat on a rock close to the stream's source, the bank behind them thick with whortleberry growths over the pale flowers of which the night moths hovered. From the high tor behind them a vixen screeched and was answered distantly by her mate.

Bada said, 'Inbar says that he will stand and give you answer only by arms. By your long absence he declares you have forfeited the right to lead our people.'

'And what do the people of the Enduring Crow say?'

Bada smiled. 'Had they been for Inbar they would have taken sword and spear and you would not have rested peacefully here tonight, no matter that you come with open warrant from the Prince. Inbar will await you on the fighting ground and gives you choice of weapon, spear or sword.'

'I take the sword.'

'So be it.' Bada was silent for a moment or two and then with something like a sigh shrugged his shoulders and went on, 'You were good friends once and shared many trials before he wronged you. Should it come to it, there is a strange goodness in him which might stir you to mercy.'

Baradoc's face muscles tightened. 'No . . . When he lies disarmed his heart shall know my blade.'

'So be it.' Bada rose, touched his forehead in farewell and began to move down the stream side.

Later as Baradoc lay by Tia's side under the rough canopy which made their shelter she said quietly to him, 'You remember Mawga?'

'A little. But her father more. He taught me the art of braiding horse-hair to make fishing lines.'

'She was good to me when I needed help.'

'For that she shall have a reward and high place among us.'

'What reward or high place will heal the grief in her heart if you kill Inbar — as kill him you know you can with all your years of fighting skills such as I have seen you display at practice with the guards in the Prince's yard?'

Baradoc said coldly, 'He and a companion strung me to an oak to die. He would have dishonoured you and killed my son in the fulness of time. Only his pride and the shame of being branded coward makes him stay to stand against me. For that, at least, the gods may give him some small regard when I send him to them. Sleep now, and trouble yourself no more.' But it was long before Tia found sleep.

Not far away Mawga lay on her bed in the long hall with her children sleeping near her and she knew that there would be no sleep for Mawga this night or many nights to come. Love Baradoc as she did, and still cherish undiminished her joy at his return, she knew that once his mind was made up there was no turning it by any plea she could make. A man's pride was beyond the knowing of a woman, shaping Baradoc to mercilessness and . . . *Aie*, the gods help him . . . Inbar to stay and stand against him without hope of victory. For all the shame he would have done to her there was no stilling the hope that had been in her that Baradoc would find some pity once it lay within his gift to kill or spare . . .

Unsheltered under the stars against the dew Arturo lay sleeping with Anga curled between his drawn-up knees and arms and his sleep was untroubled by dreams for Arturo rarely dreamed by night since his days were oversurfeited with them. Long before the first sunflush in the east roused the larks to rise and sing he came awake and walked with the hound puppy to the stream. He stripped himself and washed in the cold water and then sat on a boulder and stared down the long valley whose turns and twists hid the settlement and the sea from him. Proud he was, he thought, to be coming back with his father to the settlement; a father who had travelled far, seen many wonders, and fought under many commanders, a father who spoke now the tongues of Romans, Greeks and the dusky-skinned men of the African Vandals' lands, a father whose skill with sword and spear, aye, and throwing axe had amazed him when he had seen him (not without pride) display them in the Prince's yard. The only fault he could find in him was that adequately as he sat a horse, man and steed were never completely one. Though today held the coming excitement of the fight between his father and Inbar (and Inbar would fight well but must finally be overcome) he wondered what excitements could really exist for him in the settlement when all was put in order under his father. He had the feeling strongly that he would soon miss the work with the Prince's horses, the smell of the stables and the blood-stirring gallops and tussles with wild, unruly mounts in the breaking pens

. . . *Aie*, and the good companions of his own age with whom he worked. Here, his father could school him to the chieftainship which would eventually be his, a future which held no relish for him unless first he had proved himself in lands and countries far beyond this Dumnonia. There was, out there, to the east, north, west, and south, so much to be seen and tried, a feast of adventures and discoveries and challenges of all kinds to test him into full manhood. No, something told him that, patient as he might try to be, his father could never succeed to shaping him into ways that would chafe his spirit. The tattoo of the red-legged chough on his shoulder was no brand to mark ownership. No, when the time came he would go so that men everywhere would know his mark and think deep before they stood in his way.

Footsteps sounded behind him and he turned to see Galpan carrying his drinking bowl to take water from the stream. The old priest dipped and drank and then, squatting on his hunkers, the edges of his rough robe trailing in the water, looked up at him and said, 'How was my once good friend Leric?'

Arturo grinned. 'Scholarly and in good health when sober, but unruly as a drunken pig when not. He sent you greetings.'

'Which I may not welcome.' Galpan spat

into the clear stream.

To tease him Arturo said, 'He taught me about the Christ religion. I did not know that once it was so strong in this country.'

'Aye, with the strength of bindweed which under a canopy of white, innocent-seeming flowers throttles all that grows. Now the land is hoed clear of it in most places. What did you think of its teaching?'

Arturo shrugged his shoulders. 'Nothing. It is a religion for women, not men.'

'Aye, and Rome learnt that too late.' Galpan rose, rested a hand briefly on Arturo's shoulder and added, 'You are a good youth, though a little too full of spirit. It may be that our gods have marked you for great things, but let that not blind you to small things. Your hound dog's ears carry sheep ticks which suck its blood and you have not seen them. In the days which may come make sure that before you venture into great affairs or affrays you have not been blind to the small galls and frets that fill life. There is no trust or truth to be found in the line of an arrow with worn flight feathers.'

He moved away and, after watching him for a while, Arturo called to Anga and began to nip free the swollen sheep ticks in his ears, whistling gently to himself. Priests were all the same . . . Galpan and Leric . . . full of mysteries and prophecies which he was sure they invented to mark their own importance. Sometimes he had wondered whether they had not invented all the gods themselves, too, in their imaginations. Anyway, he had known before they left Isca that Anga, moving through the moor grasses, would get sheep ticks, had pinched them clear before setting out on the morning of their second day, and had been on the point of doing so when Galpan had come to him. As he finished clearing Anga's ears the voice of Baradoc called to him from up the slope. He rose, stretched himself, and went to him. Today, he thought, Inbar would die. For a brief moment the stir of some emotion disturbed him . . . there had been things about Inbar that he had liked. One thing at least had to be said for him, evil at most he might be, but he did not lack courage to stand and face his father. The gods would show him some kindness for that, maybe, when he went to the Shades.

*　*　*

Baradoc and his party rode down the valley to the rock-paved open space before the long hall. The sun from a cloudless sky gilded all with its brightness, and charged with changing colours the spray of the stream's

128

falls. Baradoc drew rein before the silent tribespeople who had lined themselves in a great crescent between him and the path to the sea. They gave him no greeting or raised arm welcome. For the moment Inbar's challenge lay between them and the joy in their hearts at his return. Why, too, should they greet the one they loved with noisy acclaim if in a little while the Fates should throw their knuckle bones against him and so leave them to the wrath of a victorious Inbar? Baradoc understood this and tightened his lips against the turn of disdain in him at their waiting on chance to save them venturing their own skins by any show of favour to him. Over the heads of his people he could see the sharp cleft that opened the view to the beach and the sea, the beach from which, boys still, he and Inbar had by the treachery of visiting traders been snatched to slavery. He watched for a moment or two the white, combing curl of the breakers and his eyes followed the flight of the seabirds, low coasting shags and puffins breasting the waters and the gulls screaming high while on the dark cliff crags he caught the quick, restless foraying of his tribe's bird, the black chough with scarlet legs. High above all a pair of sea eagles circled on an air current. *Aie* . . . he thought, he had been long away, gone as boy and returned now as man. These people were as children to him. There was much they would have to learn . . .

The horse party dismounted and a group of boys and youths came forward and took their mounts. Bada came from the crowd to Baradoc and said, 'Inbar waits on the trying ground.'

Baradoc nodded and, as Bada turned, he followed him. The crowd parted before them as they took the path to the clifftops and then followed behind them. They climbed the track through gorse patches where bees and flies feasted on the golden pollen, across the sheep-bitten grass fragrant with milk-wort and marjoram to the high headland which thrust its steep fall into the restless waters below like the prow of a questing sea-raider's craft.

On the flat turf, his back to the sea, Inbar waited for Baradoc. He wore short leather breeks and his feet were bare to give him true fighting grip of the ground. From his waist upwards he was bare, his torso and arms brown by the sun, the wind stirring his dark hair and beard. He held himself tall with a new dignity which came strange to all who marked him now, and although his lean, thoughtful face was firm set there was the twist of a bleak smile about his lips.

A few paces in front of him there lay on the grass two broad-bladed long swords and two small fighting shields, wooden framed and covered with layers of stiff, hard-cured leather. In the centre of each shield the sun struck dull fire from the high rounded bronze bosses. As the tribespeople made a wide crescent behind Baradoc to enclose from cliff-edge to cliff-edge the fighting space, Bada went forward and stood over the swords and shields. But for the moment Baradoc was unaware of Bada. He halted a couple of spear-lengths from Inbar and looked at him. If there were to be speech between them he knew that by tribal custom it could not come first from the man who claimed to have been wronged. At first, since no word came from Inbar, Baradoc slowly stripped himself of his belted tunic and the coarse shirt he wore below it. As he tossed the shirt away Inbar's eyes marked his naked, weather-tanned and hardened body and saw too the puffed lines and pale furrows of battle and slave-whip scars.

Seeing these, there was a strange, sudden stirring in Inbar that roused the sharp memory of their old friendship when as youths they had served as slaves to the same wise master who had been butchered to death by the axes of drunken Saxons at Durobrivae

131

long ago, and in his heart he felt regret at the shifts of his own ambitions and greed which had finally brought him to this trying ground. Raising his eyes he saw beyond Baradoc on the edge of the waiting crowd, the figures of Tia and Mawga, standing close together. His eyes passed quickly from Tia to Mawga. The golden-haired beauty of the Roman girl who had once stirred him to lust meant nothing now for over the years Mawga had moved into his heart, and Mawga, her eyes moist with waiting tears, lowered her head as though she would not with her womanly fear dull the edge of his courage.

Inbar's gaze came back to Baradoc and in a steady voice he said, 'It is long since we met last. The gods ruled that day as they rule all days and gave its outcome. Now I am content that they shall judge this day and give life to rest with him who shall be proved to hold their favour.' He stepped back a pace and nodded to the weapons which lay between them.

Baradoc said evenly, 'So be it.'

He stepped forward, picked up one of the small shields, slipped his left forearm through the thonged loop on its inner side and grasped the wooden hand-hold on the far side. Then he took up from the ground the sword nearest to him, swung it once or twice to get its feel and balance, and then stepped back and watched Inbar ready himself with shield and sword.

From the edge of the crowd, his throat drying already, Arturo watched them, saw them raise their swords high to one another and then spring back and half-crouching begin to circle warily. The shock of their first meeting took him by surprise for suddenly they were closed and the clash of their swords struck fire sparks in the bright air and the thud and hiss of sword against shield seemed to fill the morning with a noisy venom and anger which seized his own body and tensed every muscle in his limbs.

They came apart from that first clashing and, holding fighting distance, swung and cut and lunged as though they sought now only to test and prove each other's qualities and courage. Their breath grunted and sobbed from their lungs as they circled and stamped and parried and slowly over their naked torsos the sweat rose and lacquered their skin so that every movement was marked with the fierce ripple of sunlight running like fire over them.

Suddenly, without any eye keen enough to mark the swiftness of the blade that scored it, a crimson line of blood marked Inbar's left cheek. As suddenly again, as though the gods would match their favours, a great chip of leather flew from the edge of Baradoc's shield and the glancing blade of Inbar turned course and cut into the soft under flesh of Baradoc's sword arm. From then, as he fought, his forearm grew red with the blood that came from him to seep over his hand and the pommel of the heavy sword. But from the moment of his wounding it seemed that Baradoc, resenting even such a minor injury, lashed himself with some inner chastisement for under-valuing the prowess of his adversary. He became as a man demented with cold contempt for Inbar, and as a man exalted and so much at one with his weapon and so much in accord with the skills that had come to him over the years that fighter and sword were one whirling, probing, taunting, invulnerable singleness, and a low sigh of wonder came from the watchers as they saw plainly now and again as Inbar left himself open that the slashing edge of Baradoc's sword was turned at the last moment to strike flat-faced in brutal arrogance. Again and again, for further humiliation, Baradoc forced Inbar step by step back to the cliff's edge and held him there while all knew that he had the power and mastery now to send him toppling and spinning to the sea below with a thrust to his body. Yet, each time, Baradoc drew back and stood with sword point lowered while Inbar held his ground, shoulders heaving, his mouth gaping and sucking at the salt air to give him breath for fresh fight.

At such times Tia was forced to turn her head away to shut the sight from her until she heard the clash of swords again ring clear above the cries of the seabirds below. At her side Mawga had no power to turn away. She prayed to the gods either to give Inbar quick end or the gift of their favour to soften Baradoc's heart when Inbar finally lay at his feet.

Then as the swaying, breath-hungry Inbar, blind now to all but the craving to fight while he kept his feet, came forward in weakening attack, Baradoc gave ground until they were in the centre of the open space.

There, in a gesture of contempt, Baradoc slipped his left arm free, tossed his shield from him, and leapt forward. His sword drew two fine blood lines across the man's chest within his laggardly guard. As Inbar winced with the pain and his head jerked skyward with muscle shock, Baradoc smashed the flat of his sword down viciously across the knuckles of his opponent's fighting hand so that his weapon was beaten from it to drop at his feet. Inbar swayed, then fell to the ground and lay there, lost for the time from the world by fatigue and humiliation.

A great cry went up from the watching tribespeople. Baradoc, his body gleaming with sweat, unheedful of the blood that coursed down his sword, darkening the dull gleam of its blade, stepped forward and put his broad swordpoint to Inbar's chest above his heart. Then, for the first time did Mawga turn away to find Tia's arm wrapped around her and Tia's hand pressing her face gently to the comfort of her breast. By Tia's side, while the tribe sent up cry after cry for the kill, Arturo stood wooden-faced watching, loth to move or speak or by any sign betray a strange shame for his father who, despite his wound, must have known that he was always more than Inbar's match and had played with him like cat and mouse and who now, in easy victory, would show no mercy for this humiliated man in whom much that was good outweighed the bad.

Inbar, lying at Baradoc's feet, opened his eyes, felt the small bite of the sword's point against his chest, and saw the red-bearded muscle-taut face of Baradoc above him, the deep brown eyes still and dark as the darkest bog pool. Then with a slow sigh he said, '*Aie* . . . you have learnt fine skills and feints in your wanderings. But before you press home the sword and send me to the gods I pray one charity from you. Take my wife

Mawga into your house and treat fairly my sons who had no part in my doings.'

Looking down at him as he spoke Baradoc felt no pity for the man. No matter the companionship of their boyhood and the slavery of their youth this man would have left him to a slow death to make pickings for the carrion birds and the scavenging beasts. Behind him he heard the stir and low voices of the tribe and he said aloud so that all should hear clearly, 'Though you would have dishonoured my wife, yours shall live under my roof in peace. Though you would have killed my son when yours were well-set, your sons shall live and serve with the tribe without fear of me.'

Inbar said, 'I am content. So now, send me on my way.' As he finished speaking he closed his eyes and lay waiting.

Baradoc stood above him and his hand firmed on his sword to make the thrust true and clean. But it seemed to him then as though some power beyond his control was slowly possessing him, staying his sword hand and, against his will, invading his whole mind and body. Through their dead fathers they shared blood, he and this man, and their fathers had only known love and comradeship with one another. Then, as though not he but some other voice now lodged in him spoke, as

137

though not he moved but some inexorable will commanded him, he knew himself to raise his sword point. He stepped back from Inbar to the close-by Bada and said, 'I rest it in the hands of the gods who suddenly move within me. Let him make the cliff run, but if he have not courage for it, let him be stoned for he is not worthy of my blade.'

Almost before he had finished speaking, a great shout went up from the crowd. 'The run! The run! Let him take the run!' While they still shouted Baradoc turned away from Inbar and moved through his people, seeing for a moment Tia's face, her eyes moist with tears, and by her side Mawga who would have moved to him but was restrained by the hand of his wife. He walked alone down the cliff path, hearing the shout of voices and the stamping of feet behind him as all was prepared for Inbar's run. He climbed the stream-side path to the long hall and entering called to an old, half-crippled woman servant who served the cooking booth to bring him water and cloths to clean and dress his arm wound. As he sat and was tended by her he heard distantly a great shout arise and he knew that Inbar had taken the cliff run. Once, as a boy, he had seen a tribesman take it and go to his death. In the living memory of the tribe out of a score of men to make

138

the run no more than two or three had been known to live and escape to banishment from all the tribal lands of the Cornovii here or with their cousins in the far north of the country.

Some time later when Tia and Arturo returned to the long hall and Tia was insisting on re-dressing his wound after her own fashion with a salve of healing herbs and the whites of fresh eggs, he said, 'He took it. I heard the great shout.'

When Tia made no answer, Arturo said, 'Yes, my father. He took it. But though we waited he did not show.'

Tia, finishing his fresh bandaging, said, raising his right hand to her lips and kissing it, 'I was glad in my heart that you found that mercy for him.'

Baradoc grunted. Small mercy it had been and that never lodged knowingly in his own heart. He said, 'Where is Mawga?'

'For tonight she keeps her place with her children on the cliff to mourn Inbar. She will come here in full time.'

That night, lying on his bed, the window slit above him unboarded to let the cool air in, Arturo lay thinking about Inbar. The crowd had formed a long open lane which led to the cliff's edge. Inbar had stood at the end of it while two tribesmen stood a spear's length behind him armed with the broad-bladed fighting swords. Once a man began the run along the lane to the cliff brink from there to take the outward jump and the long drop to the sea below there was no holding back except to be overtaken by the following swordsmen and to be hacked to death. There had been no hesitation in Inbar. He had run outpacing the followers and had leapt clean and far out. Arturo could see him now . . . dropping feet first and then, as the wind took him, cart-wheeling and sprawling while the dark sea rushed up to meet him and the cliff birds rose from their roosts in their hundreds, their cries drowning the shouts of the tribe as they lined the cliff and watched. Far below as Inbar had hit the water a plume of foam had spouted and been ragged and teased to nothingness by the wind. Inbar had gone under and had not shown again. Had he shown none would have helped or hindered him. The tribal law was that he must go where sea and tide took him, but seek the shore he must not until darkness came. If the gods gave him that grace then he must pass out of the tribal lands, out of all Dumnonia and never return. But Inbar had not shown. Few men ever had, though often their broken and battered bodies had been recovered days after when the tide washed them ashore.

That night, too, as Tia lay alongside Baradoc it was long before sleep came to her as she thought of Mawga with her children keeping vigil on the clifftop. The grief which she knew clouded Mawga's mind took from her the secret joy which she, herself, had come to know in the last few days. She was with child again. Although she had waited to be certain before telling Baradoc she knew that it would be many days yet before she would speak to him. He had been as merciful as tribal law allowed him to be towards Inbar and for that she honoured him, but she wanted no telling of her joy while Mawga dwelt in the first dark shadows of loss and despair from Inbar's death.

At her side Baradoc mumbled in his sleep and then, groaning a little, clutched at his bandaged arm with one hand as the pain of his wound invaded his dreams.

During the next two years Arturo never left the tribal lands. He grew in strength and height and in longing for the life which he had known at Isca. On the few occasions when Baradoc went to see Prince Gerontius he was refused permission to go with him. There were times when he sat alone on a cliff top staring out to sea, brooding over his grievances and the dullness of life in the settlement. Even the Scotti raids had now

141

grown few and far between so that there were only rare times when, sword in hand, he could join the tribesmen in their stand on the beach at night or early morning to beat off the sea attacks. Sometimes he wondered whether Baradoc's firm refusal to allow him to go back to Isca came from his own, though never expressed, bitterness at the loss of his fighting powers. The wound which Inbar had given him which he had at first treated as of little account had refused to heal properly. It had festered and sent him into a fever for many weeks. Tia and Galpan had treated him, but when with the passing of the months the wound had finally healed it was only to reveal that the arm muscles had wasted so that he could no longer wield a heavy sword. Baradoc had made light of it, no matter what his inner feelings might be, and had trained himself to use his sword lefthanded but with only a shadow of the dexterity and skill he had known before.

A man so burdened, Arturo guessed, must always know bitterness or regret, and — he was honest enough with himself to see this — would want to keep a growing son, his heir, close to him, to fight at his right hand against the Scotti. *Aie* . . . he thought, watching a peregrine stoop from on high above the cliffs to take a rock dove, but what of the son? Each day here, except for the changes of weather and season, was the same as another and his body and mind itched for the excitements and adventure of Isca and all the lands beyond.

So it was that out of boredom and restlessness as he reached his seventeenth year Arturo began to find himself more and more in trouble with his father. He would steal out at night to meet a girl and then have to face Baradoc and an angry father. If one of the other youths spoke to him carelessly he would waste few words but take to blows and then accept stoically a beating from his father for brawling. Once he stayed away for three days high up on the moors, hunting and roaming with only the now full grown Anga for company. When he came back he stoutly maintained that he had been bewitched and held captive in a cave, and went on to invent some fanciful story which even made Baradoc secretly smile to himself. Of words and inventions to excuse or defend himself Arturo never had any lack.

One day as he sat on the cliff, brooding over his pinioned life, Tia came to him. She sat beside him, holding in her arms the girl-child, Gerta. Arturo leaned back on his elbow and stroked the warm cheek of Gerta and said, 'She has your eyes, my mother, like the blue flower that grows among the corn, and your hair, brighter than the bunting's breast. One day she will marry a great chief and men will sing about her beauty and her goodness.'

'That she be a good wife to some man is all I ask,' said Tia.

'And what do you ask for me?'

'That you pleased your father more.'

'So I would if he gave me liberty to do what I must. And if he does not give me that liberty then soon I shall take it for the gods command more obedience than any father.'

Tia laughed. 'Now you begin to talk in your riddles again.'

'No. I say only what has been said. In the cave where I was held on the moor by enchantment the gods spoke to me plainly.'

'Arto!' Tia shook her head, smiling. 'You dreamt with your belly empty from hunger.'

'No. I have few night dreams. I saw and heard. The gods have put their mark on me and, when the time comes, I must obey them.'

'And do they tell you to chase the maidens here and brawl with your companions and —'

'No.' Arturo sat up. 'They tell me only that when the sign is given I must go.'

'And what is the sign?'

144

'I shall know it when I see it.' He plucked a grass stalk and began to tickle the nose of Gerta, making her crow with pleasure. With a glance at his mother, he said, 'You do not believe me? You think I am no more than a fledgling whose growing flight feathers begin to itch and make it long to take the air? No. It is more than that. There are things for me to do.'

'What things?'

'The gods will show.' He rolled over on his back and stared at the sky. 'You have all power over my father. Ask him to give me leave to go . . . back to Isca and then when the sign comes to where the gods will.'

For a moment Tia said nothing. She was thinking of the old Christian hermit, Asimus, who had placed the sacred silver chalice in her hands and told her that one day held by the right hands it would blush crimson within to mark one — the words of Asimus rang clearly in her memory — *who is marked for great and noble duties, someone whose name will live for ever, to be praised by all true and just people* . . . Often, since he was now grown almost to manhood, she had thought of telling Arturo this but had decided against it for it would have only increased his longing to be away from the settlement. Yet now that he had begun to talk of signs from the gods himself, and she herself had once seen the chalice cup blush pink as his baby hands held it, she wondered whether there was not a duty in her to tell him. The temptation was strong in her this moment, but she suppressed it for she knew that it would only strengthen his discontent and, maybe, push him to some rashness which would bring down on him the anger of his father and the Prince of Dumnonia.

Standing and cradling Gerta in the crook of her arm, she said, 'Carry yourself patiently and keep from all wildness until the winter comes and I will speak to your father for you. But expect nothing from me if you once play the hellion or the bully or — ' her lips tightened to hide an impulse to smile, ' — seek to frolic with any maiden in the bracken.'

Arturo jumped to his feet, seized her hand and kissed it and cried, 'I shall be as patient as the plodding ox, as forbearing as a priest . . . aye, and as untouched by any maiden's charms.'

So, through the rest of that summer and autumn until the first of winter's gales pushed great curling combers far above the summer drift line on the beach, Arturo was of good behaviour; though sometimes to give ease to the pent-up longing and excess of natural spirits in him he would get leave to ride on herd duty on the moor. Then, with Anga at heel, he would set his pony to wild galloping among the tors, and sing and shout to himself like a madman. But also, too, when he was on the moor he would spend time with old Galpan and make him tell all he knew of their country and draw maps with a stick in the heath sand of all the tribal lands that divided the country. So great was his demand for knowledge that there were times when Galpan, squatting with his back against a rock in the sun, would lose his words in a mumble and drop off to sleep. Then Arturo would lie back and stare up to the sky and watch the great clouds drift in from the west and, of all the places of which Galpan had spoken, his mind would go flighting north-wards to Lindum and he would remember Daria, the black-haired daughter of Ansold the swordsmith. One day, he told himself, he would ride into Lindum and find them and Ansold should make him a sword that all men would fear. Then he would take Daria to be his wife and somewhere carve himself a domain and a kingdom so that all men should call her queen and bow their heads to him for permission to speak just as all men did to Prince Gerontius and that old windbag Ambrosius and to ailing Vortigern. *Aie*, and maybe the day would come when the long kennelled Angles, Jutes and Saxons of the East should have their days numbered and be driven into the sea. That, at least, would give his father pleasure.

* * *

On a night of hard frost when the stars seemed fixed like chips of ice in the sky and the winter grasses were so hoared with rime that the clifftops looked as though they were snow-covered, Tia spoke to Baradoc about Arturo. She had chosen her time well. That day she had told him that she was certain that she was with child again, and also a messenger had arrived from the Prince of Dumnonia calling him to a counsel at Isca.

Baradoc listened to her patiently, watching the firelight play over her face and draw sharp glints from her fair hair, and sometimes took no heed to her words as he remembered the early days of their meeting in the forest of Anderida. Their love now was mature and abiding and he knew that she spoke as she always had done from their first meeting with commonsense that came from careful consideration.

She finished, 'He has curbed his ways and shown all patience. To be a man among men he must now go from here. Take him with you to Isca and leave him with the Prince. Things are afoot there and I ask nothing about them. That you show openly now little of your old hatred of the Saxon kind means only that your anger is now appeased by some great hope for the future. Make Arturo part of that future. Although I think he talks too easily of signs and miracles which live only in his imagination, maybe that is how the gods work. But with my own eyes I saw the water in his silver bowl turn crimson as he held it.'

Baradoc smiled. 'It was but the reflection of the red sunset.'

'No. It was mid-morning, and you know so for I have told you the story often.'

'I tease you.'

'Then please me also. Take Arturo with you.'

Baradoc reached out and took her hand. 'It was already in my mind. He shall go.'

So Arturo rode to Isca with his father. But before he went Tia took him aside and told him of the silver bowl and the words of the good Asimus and how, as a babe, he had held it and the water had flushed with crimson from the blood of the Christ who had died on the cross, and she gave him the bowl to take with him since it was rightfully his.

Looking at it as he held it in his hands he

said his thanks and then added thoughtfully, 'I would it had been one of our country's gods.'

'There are many in this country who claim him as the only god.'

'So I know. But for my taste there is over-much gentleness and forbearance talked about him unless, of course — ' he gave her a quick grin, ' — he uses that as a cloak to hide his real strength and power. *Aie* . . . maybe that is it. He waits for the day when, perhaps through me, his true majesty and power shall be shown to all. Maybe, too, this is the sign the other gods have chosen to test me. Instead of Badh I have this Christos for they know that one day he will be even greater than Badh.'

When Arturo was alone he filled the bowl with water and cupped it in his hands. He held it until the silver was warmed by his palms but there was no flushing of the water. He gave a careless shrug of his shoulders, tipped the water to the ground, and then stowed the chalice away in the baggage pack he was making ready for his trip to Isca.

The Road to Corinium

Arturo sat at a bench in the tavern courtyard, elbows on the rough table, staring at the sparrows which quarrelled over a scattering of scraps which Ursula, the tavern keeper's daughter, had just thrown out of the door. Spring sunlight filtered through the leaves of the ancient elderberry tree which grew against the courtyard wall. Anga lay in the shade under the table snapping at the flies which teased his muzzle. Discontent and boredom showed plainly on Arturo's face. If anyone, he thought, had told him almost three years ago when he came here that he would be tired of Isca so soon he would have laughed in their face. He was, too, he knew, out of favour with the Prince for his occasional bouts of brawling and outspoken comments on military affairs. The Prince, he felt, with all the men and horses at his command should have moved east long ago. The minds and spirits of the cavalry men yearned for action and being denied it they grey bitter and sullen — though not so outspoken with their discontent as he.

Ursula came from the tavern and set before

him a jug of beer and a beaker. She was a dark, tall girl of his own age, her cheeks the colour of ripe spindle berries, a strong, large-breasted girl who knew how to look after herself when the young men of the Prince's household grew over bold from drinking. But with this Arturo she had never had trouble . . . more the pity for everything about him found favour with her. In his twentieth year, broad-shouldered and tall with a closely cropped beard and his pale hair fired with red glints, a young man to make any girl's mind flower with romantic fancies, he had it seemed only two loves, the ageing hound which lay at his feet and the horses of the Prince's pastures.

Arturo fumbled in his belt pouch and dropped a small silver piece on the table. It was one of the coins which the Prince had started to mint in the last year for the use of his household in Isca and the surrounding country. Because he pretended to be or really was — no man could say for sure — descended from the old Belgae people who had come to the country now held by the Atrebates and the Dumnonii and had spread north to colonize the Sabrina basin, Prince Gerontius had copied a pattern from their old coins. On one side was a barbaric design of a horse with a triple tail and on the other a

152

primitive shape of a thorn tree which the townsfolk said resembled more the skeleton of a flat fish.

As Ursula picked up the coin Arturo said, 'Bring another cup. Durstan joins me soon.'

Durstan came into the courtyard before Ursula returned with the extra beaker. Thickset, dark-haired, sharp yet smiling brown eyes deepset in his weathered face, he was dusty from exercise in the schooling pens. Of the same age as Arturo, he was much shorter and seldom given to brooding. Life for Durstan was a brightly moving pageant which gave him constant delight. It was said that where others sometimes groaned and talked in their sleep Durstan always laughed.

He sat down opposite Arturo, reached for Anga's lifted head and briefly fondled and teased the hound's ears. Then he filled the single cup and drained it in one long draught, his adam's apple working against the throat.

Putting the beaker down, he said cheerfully, 'You look like a crow in moult, Arto.'

'Who would not when life here is the same thing every day?'

'Nay, the day will come.' Durstan turned and grinned at Ursula as she brought the second beaker and pinched her bottom as she turned away, though ducking swiftly to avoid the backhand swing of her arm.

'The day has come and gone. How many times has the Prince sent the Count Ambrosius's plea-men — who came to ask for more men and horses — away with an empty answer? I think he means not to join any fighting but to make all secure here and stay within his bounds until — and then it may be too late — the fighting comes to him. Meanwhile, what do we do? We breed and break horses and drill and sharpen up our men — and then give them nothing but exercises in mock attacks and battle skills. And when we have finished with one lot we send them back to their tribes where they soon forget what they have learnt while we go to work on a new lot of levies. Do we sit here for ever, fighting imaginary battles?'

'And is this the feeling of your good father, Baradoc?'

'I know nothing of his thoughts. He keeps them as secret as does the Prince. Once it was well known that his hatred of the Saxon kind was like a fire in his belly. And now, so Leric has told me in confidence, the Prince has sent for him. He arrives in a few days, and it is in my mind he comes to take me back to the settlement.'

'Why so?'

'Because I have asked the Prince to give me

a horse in return for my services here and leave to ride to join Ambrosius — and have been refused.'

Durstan laughed. 'Then go without a horse.'

Arturo frowned at him. 'How could I? I am the son of the chief of the tribe of the Enduring Crow — '

'Now in full moult.' Durstan laughed.

'Aye, maybe. But Ambrosius would do me no favours if I arrived without horses and without men. He would do me no honour since the Prince has refused him more help to take arms against the Saxons.'

'The news is that they sit quietly, content with what they have. Why stir up the hornet's nest?'

'No Saxon sits quietly — except to let his wounds heal — when over the hill there is plunder and land to take. In this, for all his vanities, Ambrosius is right. Do you tell me that you are happy to be here, sweating and riding and shouting all day at sour-faced tribesmen who come only because the Prince has ordered their levy. Not one of them but longs to get back to his home grounds.'

Durstan shrugged his shoulders and filled his beaker. 'No, I am not happy. But I take care not to show it openly. But I am patient, where you are not. Here there is good living, horses and work, and drink and girls in the evening. When the gods will it, then things will change.'

Arturo smiled suddenly, and said, 'Sometimes the gods feign sleep, I think, to give us the chance to arrange our own lives for a while.'

Durstan was silent, but his eyes were on Arturo. He had the same discontent as his friend, but more patience and, for all his carefree manner, more caution since, where Arturo was the son of a chief who was close to the Prince, his own father was long dead and had never been more than a horse trader from neighbouring Lindinis in the country of the Durotriges. Only his eye for and skill with horses had brought him to the Prince's service.

Finally he said quietly, 'So the gods sleep. How would you have us arrange our lives?'

'We have our own arms and the right to carry them. We buy two horses at the next trading fair and then go north to Ambrosius.'

'But he would give us no welcome. This you have said.'

'Not us alone — but with men well mounted he would. Twelve men, nay six, well horsed and armed he would accept.'

'And where would we find these others and their mounts?'

Arturo sipped at his beer, and then said, 'The gods must wake some time and give us a little fortune. You think that between here and Corinium or Glevum there are none such as us waiting for the prick of comradeship to bring them forward? No horses to be found or plunder to be taken to pay for them? We shall come as no ragged band. You and I between us can train them and when Count Ambrosius sees us there will be no heart in him to turn us away. He needs fighting men.'

'The next trading fair is but three days hence. When we have these horses where do we keep them so that none knows they are ours?'

Arturo nodded to the tavern. 'Ursula's father, Durno, will stable them and say he has bought and holds them for resale. Which he often does at fair times.'

'The Prince will make trouble for him when we are gone.'

'No. He will say that we stole the mounts.'

'You speak as though you had already arranged all this with him.'

'I have, Durstan.' Arturo grinned.

'And he does this out of friendship for you alone? Or maybe you have promised to marry his daughter?'

'I make no promises, nor does he deal in them. You go to the fair with him. You pick

157

the two horses and he buys them and holds them until we are ready.'

Durstan shook his head. 'All this is wild talk, Arto. You live in a dream. With what are these horses to be bought? Here in Isca the Prince's demand for good mounts sets the barter price high.'

'I have that which will get us two good horses and also leave enough to pay Ursula's father for his trouble.' As he spoke he reached into the loose front of his tunic and brought out the silver chalice which his mother had given him. Seeing the look of astonishment on Durstan's face, he said, 'It was a gift from my mother and is mine to do as I wish with. Take it and hide it until fair day.'

Durstan picked it up and turned it about, examining it. Then whistling gently as he put it under his short cloak, he smiled at Arturo and said, 'For this we should get two good mounts and Durno be well satisfied with the barter balance.'

'Aye, he can use it as a dowry for Ursula.'

'For myself I would take her without dowry.'

'For yourself, Durstan, there will be no marriage for many years. A little love-making in the bracken or heather now and then, but no marriage. I want no men with me who are thinking always of home and wife and

158

children. Such thoughts clog the eyes and make the shield arm slow to drop to counter a sword thrust to the gut. All those who join my company must be free to fight without care except for themselves and their comrades . . . '

Durstan said nothing, but his eyes grew round and a smile faintly touched his lips. Arto was away again . . . and without benefit of a beaker too much of beer or Gaulish wine. He turned away to seek Durno and briefly found himself wondering whether for all their friendship he was wise to link himself with this venture. For all that the Prince refused at the moment to give Count Ambrosius any help there was a bond between such men that held them in smaller matters. Neither would give sanctuary in their lands to any man the other had outlawed. And for all he knew it could be that both of them let it be known that the Prince refused all help to Ambrosius purely to tempt the Saxons into some advance which, by the unexpected intervention of the Prince, would bring disaster on them. Men like Ambrosius and the Prince followed high and secret policies that few were privy to. The one thing he was sure about, no matter what Arto said, was that all that went on in Isca and its surroundings was not concerned simply with the protection of their own lands alone. The levies and tributes laid on the merchants, traders and common people were too high for that.

As he went through the tavern kitchen to find Durno, Ursula, bare-armed, was mixing flour in a great bowl on the table, her back to him. He pinched her bottom and darted through the far back door to the rear courtyard and the stables where he knew he would find Durno.

* * *

On the first day of the horse fair Durstan went with Durno and the two horses were bought. One was a black stallion of seven or eight years, well schooled, which had been shipped from Gaul two years before, and the other a grey mare, older than the stallion but smaller with a touch of dun and mealyness about the ears and muzzle which showed some not far distant moorland strain.

They were lodged in the big courtyard behind the tavern and kept there for three days. Arturo and Durstan made their preparations to leave on the night of the fourth day. Since the tavern was well outside the fortress area and on the southern side of Isca, the two had decided against the risk of riding north through the town. They would

160

go south down the river road and, when they were well clear of Isca, begin to make a wide semi-circle to the east which by daybreak would bring them around to find the north-easterly road running up to Lindinis. They left their lodgings in Ricat's house just before curfew. Not risking a noise on the stairs they dropped from the window of the room in which Tia had once been lodged to the softness of the freshly turned rose bed below. Both wore their long cavalry cloaks over their leather tunics and trews and their thick belts from which hung their swords and side daggers The weather had blessed them by bringing an evening of soft rain with a fair breeze so that there was nothing odd seeming in being abroad heavily cloaked.

But if the weather had blessed them the gods — perhaps waking from their sleep — had not. Durno had betrayed them, following the prompting of his own fears and wisdom. He was a prosperous tavern keeper, but the worm of anxiety had eaten into his mind, growing more active as with each hour he foresaw the strain that would be his when the Prince's men began to question him and the horse trader who was still in Isca. Maybe the worm would never have stirred had it not been for a remark of Durstan's when he had handed him the silver chalice.

When he had admired it Durstan had told him — there was never any subtle bridling of his tongue for his nature was too open — that it had been a gift from Lady Tia to her son. The horse trader, under questioning, would produce the chalice and he knew that the Prince, or Ricat or one of Arturo's companions would recognize it. So that morning he had gone to the castle and told all and in return had been given his part to play.

When Arturo, with Anga at his heels, and Durstan came into the darkened yard Durno was waiting for them, holding the two horses. The only light came from a pine faggoted torch thrust into a wall bracket, its flame flattening and swirling in the breeze.

Durno held the stallion while Arturo mounted. But, as Arturo settled to his mount, three men came swiftly out of the stable, all armed with drawn swords. Two of them moved to Durstan who was still unmounted and the other came swiftly to take Arturo's horse by the reins while he held his drawn sword ready to strike. His back to the others the man said, 'Sit firm, my master, and no harm comes to you. It is the Prince's order.'

As he spoke there came the first clash of swords as Durstan was backed against the stable wall and faced the two other guards. Arturo sat firm, knowing that one movement

162

to reach his sword would set his guard free to strike. Helpless he watched as Durstan, back to the wall, fought the two guards. Durstan gave no cry for help, no look towards Arturo. He was a good swordsman and for a time kept the guards at a distance, but for Arturo watching it became clear as the courtyard danced with the leaping shadows from the wall torch that the two were taking their time and enjoying themselves a while before finishing their business. If became clear too to Arturo that Durstan was to be sacrificed because he was nothing, the son of a dead horse trader, a man of no importance. Durstan was marked for death — but he, since he was Baradoc's son, would be spared, and sent back in disgrace to the tribal lands. In that moment, also, he realized that only because the Prince needed his father was he being spared. A black fury suddenly possessed him. He drew breath and shouted angrily, 'Saheer! Anga — Saheer!'

From the courtyard shadows behind the stallion which suddenly curvetted and moved nervously came Anga, his hound, like a great shadow, swifter and truer than any of the dancing torchlight shadows, rising in a long curve from the ground beneath the guard's raised sword arm to take him in the throat. Man and hound rolled to the ground together and the scream in the man's throat was brief lived.

Arturo swung the stallion round, drew his sword from under his cloak, and rode down on the two guards who turned to meet their death at the noise of his coming, one from a thrust in the back from Durstan and the other from the sweep of Arturo's blade slashing into the side of his neck.

Holding in the stallion only for time to see Durstan swing himself on to his horse, Arturo called to Anga and rode hard for the open yard gate. He went sweeping out into the rain and wind, riding fast through the maze of hovels and huts that fringed the southern side of Isca. Behind him he could hear the sound of Durstan's mount following hard.

They galloped in single file without halt or speech between them and took the road along the left bank of the river which led to the sea, but three miles from the town Arturo swung his horse off the road to the left. Dropping pace a little, he began to thread his way through a broken country of small, stream-lined valleys and over the rises of the sparsely forested hill tops to make a half circle which should take them round well to the north and east of Isca.

They both knew this country for they had ridden over it at exercise many times and on

164

their free days had hunted boar and deer here with the Prince's hounds. As he rode Arturo carried in his mind a picture of the maps which old Galpan had drawn for him in the sand and, more accurately, those which Leric treasured in the Prince's chambers limned on faded and brittle papyrus. Lindinis was forty miles from Isca on the old legionary road which ran north-east through Aquae Sulis and on to Corinium and further Glevum, and beyond, if fortune and the Prince's and Count Ambrosius's displeasure forced them to it, there were roads that ran north to Lindum and Eburacum. But there was no wisdom in taking the Lindinis to Corinium road yet for they had killed two, maybe three, of the Prince's men and the warrant against them would be passed from post to post quickly.

Pulling up to breathe their mounts, they sat side by side, the steam and sweat of horse hide strong in their nostrils, and for the first time they spoke. Their cloaks were heavy with the soft rain and their baggage rolls lashed behind their thick felt saddles hung limp and bulky like badly made hogs' puddings.

Durstan wiped his face and eyebrows with his hand and said lightly, 'Arto, my thanks.'

Arturo nodded at the ageing Anga who lay flat on the wet ground panting. 'Give me no thanks, but you owe a cut of good venison to Anga.'

'He shall have it.' Durstan sighed slowly, shook his head and went on, 'By the gods, the Prince is a fox.'

'And Durno a serpent.'

'Nay, a frightened man, tempted by silver and then made sleepless by fear. Your true villain makes a bargain and sleeps sound. There will be no welcome for us from Ambrosius.'

'That is to be tried.'

Durstan shook his head. 'No. It comes to me that there is something between the Prince and Ambrosius which they only know. Against it, you and I are nothing. The Prince would have had me killed and you sent back to your people. Now the word will be out against us. I am for death and you to go back and serve your people and stay fast within the tribal boundaries.'

'Be the Prince what he may. The gods serve those who serve themselves. If there is no welcome for us at Glevum then we will find a welcome elsewhere. But for now you are right about the Lindinis to Corinium road. We go farther east to Sorviodunum and then north through Cunetio and Durocornovium. For a time we ride by night and rest by day.'

'And draw our belts tight when our bellies grow empty.'

Arturo laughed. 'That never while we have Anga.' He pulled his horse's head around and began to move off at a walk, heading more sharply east. There was no need for hard riding or haste for they were going into a wild, thinly peopled country of few roads, a country valleyed and moulded by the headwaters of the rivers that ran south and finally found the sea between Durnovaria and Vindocladia, the main townships of the Durotriges.

★　★　★

The next morning Baradoc, long since summoned by the Prince, arrived in Isca. Tia had come with him and they were lodged in Ricat's house. He stood now in the sunlight by the open window of Gerontius's audience room and the anger in him against Arturo smouldered still. Smoke rose in the still air from the homesteads below the castle. A skein of swans came in heavy flight from the river and the jackdaws quarrelled over their nesting sites along the broken ramparts.

He turned to the Prince who, red robed, heavy-eyed, sat in his chair, one hand drooping to scratch at the head of the hound which crouched at his side.

Baradoc said, 'Withdraw the warrant. Have

167

him back here. Have them both back. They have had their lesson and will come to heel.'

The Prince shook his head. 'Two of my men are dead. The warrant stays. The word has gone to Count Ambrosius. Against Durstan I would withdraw it and he would stay kennelled. But there is no taming Arturo. Time or the gods must do that. There is no place for him in the matter we both cherish while he stays as he is.'

'And if he is killed and someone claims the head price?'

'He shall have it.'

'How then shall he free himself from the warrant?'

'Can I read his future? If there is a way, then the gods will show it. That two of my guards are dead is nothing — but too many of the young men are restless against the discipline and the long wait. Many of them have felt as Arturo did, but would have stayed content. But now they have to be gentled again to a patience which is not in their true natures. There is no place for Arturo in this matter. For you, my good Baradoc, I would do much. But two men are dead, and their price must be paid or I shall have my hands full of further trouble from their comrades.'

Baradoc's lips tightened. Behind the firmness in the Prince's voice was also the echo of arrogance. Not for the first time Baradoc found himself wondering which of the two men, Ambrosius or Gerontius, held mastery and called the tune for their followers to dance. At this moment his feeling was hard in favour of Gerontius. Ambrosius was older, and vain for the day when a campaign could be fully carried against the now quiet Saxons who, except for a few marauding, plundering bands that forayed the border lands, kept to their own enclaves in seeming peace. Ambrosius looked only for the day when his dream of wearing the purple of an emperor should come. On that vanity Gerontius played with skill, he was sure, but this Prince had his dreams too, though he babbled them to no man in the way Ambrosius did. For the time being Gerontius gave service and precedence to the older man while here in Isca and the western lands he built slowly to a strength in men and horses that could come to his call and be made ready in weeks when the time was right.

Now, once more, for the sake of his son, he said stubbornly, 'Count Ambrosius can refuse you nothing. Call back the warrant. Banish Arturo from your lands for a term, but let the Count Ambrosius know that he can take my son into service. He will weather in time and he is the kind men will follow when the years

169

have steadied him.'

Gerontius shook his head. 'No. To do so would encourage others into impatience and rashness. But for you, out of my love — aye, and also my need of you, good Baradoc — for there is only frankness between us — I make the warrant of outlaw for a term of three years. After that your Arturo, if he lives, is free to come and go and serve either here or with Ambrosius. More I cannot do.'

'And Durstan?'

'Is he then also your son from some happy chance?' The thin lips curved slightly.

'No. But he is Arturo's man, and Arturo will not accept for himself that which is denied his comrade. This I know.'

'Then Durstan shall be given the same grace.'

'I thank you, my Prince.'

Gerontius nodded and then, rising from his seat, walked across the room and took from the long table on which stood a great bowl of pink apple blossoms a cloth-wrapped bundle. He came to Baradoc and handed it to him.

'You have someone who will find Arturo?'

'Yes, my Prince. Myself.'

'Then take this to your son and give him this message. In three years' time if he brings me the bowl which is wrapped in that cloth he is a free man. Until then death waits

170

for him in my lands and those of Count Ambrosius. Also, since you are his father, you will pay the death price to the families of my two guards who were slain.'

'So shall it be.'

Baradoc slipped the wrappings from the bundle, but already he knew well what lay within, the silver Christos chalice which old Asimus had given to Tia and himself over twenty years ago.

On his return from the Prince to Ricat's lodgings where Tia waited for him. she said, 'Who will you send to find Arturo?'

'I go myself with two of my men.'

'How will you find him?'

Baradoc smiled and reaching for her hand said, 'He is my son and though wild and without sense his mind when his skin is at stake works as mine would. I shall find him.'

'The gods protect him.'

Holding down a sudden movement of bitterness, Baradoc said softly, 'Why should they not? Already he talks with them like a familiar. The otters will feed him with fish and the ravens bring him meat and the sparks from his flint will kindle wet tinder to give him fire and warmth . . . '

* * *

Two days later in the early forenoon, while Arturo and Durstan rested their horses just off the old track that ran up to the north from Sorviodunum to Cunetio, Baradoc rode up to them, leaving his two companions on the track below. Both Arturo and Durstan had long since seen the party approaching but when Durstan had looked inquiringly at Arturo he had merely smiled and shaken his head, saying, 'It is my father.'

'How can you know?'

'The gods told me as I lay awake last night with my belly rumbling from half-cooked pig meat.' But the truth was that he could pick out his father riding a horse from a far distance because of his stiff right arm which he liked to ease by thrusting it into the front of his tunic to hold it like a sling.

Durstan grinned. 'Did the gods tell you how he would find us and why?'

'They had no need. He would read my mind and know we would never take the Lindinis road. Each day it has rained and the tracks of two horses and a hound have given him our line.'

They stood at their horses' heads as Baradoc rode up to them. When he halted Arturo gave him greeting and Baradoc acknowledged it, grim-faced, with a nod. He said, 'For two who have a blood-price on

172

their heads in all the lands of Prince Gerontius and Count Ambrosius you travel leisurely.'

'A man without destination has no need of hurry, my good father. That there should be a blood-price is unjust for arms were drawn against us and we had the right to protect ourselves.'

'I am here for no dispute. The warrant runs for three years. If you are alive then you are free of the now forbidden lands.'

His face tightening with sudden stubbornness Arturo said, 'We are free of them now if we care to take the risk. There are many who live so . . . aye, both Saxon and British.'

'I give you no counsel but this. To live you will need companions. Pick them well for the blood-price is high and a temptation. Your mother's heart sorrows for you. Mine knows only stiffness. The Prince from some fancy of his own sends this.' Baradoc tossed a cloth-wrapped bundle to Arturo. 'At the end of the three years there is no pardon unless you return it, so guard it well.'

Arturo loosened the cloth and took from it the silver chalice. Then, seized by pride and deep anger, he said with deliberate contempt, 'Your Prince, my father, is a man of windy fancies and little action. He plays at war with his horses and men but sweats with fear at the

173

thought of a wound. For him even the quick buzz of a wasp is too like the feathered hiss of an arrow for comfort. Against him pompous Ambrosius is Mars himself. So speak thus to him from me — for the gods have said so — that one day he will sue me to return. Aye, the day will come when this country will cry for Arturo and his voice and that of Ambrosius shall not be the least among them in clamour.'

For a moment or two Baradoc said nothing. Emotion played within him like summer lightning. Anger, despair and bewilderment and the faint flicker of pride possessed him. There was a madness, he felt, in Arturo that made him stranger not son, and against all common-sense he wondered whether there was not some other creature inhabiting him deeply who now and then woke and rode him to wildness.

Then, in a weary voice, Baradoc said, 'If I live to see the day that Gerontius or Ambrosius sue for your return, then I shall have lived into the age of miracles. Yet, because you are my son, and for your own sake, I pray the gods to bring you to reason.' With a jerk at the reins with his left hand Baradoc wheeled his horse away and called over his shoulder, 'Until today I had a son. Now I have none.'

174

Arturo said nothing. He watched as his father rode away to join his companions on the trackway and they turned and put their horses to a steady trot, and he watched still, his face grim, until they disappeared over the smooth shoulder of the chalk downs. He knew quite clearly that he had been boastful, arrogant and vain with his father and there was no pleasure in him from it. He knew, too, that the warrants of outlawry would make life hard and dangerous for himself and Durstan. But there was no turning back now. He was in the hands of the gods who would show him no favours unless they saw him proving himself . . . *Aie*, and maybe then not give their help too readily at first for they knew too well that the early spring of courage could be the false growth of anger and pride. No, he and Durstan were with each day in peril of their lives. To survive would call for the patience of a stalking wildcat, the cunning of the hunted hill fox and the bravery of the cornered boar that savages a way to freedom through armed men and bloodlusting hounds. More too he would need — the wisdom and the exemplar of a true leader to bind men to him in loyalty and service without question so that he could make good his hastily flung vaunt that one day both the Prince and the Count Ambrosius would call for his aid as an equal and without condition. For a moment, as brief as the flick of an eyelid, he wished he were safely back in Isca, dust and dung and horse flesh smells about him as he rode to exercise or drill. Then the wish was gone, leaving a dying ripple on his mind like the fading water ring where a swallow stoops its breast to the stream in swift flight.

Behind him Durstan said quietly, 'And did the gods truly say that one day our lords of the West would sue for your return?'

Arturo turned, smiling, and shook his head. 'No. But they will.'

They turned their horses' heads northwards, moving towards the distant sanctuary of the forest and marsh lands about the headwaters and upper valley of the river Tamesis, a lawless land between the Saxon East and the sprawling enclaves of the West, a land of low-caste men of both sides who tilled their patches, tended their cattle and when times or seasons grew bare took to plundering their neighbours Here, forest and downland and meagrely cultivated valleys had been fought over again and again in the last sixty years, and was now a refuge for robbers, outlaws, traitors . . . hard, vicious men who would cut a good man's throat to rob his hen roost and then the throat of his wife when they had dishonoured her.

As the light began to pale in the western sky they came over a smooth curve of the downs and saw before them the great ring of standing henge stones which men called the Circle of the Gods. They came to it unexpectedly for neither of them knew this country except by repute, but Arturo recognized the place at once from his mother's stories of the great journey she and his father had made over twenty years ago when the country had been torn with civil strife following the ravaging westward movement of the Saxon armies.

They spread their pack blankets and made camp outside the circle and ate what remained of their cold pig meat. They lit no fire for the night was mild and they had nothing to cook and no desire to draw attention to themselves. Lying on his back, staring up at the brightening pageant of the stars, Arturo found it strange that he should be here where all those years ago his mother and father, not so old then as he was now, had made a shelter and slept. A little way from him Durstan lay with his head cushioned on Anga's flank and played on the small elder-wood pipe he always carried with him the slow, lazy tune of a stable-yard song. He broke off as Arturo suddenly stood up and began to rummage in the loose pack at his side.

Arturo took the silver chalice from the pack and then drew his dagger from his belt. When Durstan raised an eyebrow questioningly he said, 'Where we go and what we do — how long should we keep a silver bowl safe?'

'There are those who would slaughter a handful of homesteaders for it. Aye, or murder their mothers, fathers and brothers.'

'This place is under the protection of the gods. Come.'

Durstan rose to his feet and, followed by Anga, they moved between two of the great cross lintelled henges into the cricle. At the foot of one of the great stones against whose side a fallen lintel leaned half propped Arturo buried the chalice, cutting a square of turf clean from the chalky soil and then digging the hole deep with his dagger and hands. When he had finished and stamped the turf back into place Durstan said, 'The gods have it in their keeping. Would that they could name to us the day of its recovery.'

'No matter the day. It will come in good time. I ask the gods only that on the day we shall both be together.'

Arturo looked up into the star-scattered sky and Durstan smiled to himself, knowing that his companion looked for a sign from the gods of their approval. *Aie*, he thought, the smallest of shooting stars would do, or the slow drift over the stones of a pale winged owl, that bird of omens. For his friend's comfort of mind he hoped that chance would favour him. But there was no open sign from the gods.

The Villa of the Three Nymphs

From the Circle of the Gods the two went north-eastwards, travelling slowly, following the line of the old road to Cunetio but keeping some distance from it wherever they could, though they were forced to take to it to pass through the great forest to the south of Cunetio. The town, lying on the far slope above a tributary of the river Tamesis, was largely in ruins, and almost uninhabited. Only a handful of old people existed miserably among the abandoned and despoiled houses.

As they left the town and began to climb the slopes of the downs beyond it on a line which would take them to the river Tamesis, Arturo fell into a silent mood, riding ahead of Durstan with Anga at his horse's heels. Durstan made no effort to break into his companion's solitariness. There had been a time when he had sought to break through these periods of withdrawal by talking cheerfully or playing his pipe, but he knew now that there was nothing to be done but to keep silent and wait for the mood to pass. Out of loyalty to him and to save his life Arturo had altered the whole fashion of his

180

own life. He, Durstan, had little to lose for he had never had much to protect or treasure, but Arturo was the son of a chief who was close to Prince Gerontius. He was high born and, from his father's closeness to the Prince, would in time have come to rich honours and important commands in the Dumnonian army . . . though the gods knew that there had been little sign of the Prince ever wanting to commit his men to any eastward move against the Saxons. And now, Arturo was outlawed, which made him prey to any man eager for his head price. Arturo had spoken defiantly to his father, but now he was digesting his rashness — not regretting it, Durstan was sure, for when Arturo committed himself he accepted all the consequences and soon found reason or excuse or the spur of divine intervention to justify his acts. But now he was concerned with the shaping of the life that lay ahead of him and the common-sense way of dealing with it. This he must do by himself because only so would the gods still keep him in favour. A whine of self-pity grated on their ears, and a turmoil of regrets in a man's heart left them unmoved.

So they rode for a long time while the midday sun began to slide down the sky. Then, as they crested the long curving shoulder of the downs, Arturo pulled up his horse and waited for Durstan to come up with him. Without a word he pointed to the valley below where from a clump of thorn trees a billowing of thick black smoke rose into the air. Some of the land around the trees had been cleared and was now bright with the green of growing crops. As they watched an old man came stumbling and running from the thorns pursued by another man who in a few paces overtook him and felled him to the ground with one sweep of the sword he carried. The old man screamed and the noise carried faintly to them on the wind. Then the noise was gone as the swordsman thrust his blade into the man's throat.

Arturo said, 'To help others in trouble is the best way to forget one's own. Come.'

He drew his sword and began to ride fast down the valley side, and Durstan followed him. The swordsman below saw them coming and ran back into the thorn trees. With Anga racing at their heels the two swept down to the trees and, dividing, went one round each side of them to come galloping into a small hollow in which flames and smoke roared up from the burning of a brush-thatched hut. Beyond the hut two men, with their backs against a small cart, were fighting off the attack of four other men, using spears against the swords of their attackers.

As Arturo and Durstan rode into the fight from either flank the men turned to face them. They were Saxon outcasts, wearing sheepskin tunics, short trews, and armed with scramaseax swords and daggers. As Arturo bore down on his man, the Saxon began to run quickly, hoping to get under Arturo's sword and find a way to take him in the groin. Arturo wheeled away to escape the threat and flat-bladed him with a backhand sweep that sent him to the ground. One of the men who were being attacked jumped forward and thrust his spear into the man's heart. Another Saxon ran at Arturo, seeking to get under his guard and chop at the horse's forelegs to unseat him, but this time, anticipating the move, Arturo levelled his sword at the man's throat, riding hard down on him until the man was almost under his guard and then, thrusting the sword point into his throat, sent the man toppling away, screaming in a strangled death agony.

In a few moments the whole affray was over. Two of the Saxons lay dead on the ground and the others were racing fleet-footed up the downside, choosing the steepest scarp where the horses would have been hard put to follow them. Arturo watched them go, but his attention was less on them than on the significant and always to be remembered fact that he had killed his first Saxon.

From behind him a voice said, 'The good Lord give you thanks for coming to our help.'

Arturo turned as the man, one of the two whom they had rescued, finished speaking in time to see him cross himself and knew that he was one of the Christos followers. He was a young man, lightly bearded, wearing a long shirt whose ragged hem fell well below his knees. He had a pleasant, open face, the deep brown of his eyes the same colour as his long hair.

Arturo said, 'Who are you? And why do the Saxon men attack you while the crops are still in the ground?'

'My name is Marcos. And this is my brother Timo.' He nodded towards the other man who was the shorter of the two and looked also the younger. He had the same hair and eyes as his brother, but his face was solemn and tight-lipped. Marcos went on, 'He, too, would thank you, but he has no speech though he understands all that is said.' At this Timo nodded though his face remained unchanged. 'As for the Saxons . . . there is one crop they can gather all the year round. They came to take us for slaves. Many of our kind have been taken down the river and sold to the people of King Hengist.

184

They need slaves since for the barbarians the only work worthy of a man is fighting. To follow a plough and raise crops is the work of slaves and women.'

Arturo looked at the now smouldering remains of the thatched hut. 'This is your home?'

The lips twisted ruefully in the pleasant face. 'Was.'

'And the old man who lies dead beyond the thorn trees?'

'Our father.'

Arturo nodded and then said quietly, 'We remain here tonight. Go bury him.'

Marcus nodded and then turned to his brother and said, 'Come.'

Still sitting their horses Arturo and Durstan watched the two brothers go to the rough cart to which a small, sturdy pony was yoked. They took a well-worn wooden spade, its blade iron tipped, and an axe from the back of the cart and made their way to the thorn trees.

As they disappeared Durstan said, 'We have given our help. Why stay here tonight? The Saxons will not return.'

For a moment or two Arturo said nothing. He watched a kestrel wind-hovering above the downside. It had been there when they had ridden down to attack the Saxons and it was still there. It was an inhabitant of another world than the world of men; and above and beyond the world of the kestrel was the world of the gods who marked and controlled all life . . . the movement of a vole in the short grass below the kestrel and the movement of chance and time which had brought them to the aid of Marcos and Timo. But only men of small vision called it chance and time. Life was patterned more intricately than the interknotted serpentine designs of a jewel-maker's brooch and the gods ordained the pattern of men's lives.

He smiled suddenly and said, 'These two are homeless and dispossessed. So are we. A single stick breaks in the hand easily. Bind ten together and they defy the strength of most men. They owe us their lives so they would never sell ours for a handful of blood money.'

'True — but what can you offer them? This is their home. We have nothing.'

Arturo smiled. 'But we shall have, Durstan. If they agree we shall be four bound together . . . the gathering of strength begins. First men and then — ' he nodded towards the dead Saxons, ' — their arms and their clothing, though the gods know it will take hard washing to clean the stink from it. And in the cart there I see tools, hoes and axes and homesteading gear. The pony, too, is young and well-fed so they are no men to neglect their animals. With all this we need but a place to settle and soon others will come to us.'

'And you will tell them who we are and why we are without any true state?'

'Is there any enduring companionship and faith built on other than the truth?'

Durstan smiled and shook his head. 'And, so, in the end you will have a comitatus, a gathering of companions, that will grow into an army which will one day bring both Count Ambrosius and Prince Gerontius to sue for your help? You dream, Arto — but I like the dream.'

'Everything in life begins as a dream. That is how the gods speak to us. First the dream and then the reality. Believe that and work for it and then the gods are on your side. Today I have killed my first Saxon. It is a day of portent. I should ignore it at my peril. Now let us go strip the carrion there of their arms and clothes and leave them to the foxes and kites. Later I will talk to Marcos.'

They ate that evening with the two brothers who produced eggs, cheese, cabbages and two chicken from their cart, and a bronze cauldron for cooking with water that came from the still running source of a winter bourne that flowed away down the valley

187

from the edge of the thorn brake. When they were done Arturo spoke frankly to Marcos, first of the state in which he and Durstan found themselves and then of their need for comrades, of a great company of comrades which should eventually grow into a great army to be the envy and the awe of all men.

At first, Durstan noticed, the two men were plain-faced, showing nothing of their feelings, but slowly the spell of Arturo's words began to touch them. For the first time, too, Durstan found himself listening to an Arturo he had never heard before. Although he stayed quiet-voiced there slowly grew an enspelling magic about him, an undeniable display of his utter belief in the destiny which the gods spelled out for all men who were ready, without questioning, to follow the gods' beckoning and make their faith work for them so that dreams should become life. Never in all their time in Isca had he known this Arturo and never before — since there had always been an edge of amused disbelief (not frankly revealed) in him for Arturo's flights of fancy — had he found himself, as now, won over to the slow, powerful faith which Arturo had in his own destiny . . .

When Arturo had finished speaking Marcos said, 'Our father is dead and neither Timo or myself are married. Living here grows more dangerous for — ' he nodded to the distant bodies of the dead Saxons, ' — more and more small parties of the men of the South Saxons come up the river valleys since they can find neither living space nor good plundering in their own kingdom. When you arrived our cart was loaded for we were going to abandon our young crops and move away. But where we move and whom we serve rests not with me. My brother and I are as one. I go nowhere nor accept any service unless we are together. For myself I would join you.' He looked at Timo and said, 'You have heard the words of this Arturo How do you find them?'

For a moment or two Timo gave no response, but slowly the corners of his solemn mouth moved to a wry smile. Then suddenly his hands came to life, fingers touching palms, fingers playing against each other, and sometimes a hand flighting to make some expressive movement about his forehead, and all done so rapidly that to Durstan watching it seemed like a flight of two wide-winged birds steepling and playing together in some intricate courtship display. Then, abruptly, his hands collapsed and lay still on his knees.

Arturo said, 'What does he say?'

Marcos smiled. 'That we are fatherless, and you shall be our father. That we now seek a home and a new life and the bond of

189

comradeship, and that he is ready to serve you. But he says also, and so do I, that we serve only one god, while you serve many. We are Christos men and must remain so.'

Arturo answered, looking directly at Timo, 'In my camp all men shall be free to serve their gods, be they one or many. We swear but one oath. That of comradeship. He who breaks it shall himself be broken.'

So Marcos and Timo joined Arturo and Durstan. They slept that night in the open close to the warmth of the slow-dying embers which were all that remained of the hut. But Arturo lay awake for a long while before sleep came to him. Today was a beginning, but he was wise enough to know that the passage of a dream into reality would be a long slow birth. Before men could be drilled and shaped into a fighting force they must eat to live and not all the hunting skills of a band of comrades could feed them. Both Timo and Marcos were good husbandmen and with time their fighting skills could be sharpened. But it was for now as sowers and reapers of crops that he needed them most; and before any ground could be turned or cattle herded a place had to be found where they could dwell securely. From talking to Marcos he knew that only in the nomansland around the source waters of the Tamesis far south and east of Corinium and Glevum, where Count Ambrosius's mandate did not yet fully run nor the slow up-river creep of small Saxon bands yet reach, hope lay of some haven which would give them and, with the help of the gods, others to come, shelter and time to grow into an ever-increasing company.

At his side Anga growled softly, catching the scent of the marauding foxes about the bodies of the dead Saxons on the hill slope. From the thorn trees a little owl shrieked suddenly and, for a moment, the noise echoed the dying scream of the Saxon he had killed. Everything about this day, the thought as sleep began to take him, had been touched by the gods. In the years to come when the story of the companions of Arturo came to be told, the seed and growth of their renown, springing from this day, would be hailed as the work of the gods.

★ ★ ★

Two days later having crossed the weed-grown, slowly breaking-up Londinium-Calleva-Corinium road close to Durocornovium they found a ford over one of the tributaries of the Tamesis. Some miles to the north of the ford in a small valley they discovered an old abandoned Roman villa. It lay at the head of the valley, screened

191

by a new growth of trees and bushes. Its large courtyard was surrounded on the west side by the ruins of the steward's office, the kitchens and the latrines. Linking this on the north side to the east wing were the weed-and bush-covered remains of the foundations of the hot and cold bath houses. Only the east wing with the old reception room and a series of private rooms fronted by a covered corridor remained partly roofed. Here from time to time travellers or temporary settlers had made a home. Much of the villa had been pillaged for building stone and roofing tiles and all the wooden and iron piping long since taken.

At the side of the courtyard a spring — the source of the stream that ran away down the valley — broke from the steep hillside to cascade into the overflow from a circular basin of marble. This was backed by a pillared and arched shrine holding the figures of three nymphs.

Riding into the courtyard, followed by his companions, Arturo drew up and looked around him. Broken stones and burnt rafters lay about the weed-covered courtyard. The villa was hidden from the lower valley to the south by screening trees and from the north by forest land which came right up to the back of the old bath houses. As he sat on his horse, his eyes going over the litter of shattered red tiles, the rubble of broken masonry, the air full of the sound of the spring water flowing from the marble basin, he saw not the ruin before him, but the villa as it must once have been, and the thought came to him that this was the kind of dwelling place which his mother's people had once known. All over the country lay such ruins, shabby, broken and despoiled reminders of the now faded and shrunken Roman Empire. Well, empires flourished and died, but empires could spring again from their own ruins. Greatness was never dead. It languished here still and all over the country waiting for the restoring hand and the undying spirit of man to bring it back to the glory it had once known. Surely it was for this that the gods had directed his steps this way? Here was a refuge and a beginning, here was a place and a moment opened to him as a challenge from the gods. Bracing his body proudly as he sensed the truth and significance of this moment, he looked for the sign which he surely knew the gods must make him.

And the sign came. The black stallion he sat suddenly moved restlessly under him, curvetted, and called for all his strength to hold it. The horse threw up its head and neighed, setting the echoes beating back from the surrounding trees. From the trees beyond the ruined line of bath houses came an answering whinny and out into the sunlight, stepping proudly, her head turned towards them, came a white mare, neck arched and mane flowing as she broke into a gallop across the tree front and then, with another whinny, disappeared into the forest.

Calming his restless mount Arturo turned to his followers and said, 'This is our place for the goddess Epona has marked it with her sign. There is water for all our needs, wood in the forest for our fires, sun-facing ground in the valley to break for our crops and — ' he smiled, ' — a roof over our heads from the simple task of picking up these fallen tiles.'

So, the villa of the three nymphs became their home. Although it was growing late in the season they broke the ground on the south facing slope with the simple plough of Marcos and Timo and sowed the little that remained of their barley seed. They all worked through the lengthening days from morn till night re-tiling and refurbishing the east wing into living quarters and a secure stable for their mounts. At night they stood guard duty in turn, but for two months none disturbed them. Arturo and Durstan set up a small shrine at the end of the pillared corridor to Epona and welcomed with grace the homage Marcos and Timo made to their own god when they carved the Greek letters *Chi Rho* above a niche outside the door of their room and kept the niche adorned through the seasons with wild flowers. And their gods seemed to favour them for the crop lines showed quickly and they were lucky enough, or god-graced, to round up four sturdy winter lambs and a milch cow which they found straying in the forest. A hen they had brought with them, squired by a great black cock, sat a clutch of twelve eggs and brought off eight chicks. There was pasture in the valley for their hobbled horses and the rich promise of hay to be made which would see the beasts through the coming winter. In Marcos and Timo they found two men of skills which they envied. Marcos made a turf-covered charcoal burning stack in the forest and a pair of deerskin bellows to fuel and work a small forge where with heavy hammer he repaired broken plough shares and hoes and grubbing picks and mattocks. In the rubble of building material he found an old sharpening stone so that their weapons and the Saxon seax knives and scramaseax swords they had brought with them never lacked a bright keen edge. Timo, too, had his skills for he made hunting bows and knew the right wood to shape fire-hardened throwing

195

spears and he was a true herdsman maybe because his dumbness reached out and gentled the dumb animals in his care. His hands, too, with which he spoke — and whose language Arturo and Durstan began slowly to read — had a deftness with which he shaped fish hooks from bones to take trout from the broadening valley stream and horse-hair lines not only for fishing but to fashion bird-nets which they hung like a fine, faint mist between trees to take pigeons and doves and wild geese and ducks in the marsh at the far end of the valley. So, as the days passed, they moved from short to good commons and from poorly to well lodged, and their beasts and poultry thrived and the milch cow proved to be in calf which, dropping at high summer, brought milk for all and a store of cheeses to set against the coming of winter.

All this time they lived without going far from the villa. They had their own small world to make before there could be any far venturing beyond it — though there were times when the itch of impatience took Arturo like a fever and he longed for the blood stir of a more manly work than careful husbandry. When these moods came on him he would go through the forest to its limits and sit overlooking open country and the dim shape of the hills that lay to the northwest knowing that there lay Corinium and Glevum and men and horses and weapons without which the design of his life which the gods were slowly patterning could never be completed. Though it was hard for one of his nature, he schooled himself to patience, telling himself that these days were being set for him by the gods to temper the iron of his ambition.

Then, on a day when autumn was whitening the forest glades with the fronding curls of willow herb seeding and the red squirrels worked the hazel branches collecting the loose capped nuts to store against the coming winter, Arturo came into the courtyard in the early morning as his companions readied themselves for the day's work. He was dressed in rough cross-gartered trews, wore open shabby sandals on his feet and a long, belted tunic which had belonged to one of the dead Saxons, a dagger in the belt, and a short cloak caught at the throat with a rough circular brooch which Timo had found in the ruins and repaired. Over his shoulder he carried a small store of provisions in a knotted cloth.

Seeing him and marking his dress and provision sack Durstan said, smiling, 'So the time has come?'

'Yes. Last night the gods spoke to me in a dream.'

'You — who so seldom night-dream? They must have waited long for the chance. What did they say?'

'Go north to where the hills fall away into the great valley of the Sabrina. There one waits for you.'

Durstan would have smiled more broadly but he deemed it wise, sensing Arturo's stiff mood, to keep his face unmoved.

'Just that?'

'No more.'

'You take your horse?'

'No. Nor Anga.'

Marcos said. 'There is a price on your head and men may recognize you.'

'No. I ride no horse. I dress like a peasant. Who is to recognize Arturo, son of Baradoc of the tribe of the Enduring Crow and a troop leader in Prince Gerontius's cavalry? Besides, I fancy that after all these months men will long have marked us as dead or murdered by Saxons. There will be none who watch still with hawk-eyes for Arturo and the chance of blood money.'

Timo stirred and looking at Arturo moved his long thin hands in a brief flutter of his finger play.

Arturo, his mood changing suddenly,

laughed and said, 'Good comrade Timo, if by ill-fate I am killed then that is the will of the gods and this place will be yours for the grace of a prayer for my soul. But that time is not for now since the gods in my dreams, though they spoke no more than I have said, held up before my eyes a red banner on which was blazoned a white horse and the white horse carried a rider, fully armed and capped with a war helmet, and the face of the man was my own face. Would they have shown me this if I am to die in the near future?'

Marcos said, 'There is no doubt in my mind that your gods have spoken so and shown you this sign. But you go into bad country. So I tell you this. If he still lives my father's brother, Paulus, who is a carpenter, settled in Corinium. He lives near the east gate. If you should need help or shelter go to him and say that you are the good comrade of Marcos and Timo, the children of his brother. You will not be turned from his door.'

Arturo nodded. 'This I will remember.' He bent and fondled the ears of Anga who stood at his feet, then gave the hound a word of command. Anga hesitated and then moved from him and went to Durstan. With a farewell movement of his hand Arturo turned and made for the forest boundary beyond the west wing of the villa. As Arturo disappeared into the trees Durstan, with a shrug of his shoulders, turned and followed the others who were already moving to their work.

When he caught up with them Marcos said, 'I have nothing but honour and gratitude to Arturo — but do you believe the gods truly speak to him and show him their signs?'

Durstan shrugged his shoulders. 'You saw the white horse when we first came here?'

'Aye, and have seen the mare since for often she grazes in the lower valley. She is as wild as a hawk and no man could come near her. What has she to do with the gods?'

'Does your god never give you a sign?'

'Yes, but it is nothing that the eye can see. When I pray I feel him move in my heart and thoughts, and I feel his strength comforting my weakness.'

'From each god his own way of revelation. And for each man his own way of marking the shadow which his god casts.'

For a moment or two Marcos was silent. Then casually, he said, 'A white horse on a red banner. White and red, those are the true colours of Christos.' He nodded to the villa. 'It would look well flying from the roof-top yonder.'

'But better carried before a well-armed host.'

Arturo travelled for five days without haste, and each day he moved into more settled country where men worked their fields and tended their herds in peace. Seeing him come, armed only with a dagger and poorly dressed, he was given welcome and food and shelter for the night. None asked him from whence he came or where he was going for if a man made no move to explain himself then all knew that he remained silent out of good reason.

He passed through the deep valleyed country well south-west of Corinium and on the morning of the fifth day came out of a thick wood that covered a valley ridge to find before him a great fall in the land. The ridge side plunged steeply away from him, dropping almost sheer in places to a wide plain far below. Through the clear air of the autumn day a vast panorama was spread before him and he saw it as though from the eyes of an idling falcon borne up on a steady air current. Beyond the plain ran the broad, snaking ribbon of the Sabrina river in full tide, the sun taking the silver of its waters with a keenness which hurt the eyes. Far to the north-east it ran until it was lost in the encroaching folds of the long ridge line on which he stood. To the south-west it broadened slowly and was swallowed by the sun sparkle from the waters of the sea into which it ran. Beyond it, purple and mist-hazed, rose the hills and mountains of Cymru and Demetae. He stood for a while, letting his eyes rove over the great spread of river and country, seeing clearly in his mind the sand maps drawn by old Galpan and drunken Leric. Beyond the river lay Venta and the Isca of the Silures, and far away up the river on his right hand, hidden from his sight, the Sabrina waters came down through Glevum. For the first time, since he now saw it as a high-pitched falcon would see it, he became aware of the vastness of his land, and the immensity moved him, drying his throat and waking an unnameable stir of emotion in him. All this, and more and more to the north and the east was Britain . . . a country torn and divided by the quarrelling of the tribes of his own kind, harried by Scotti and Pictish raiders, and threatened by the slow, barbarian march of the Saxon warriors and settlers from the West.

He sat down and began to munch on one of the wild apples he had gathered in the wood, melding their sharpness with goat's cheese and flat bread which he had bought from a homesteader with one of the silver coins from his still-remaining store of Prince Gerontius's money. As he ate he was slowly seized with a dullness of mind and lack of spirit, rare for him, and which he would never have confessed to any man. For the truth was that now he was here he knew that he had come, not at the bidding of the gods, but because he had girded at the tedium which had grown with him week by week at the villa of the three nymphs. Homesteading gave him no joy, no fulfilment. When he had lain awake there at night there had been a confusion in his mind which had made it easy for him to imagine, or to wish, that the gods would speak to him or make some sign that would give him their sanction to leave his comrades. But the truth, sharp in him now, was that he had gone a-wandering for his own pleasure and relief. If the gods held any favour for him, then truly it would be a miracle if watching him they should trick time and chance and make real what was only a self-wrought fancy in his mind. True, he had dreamt of the white horse on the red banner. But such a dream could easily have arisen from his longing for warlike action.

With a sudden spate of self-disgust he threw his apple core out into space and heard the sharp click of bursting seed-pods as it fell into a broom bush. As he reached for another apple, a long shadow fell across the grass at his side. He looked round to see a short, strongly built man, dark-eyed and with long black hair, who wore a rough, long brown robe girdled with a thin belt of plaited leather thongs and carried a well-seasoned ash stave.

The man smiled at him and said, 'Greetings. 'Tis a long time since we last saw one another.'

Frowning slightly Arturo said, 'We know one another?'

The man sat down, placed his stave across his knees and reached out for one of Arturo's apples. 'I know you. I knew you from the time of your birth until I last saw you as a bare-bottomed infant splashing in the sand at my feet on the day I left your mother and your people. My name is Merlin.'

'Merlin? Ah, yes, of course. My mother often spoke of you. You are the — ' Arturo broke off for fear of offending the man.

'I am the ageless, the wandering one. Or so men say. But then it is seldom that I agree with what men say. And what do you do, brooding here like an eagle on its eyrie?'

Arturo hesitated for a moment or two. He had heard many tales of this man, knew too that he had been overkind to his mother and had brought her and himself as a babe from Caer Sibli to the settlement of the people of the Enduring Crow. But mostly he knew that it was said that Merlin spoke like a brother to the gods.

He said bluntly, 'I was outlawed with a companion by the Prince of Dumnonia with whose cavalry I served. I have been hiding for many weeks in a small homestead with my companions — but my feet began to itch for better occupation than following the plough and my eyes to smart for sight of new country. To the others I lied that the gods had told me to come here where I should meet a man who waited for me.'

'And what will you say when you return to them?'

Arturo smiled. 'No doubt I shall lie again, though what the lie will be must rest unknown until the moment comes.'

Merlin laughed. 'At least your frankness should please the gods. You could say, of course, that you had met me.' He reached out, broke a piece from Arturo's cheese round, put it in his mouth, and mumbled as he chewed, 'And that I had a message from the gods for you — which I have not, of course. Nor am I here by their direction. Our meeting is pure happenchance. I am on my way to Glevum from Aquae Sulis and often take this way along the ridge. So you are young Arturo who sent message to the Prince

Gerontius and the Count Ambrosius that one day they would sue for your return?'

'How do you know that?'

'The message was given in full counsel by your father. Many heard it and the tongues of man wag faster than any woman's when a Prince is so defied that he hurls a full wine cup from him in anger at the words. The discomfort of the great is ever a delight to the small. From Dumnonian Isca to Deva and Lindum the story runs . . . aye, and to Saxon Cantawarra and the island of Tanatus to make the barbarians roar with laughter over their rude mead. My young captain Arturo, the country knows you and — ' he stood up and brushed cheese crumbs from his robe, ' — now for any who pledges beyond his performance call it an Arto promise — '.

'Then the gods damn them!' Arturo was quick on his feet, standing now, his face stiff with anger. 'They shall see the truth of it one day.'

Merlin shrugged his shoulders. 'Such a truth would not be unwelcome to many. Now cool the fire of your anger. There is a foolishness about your boast that warns me, and for this I give you my own message — for sadly,' his mouth moved to a mock mournful twist, 'I am out of humour with the gods this long time and they favour me with little of their dispositions. You know the Roman tongue?'

'At my mother's knee and by the hammering of old Leric's fist between my shoulder blades.'

'Then know you suffer not alone from acedia. There are many such in the growing army of Count Ambrosius, and none more bored than in the Sabrina cavalry wing which he has stationed near Corinium. Many there grow stale with drills and manoeuvres and might be tempted from their barracks and the taverns of Corinium with an Arto promise — even if at first the promise showed no more warlike gain than petty raiding against the Saxons down the Tamesis. But remember this, speak not your heart to any man until you have proved him.'

'And how should I do that?'

'If you know not that, then you are not one to command men. Now, I thank you for the apple and cheese. I would have thanked you more had you carried a wine skin. The gods be with you.'

As he turned to go Arturo said, 'It is in my mind, for all your talk, that the gods did indeed send you to me. How else could you have recognized me whom you last saw as an infant just able to stand and walk?'

Merlin smiled. 'You could have answered

that for yourself were your mind not idle. You sprawl on the grass cuddling your cheese, your tunic flung wide open to cool yourself from walking. Need I say more since I have seen you naked many times in your mother's arms?'

Arturo smiled ruefully, and said, 'No.' With one hand he rubbed the strawberry coloured birthmark below his left ribs. Then with a frank, friendly smile, he went on, 'I thank you for chiding me. Your words will stay with me.'

He stood for a long while watching the receding figure of Merlin move away along the tree-edged ridge. When the man was finally lost to sight he turned and gathered up his gear. A glance at the westering sun gave him the direction he wanted and he set out, following Merlin's path until he should be clear of the forest edge and could make his way across country to Corinium in the east.

He reached Corinium on the evening of the next day while there was still a couple of hours of daylight left. The streets were crowded with people and the troops from the nearby camp. Market booths and stalls were open and the rutted roads were busy with the carts of country folk and packhorse-trains carrying army supplies. As he made his way towards the east gate he was with other people pressed back to make way for a patrol of cavalry moving through the city. A young man who led the party was wearing a leather war helmet, plumed with dyed horse-hair, a bronze plated cuirass taking the dying sunset light dully, knee-length boots, and was armed with a scabbarded broad sword. About his neck was knotted a blue scarf with its ends swinging freely to the motion of his horse, and the similarly coloured scarves were worn by all the men in the patrol and, too, by the dismounted cavalry men who walked the streets on leave. Arturo had no need to ask about the scarves for he knew that they were the mark of the men of the Sabrina wing of Count Ambrosius's army. He decided that when his day came all the men of his army should wear the white and red scarves of the banner he had seen in his dream . . .

A small boy, his skin as brown as sun-dried earth, wearing only a ragged pair of short trews, directed him to the house of Paulus the carpenter. It was a dwelling place that stood with its back hard against a section of the ruined city wall and was no more than one large living room and cooking quarters with a rough ladder that led to a communal bedroom above. The workshop was a faggot-thatched open shed to one side of the house.

He introduced himself to Paulus, a white-haired man in his sixties, wearing a leather working apron, the stubble of his face hoared with sawdust and all about him the sweet smell of worked wood and shavings, and told him that he came on the urging of Marcos and Timo. He was accepted at once and with few questions. Paulus lived by himself, but a neighbour's wife came in once a day and cooked a meal for him in the evening. The old man made a place for him at the table and while they ate questioned him about the welfare of his nephews. When he heard of the death of his brother at the hands of the Saxons, he said, 'God rest his soul.'

Arturo said, 'You, too, are of the Christos people?'

'Yes, and there are many in this city. It is said, too, that Count Ambrosius is one of us, but I doubt it more than pretence for the Count is ready to be all things to all people so long as they will serve his ends.'

'And those ends?'

Paulus paused from dipping a bread crust into his stew and said, 'He dreams of a conquest of all Britain with himself wearing the purple of emperor.'

'And what is wrong with such a dream?'

Paulus shrugged his shoulders, poured ale into Arturo's cup and said, 'Nothing — except the man who dreams it.'

'Men say that openly here?'

'Go into any tavern or drinking court and you will, as the night lengthens, hear many of his own soldiers and cavalrymen say it. They long for action and he gives them drills and marches and mock battle — and now that autumn is well with us it is clear that there can be no campaigning this year. This winter many men will drift from him back to their homes. It is two years since the army marched east and south. Two years — and that is a long time for warriors to content themselves with sword and spear drill. Go into the country to the villas and the farms and you will hear strong words against Count Ambrosius. Although the land is rich and is tilled in peace the crop levies to feed his men are high. I ask nothing of your business here, but take heed of your speech in this city. In drink a soldier speaks freely and nothing is done. But if a freeman, craftsman, or a farmer says aught that same soldier will whip his back bleeding raw. You like this stew? 'Tis hare . . . I have a friend who passes through often who always brings some fine gift . . . So, my brother Amos is dead, uh? And by a barbarian. Thank god they come not this way. Hare stew, I like it well. But not so well as venison — though 'tis seldom my friend brings that. Such game gets rarer the longer the army stays . . . ' The old man suddenly

211

broke off, leaned back and smiled, saying, 'I ask your forgiveness. I rattle away like a gossip from the pleasure of company for I am much alone.'

Arturo raised his cup to the old man and said, 'Talk, my friend, for there is much that I would like to know about this place and the cavalrymen here.'

Chuckling with pleasure Paulus drank with Arturo and began to talk again, never flagging, but always ready to take a new line when Arturo put a question to him.

That night Arturo lay long awake while the old man snored gently in his cot. He was in Corinium and here, and in the country around, were cavalrymen, many of them owning their own mounts, who longed for action. With money or rich barter men and horses could be bought to his side. But he had nothing to offer except a share in his dream to create a company whose fame and success would eventually bring the Prince Gerontius and Count Ambrosius to sue for his help. How many men, he wondered, would have the vision to see what he dreamed and for the sake of it go into the wilderness with him? Not many. *Aie*, probably not any — unless he found a way to play on their boredom and trap their minds with the promise of high rewards. Few men would accept the reward of simple comradeship. That was a growth which must come later. He groaned gently to himself. If ever a man needed the help of the gods to direct him he was that man.

The next morning he left Paulus to his work and wandered abroad in the city. It was market day and the old ruined Roman forum was crowded with stalls and benches on which vegetables, game and meat, crockery and pots and pans, and woollen cloths and belts and buckles and leather goods were laid out for sale. Wandering through the crowd Arturo noticed that there were few army men about. Most of them were held at stables and cavalry drills until late in the afternoon . . . the same training exercises which he, as a troop commander, had known endlessly at Isca.

Walking now from stall to stall it was clear to see that there was more for sale here, and a richer variety of goods, than had ever appeared in the Isca markets. The penned poultry and cattle were plump, the cloths and fabrics rich, and much of the pottery and bronze and iron pans and cauldrons of a finer work than the people of Dumnonia knew. Count Ambrosius, whose writ ran from the Sabrina plains north to Glevum and beyond to Deva, held in his power a fat and rich land to which tradesmen and craftsmen flocked and where farmers and settlers worked their ground and tended their cattle in peace. Maybe because of all this the Count had grown over content and was loath to stir away — but among his men there had to be those who suffered from a restlessness and a lust for war and action which full bellies could not assuage.

As he turned from a stall hung with loops of gaily coloured clay beads his eye was caught by the bright blue of a long, belted robe worn by a young woman who worked her way through the crowd, a straw-plaited basket hanging from the crook of her right elbow. A stallholder shouted some pleasantry to her and as she turned her head to reply her eyes were briefly met by Arturo's. For a moment or two, like the sudden gleam of sun between racing clouds, she smiled at him, a warm, friendly and, he imagined, a beckoning smile. Meeting it the whole purpose of his business here in Corinium was reft from him. The sharp thought went through him that it was long since he had held an Iscan girl in his arms, or felt the warmth of full red lips beneath his own. Hardly aware that sudden impulse was moving him to action, he moved forward through the crowd to follow the young woman. But at this moment the market throng pressed back upon him, trapping him against the side of a stall, to make ground for the passage of a herd of cattle being driven to the slaughterhouse on the far side of the Forum.

When he stepped free from the press at last the young woman had gone and he made no attempt to search for her. He needed no woman. Men and horses were his need. He turned away towards the north gate and left the city. A little way along the Glevum road he climbed a grassy knoll crested with two beech trees and sat down, looking across at the camp of the Sabrina cavalry wing through the air which was hazed with the dust kicked up by three troops of horse at drill. He was angry with himself for even momentarily being stirred by the sight of a pretty face. The gods had brought him here for matters of far higher import.

Horses and Men

Arturo sat on his knoll for over an hour watching the cavalry drills. He had heard that Count Ambrosius had formed his cavalry in the old Roman fashion into wings — the Roman *alae* — of sixteen troops with each troop holding thirty-two men and had even named the commander of a wing in the old style of Praefectus. From the size of the camp and the number of mounted men drilling he guessed that this Sabrina Wing was no ordinary *ala* of around five hundred strong. This seemed more like an Ala Milliaria of twenty-four troops each of forty-two men — around a thousand men in all — and no doubt commanded by a Tribunus. Maybe it was yet far from its full complement of men and horses, but it was a larger force by far than any that Prince Gerontius could muster. Clearly the ambitions of the Count ran high and matched his pride in the ancestry he claimed for himself. He was a man, full of nostalgia for the great days of past Roman glory, of Roman blood himself (though that was common enough now in this country), who longed to restore the glory of the old

216

Empire. A hopeless dream, thought Arturo
— but was it any more hopeless than his
own?

Tired of watching the cavalry and over-
warm under the midday sun, he slipped off
his tunic, made a pillow with it for his head,
and lay back, staring up at the sky. Men there
must be, he thought, drilling out there on the
plain who longed for real not mock action
and must know that it could not come this
year for it was far too late for campaigning. To
tempt any of them to his side he had nothing
to offer. Watching the small clouds slide
across the blue his face muscles tautened with
frustration. Now, if ever before, he needed
help from the gods or some sign from them
that there should be no death of hope. He
shut his eyes and silently called on them,
willing them to hear him, his teeth grinding
with his fervour as he mutely named them
. . . Epona, Nodens, Coventina, great Dis,
father of all . . . great gods and small gods he
named, battle gods and household gods
. . . Badh and his brothers, and was tempted
to call, too, to the Roman gods for surely they
held lien and interest still in this land, but
turned away from the thought for fear of
offending his own native deities.

He was brought from his silent, almost
rigid fervour, by the sound of horses' hooves

behind him. He sat up to see a man riding one pony and leading another come up the knoll and, after a brief nod to him, dismount and hitch the ponies to a beech branch.

He came across to Arturo carrying a drinking skin and sat down by him. Without a word he drew the stopper from the skin, drank, wiped his lips with the back of his hand then the mouth of the skin and handed it to Arturo saying, 'A gift is the best greeting. Drink.'

Arturo took the skin and drank. Expecting mead he found that it was wine. Handing the skin back he said, 'I thank you.' Then prompted by a wry sense of humour, he went on, mocking his own newly passed fervour, 'If you bring a message from the gods then I will give you double thanks.'

For a moment or two the man eyed him without replying. He was small of stature with a pear-shaped face, brown as a ripe chestnut and, as Arturo had noticed when he had walked across to him, bow-legged as though he had come into this world riding a pony and had seldom set foot on ground since. His eyes were as dark as polished sloes, his hair darker and tightly curled, his cheeks cleft with deep wrinkles and his thin lips, at this moment, drawn back tight over firm white teeth in an amused, houndish smile. Driving the wineskin stopper home with a quick smack of his palm, he said, 'And what kind of message wants young Arturo, son of the chief of the tribe of the Enduring Crow?' He nodded at Arturo's bare shoulder as he spoke. 'Nay, look not surprised. You would not know me, but many a time I have seen you at drill in the river meadow below Isca town. And many a mount your old friend, Master Ricat, has bought from me.'

Arturo pointed a finger at the long knife which the man wore in the belt about his hide surcoat and said, 'What charity stayed your hand as I drank? You could have slit my throat and claimed my blood-price.'

'I deal in horses, not men's lives, no matter the price. If I come from the gods then they send me without my knowledge. If they do, I thank them because it pleases me to meet one who has spoken with open challenge to Count Ambrosius and Prince Gerontius for they have often had my back laid thick with weals for horse stealing, and a few other trivial matters. But you would do well when you take the sun to keep your tribal sign and the birthmark below your ribs hidden.'

Ignoring this, Arturo asked, 'What do men call you?'

The man shrugged his shoulders. 'A hundred names, mostly vile. But seldom my own, which is Volpax.'

'Then Master Volpax — and I have indeed heard of you — the gods sent you. Knowing or unknowing by you makes no matter. They know I need horses.' He nodded towards the beech trees. 'Not mixed breed ponies like your dun-coloured mare there with a black tail.'

'You shame my mare. On a long march she would outlast many of those overstuffed, over-cosseted cavalry horses out there.' He nodded to the plain where the last of the dust was settling as the troops rode away to quarters. 'She will go six days on a handful of corn and her own foraging and meet the seventh fresh as the day she started. So you need horses? Aye, from Deva down to Isca the whole country knows that. Have you found some silver hoard that you can afford to buy them?'

'We have no need to buy them.'

'We?' Volpax's eyes widened and he grinned wolfishly.

Arturo smiled. 'The gods have sent you to an honest and reliable partner. There are hundreds of horses quartered around the barracks of the Sabrina Wing. You could work alone and take a few, or you could work with some rogue helper who would betray you when you trimmed his share — which you would.'

'It is always a temptation, I agree.'

'With me it would be different. I can betray no man without betraying myself. And we would draw no daggers over sharing for out of every three horses we take I would keep one. Remember this, too. I know a horse from an overstuffed hay bag. And, as you can, I can talk their soft language at night to gentle them and cut their hobbles or head ropes while you ride a mare in season down the lines for them to follow.'

Volpax chuckled. 'You know the tricks.'

'Why not. You probably played them at Isca against us and then sold the mounts to Count Ambrosius, only to do the same thing to him and sell them back to Prince Gerontius or some northern chief. I say, although you do not know it, that the gods have sent you.'

Volpax pursed his lips, his eyes hooding with thought and then said, 'I would not quarrel with that — for it is a sign of distinction and I gladly take your word for it. But if the gods have sent me it is beyond their power to make up my mind for me. I will think on what you say.' He stood up, the wineskin swinging from his left hand. 'You stay in Corinium?'

'I do. At the house of Paulus the carpenter.'

Volpax shook his head. 'You are too open — even with me. There is a blood-price on your head. Every man knows the taunt you have flung at Gerontius and Count Ambrosius.'

'I am open with you alone — for the gods sent you.'

'Let us from now keep the gods out of this. I have an affair which takes me to Glevum. I shall pass this way again in three days' time. Be here then at midday and I will give you an answer. Until then keep well away from this place. There are those among the blue-scarfed Sabrina men who have sharp eyes for a loitering stranger.'

'You have my promise. And I thank you for your answer, Master Volpax.'

For a moment Volpax seemed on the point of protest. Then with a slow shake of his head he turned and went to his ponies. But as he mounted the dun, he called, 'Stay close to Master Paulus. Keep away from the drinking places and wenches, and forget that you ever met me or heard my name, comrade Arturo.'

Arturo sat and watched him ride away down the Glevum road. He could have wished to be going with him for he would like to have seen the city. Then he rose and began to make his way back to Corinium. The gods were with him. There was no doubt of that. One horse in three. That meant stealing sixty to gain twenty mounts. And three hundred to have a hundred . . . *Aie*, but that was looking too far ahead. All great matters began small. Twenty mounts and then twenty men . . . almost a troop, drilled and hardened for action, red-scarfed and white-bannered and the nomansland eastwards beyond the villa of the three nymphs waiting to be claimed and ordered and tribute gladly paid for the security from up-river creeping Saxon bands which he would give to all honest folk who now lived in fear.

He began to whistle gently to himself. The gods had truly marked him. But for all that, they were stern and devious masters. Had they not momentarily tempted him that morning with a glimpse of a young woman in blue? He could have pressed after and searched for her and never have met Master Volpax. No, until he came again to the beech knoll in three days' time he would keep close to old Paulus.

★ ★ ★

For the rest of that day and the one following Arturo stayed close to old Paulus and never went beyond the workyard where the man was content to have him either helping or sitting on a stool as he worked and gossiped. Towards sunset on the evening of the second

223

day, while Arturo helped Paulus to stack a pile of rough-cut planks which had been ordered by one of the market officials for the repair of broken stalls, a voice from behind them called, 'Master Paulus!'

Arturo and Paulus turned. Standing in the open front of the thatched shed was a young woman and one glance told Arturo that it was the girl in the blue robe whom he had seen a few days before in the market. Unaware almost that he did it, Arturo ran his fingers through his sweat-tousled hair and then drew his open tunic about him and belted it.

'Mistress,' said Paulus shuffling past Arturo, 'if you come with a complaint from your father about his tool racks tell him that they will soon be ready.'

The young woman shook her head and said, 'He sends no complaint. But a summons to a meeting of the city's tradesmen and craftworkers called now because of a new demand by the Count's warden to raise the levy once again on the free work you and my father and all honest craftsmen must give to the cavalry camp.' She smiled. 'They meet now and will talk until dark and drinking time and it will all come to nought.'

'Aye, that is so. And my supper will be ruined with keeping, and I shall wake with a sore head in the morning from drinking. So be it.' He shrugged his shoulders and moved away to his house.

But when he had gone the young woman still stood her ground, her dark red lips curved in an almost mocking smile which, for some reason that baffled him, suddenly irritated Arturo so that he said, ignoring courtesy and ceremony, 'Some mornings since you smiled at me in the market place, and now you stand as though there was something you expected from me.'

Her smile broadened, and she said, 'And why should I not? Or are your promises like blowing thistledown to be carried away and lost? Have you forgotten then that once you said to me that one day you would come and woo me; that we should lie in the long grass, listen to the golden birds sing and drink the new wine? That seeking me you would ask only for one who has eyes like the blue bellflower, lips redder than the thorn berry and hair like . . . *Aie*, now that escapes me — '

'Like polished black serpentine,' said Arturo suddenly, for now memory was back with him like the sudden sweep of light from the sun breaking free of dark clouds.

'True, that was it. So why should I not smile at you in the market place — since I would know your face anywhere, or so I thought until you greeted my smile with a face as blank as a mouse-stuffed owl's? But now I know you as all folk who have heard the blood-price called against you would know you with your tunic drawn back to show your tribal tattoo and birthmark. Would you, too, have me immodest enough to lift my robe and show you the swallow's gorge mark on my thigh?'

'There is no need,' said Arturo quickly, recovering from his confusion. 'I would have known you at any time except this when — as you must know — there are other matters which bear heavily on me. You are Daria, daughter of Ansold the sword-smith. But it was to Lindum, not Corinium, that you were travelling.'

'True — but my father changed his mind when he saw the work which was here with Count Ambrosius's army. As for the matters which weigh heavily on your mind, I think you give them too little thought. You are a fool to work with old Paulus half naked for all to see your marks and so make a high blood-price an easy picking for any man who passes. Such heedlessness will never bring you the years to make good your boast to Gerontius and Count Ambrosius. Perhaps those who called that an Arto promise were wiser than I thought. None will ever sue you to come with your army to their aid. And, too, without a head how will you ever lie in the long grass and hear the birds sing and drink the new wine?'

As she finished speaking she began to turn away, but Arturo, anger rising in him, stepped forward and held her by the arm and said pugnaciously, 'You do right to mock me. But you do wrong to taunt me with talk of empty promises. They shall sue me for help for the gods have ordained it.'

Daria frowned down at the hand which held her arm and, as Arturo released her, she said, 'And the golden birds and the new wine — when shall they be heard and drunk?'

Arturo smiled. 'There will be time and place for them. You think you stand here and talk to me out of chance? Nay, even though I had forgotten you the gods had not. I take my shame for a misty memory, and accept your chiding. But it is written that on the day of my triumph you shall come riding into Glevum with me on a white mare wearing a cloak of scarlet with a lining of blue silk and about your waist a golden belt with a clasp of two singing birds. And when Count Ambrosius comes out to greet us he shall hand to you a silver goblet full of new wine, and then — '

'And then, and then,' Daria interrupted

him, mockingly, 'will be the day when pigs shall be flying and the salmon coming up the Sabrina shall wriggle ashore, their mouths full of sea pearls to lay at my feet. But for now, be wise — keep your tunic drawn and your god dreams to yourself.'

Without other word or look she turned from him and walked away. Arturo watched her go, knowing now that he would never again lose her from his mind, and wondering how he ever could have forgotten her and that rain-drenched day on the high moors when she had slipped a quick hand to the dagger in the garter sheath beneath her tunic.

He lay awake that night, long after old Paulus had come stumbling back from his meeting and the drinking which had followed it, thinking about her, knowing that he would like to seek her out at her father's house but firming himself not to do so. The gods had sent her to him and they would mark the time when either he or she would have their feet set true on the paths that led to a meeting place. *Aie* . . . and for the future he really would keep his tunic close-belted.

★ ★ ★

At noon on the following day Arturo waited for Volpax under the trees on the little knoll that overlooked the cavalry training grounds. When he arrived it was as before, riding the dun pony and leading another. He came over to Arturo carrying his wineskin and a knotted cloth in which were six cold roasted quails.

He set the food between them and this time offered the wineskin first to Arturo and began talking as though there had never been any break in their conversation.

'The affair is settled. I have a friend who keeps cattle in a valley far to the south of Corinium. He will lodge and find fodder for up to thirty horses. No more. We take no more than four horses a night — and that at long intervals — and never travel the same path to my friend's valley. Nor when the ground is soft from rain to show the hoof marks. When we have the thirty, you take your ten and I take my twenty and we go our own ways. When you have the men and need for more mounts all you have to do is to pass a message to my friend and I will come to you.'

'And how will I travel ten horses back to my homestead?'

Volpax smiled wolfishly, flicked his hand at a bluebottle which buzzed above a roasted quail, and said, 'That, Prince Arturo — for so I call you to give you heart — is your problem. Our bargain is for horses. Also from

229

today you see no more of Corinium. We stay together, not from lack of trust on my part — but for each other's safety.' He lifted the wineskin and drank deeply.

Speaking almost to himself, Arturo said, 'We shall steal our horses. Would that it were as easy to steal men.'

Rubbing a hand over his wine-wet lips Volpax shook his head, and then, grinning, said, 'You could — since you are so close to them — ask the gods for their help. If they remain silent then you must find your own way. You and I are in the business of horses. No more. But this I say — once it is known that you need men and can promise them what they want they will find a way to you.'

Arturo lay back on the grass, staring at the slow march of the heavy clouds above, and felt a heaviness, too, in his heart. Now that the moment was on him for action he suddenly felt helpless and undecided and astray. So far he had done no more than make Arto promises. Now was the beginning of the time when, gods or no gods, he had to work and scheme and make a beginning to bring to truth the words and dreams which had comforted him for so long. He sighed suddenly. 'Well, tis with one step after another that a long march is made. We will take the horses and then I will think about the men.'

'So be it.' Volpax flung a picked quail carcass into the grass. 'Be here at nightfall, fair weather or foul, and we will walk around the camp. Then tomorrow night, if the weather is kind, we will take our first horses. For now you can go for the last time to Corinium. Tell Paulus you travel back to your friends. Then, without his knowing, steal charcoal from his fire pot to blacken your face and hands for tonight.' He stood up, taking the wineskin and went on, 'I leave you the rest of the quails. But stay not overlong here. When you come back tonight give me a curlew's whistle three times. If I do not answer, then you must find some other to help you with mounts.'

Frowning, Arturo asked, 'It could happen that you won't be here?'

'Why not? I have many enemies. Is there any man who can be certain that he will see tomorrow?' He turned and walked away, rolling on his bowed legs.

Arturo stayed until he had finished the quails and then went back to Corinium. Crossing the Forum he was tempted to ask the way to Ansold the swordmaker's work-shop but held down the desire firmly. His business here was with horses and men.

That night, with blackened faces and hands, he and Volpax made themselves

231

familiar with the cavalry horse lines. Some of the beasts were penned inside wooden palisaded yards but more were hobbled and tethered to picket lines. Guard fires burned at intervals around the camp and sentries patrolled each sector of the great space which the cavalry wing occupied. They made the circuit of the camp twice to familiarize themselves with it and then, withdrawing to a safe distance, they sat in a patch of low broom scrub and watched the movement of the patrolling guards. As the night began to wear away they saw that the guards often hugged their fires and missed a patrol, and saw, too, that the guard officers were lax in their duty rounds. Inaction, Arturo knew, bred carelessness and indifference in the best troops.

Long before first light the two withdrew to their ponies which they had left tethered in a wood far up the Glevum road and Volpax led the way to a small bothy made of hazel boughs and roofed with dead bracken in a small dell deep into the wood. They slept and ate their way through the long day and there was little talk between them and no passing of the wineskin. A nearby stream gave them water to drink. When Volpax was about his business he remained sober.

The next night they took the first of their horses. Volpax left Arturo near the picket lines and went to the far end of the camp. Here, between midnight and dawn, standing in the cover of some trees he drew his bow and shot four arrows at the three guards who sat around the watch fire. The first struck the three-legged iron brazier and sent sparks and burning wood high in the air. The others thudded into the ground about the guards. The men scattered, shouting and drawing their swords. Expecting an attack, one of them blew the alarm on his horn. The blowing of the alarm brought the main guard turning out from their hut and they ran towards the danger spot. Arturo smiled to himself as he saw the two men guarding his length of picket line jump to their feet and hurry towards the alarm call. Crouching low, one hand holding his dagger and the other two stout rope halters, he went quickly to the line of horses where the animals moved restlessly. Talking softly and soothingly to the disturbed animals he slashed the hobbles from two of them and slipped the halters over their necks. Then standing between them, gentling them, crooning the love talk and caressing noises which bond all good cavalry men to their mounts, he waited. In a few moments Volpax, running low, crablike on his bowed legs, came scuttling across to the line and freed another two horses. He swung himself on to the back of one of them and rode, leading the other, out into the darkness of the night and away from the pandemonium and shouting from the far end of the camp. Close behind him rode Arturo.

By daybreak they were well south of Corinium in wooded, steep valley country, each man now riding his own pony with a haltered stolen horse on either side of him.

As the sun, glowing red through a misty autumn sky, climbed high Arturo rode with a light heart. Here, by the gods, was a beginning. Horses first and men later. And if the men were to prove more difficult than the horses, then he was content for the gods were with him. Impatience on his part would be an insult to the gods.

A week later they took four more horses, and this time without causing any disturbance since it was a night of thin brume, lying waist high over the ground under clear starlight. They worked their way on their bellies to the lines while the guards huddled about their braziers, cut the horses free and mounting galloped them away, separating and twisting and curving through the mist to defy all hopeful pursuit.

On the next foray, two weeks later, and now there was the nip of sharp frost in the air and the camp drinking troughs were plated with a thin layer of ice, Volpax and Arturo wormed their way to the pens at the northern end of the camp where unhobbled horses were quartered. Volpax surprised the single guard at the gate, laid him low with a blow from a wooden club and then freed the horses to stampede them through the camp while he and Arturo roped two horses each and rode off with them. After that they kept away from the camp for three weeks, and then made another raid using the same strategy as they had employed on their first raid.

By the time the year was well on the turn they had taken twenty horses. Since a fall of snow then made raiding unwise Arturo took two of the six horses which had fallen to his lot and riding a pony borrowed from Volpax led them back to the villa of the three nymphs where he found all in order but his friends becoming over-anxious about him.

When he returned to Volpax he brought Durstan with him so that his companion could take by turns his remaining four horses back to the villa. Now, because the weather was worsening, snow and rain often making raiding impossible for fear of their tracks being followed, Volpax and Arturo spent many a long day lodged in their bracken-roofed bothy waiting for the right conditions to favour them. Once or twice, since tedium was an enemy which Arturo was least fitted to combat, he left Volpax sleeping or nursing his wineskin and wandered off through the woods by himself, close wrapped in his cloak against the cold or the rain. Once or twice he stood at the edge of the wood and looked across to the smoke of the cooking fires rising above far Corinium. The day came when, the impulse strong and irresistible in him, he made his way there. If a man's feet itched, he found excuse for himself, then might not that be a sign from the gods? If they could colour his mind with visions why should they not as surely direct his footsteps past denial?

Avoiding the main gates he entered the city through a gap in the broken walls. A heavy squall of rain made him draw the cape of his cloak over his head. He ran across the Forum and took shelter under the colonnade which fronted the Basilica. There were very few people abroad and those that were hurried about their business. Arturo sat on a stone bench and watched the puddles forming between the broken paving of the Forum square. As he sat there his eye was caught by some graffiti marked with the soft edge of a slate on one of the colonnade pillars. A long inscription amongst them ran vertically down the length of the column. As he read it anger grew suddenly and sharply in him.

Between the empty promise of Arto and the sloth of Ambrosius where shall a warrior blood his lance?

Impulsively, heedless of any who watched, he stood up, fumbling inside his cloak for his belt pouch and went to the pillar. With a piece of the charcoal which he carried for night raids he wrote:

Arto has taken your horses. Are all the warriors of Ambrosius dormice to sleep through winter? Come south with your swords and claim your mounts.

A few minutes later, careless of whether he had been seen, he left the city and made his way across country in the gathering gloom and rain towards the forest shelter. As he went there was a sureness in him, lifting his spirits, that the gods had truly sent him to the city to read the inscription.

A few nights later with the ground iron hard from frost he and Volpax took another lot of horses, but this time things went wrong for them. As Volpax crouched, cutting the hobbles of a horse, the animal, frightened by the noise of the alarms sounding, reared and a fore hoof struck Volpax to the ground. A guard came running through the darkness, saw the two men and threw his spear from a distance. It struck Volpax in the side of his neck as he rose, tore deeply through his flesh, and then fell away from him. Abandoning the horses he would have taken, Volpax ran from the picket lines and caught up with Arturo who, ignorant of what had happened, was leading his two horses away at a fast trot. As Volpax called to him he pulled the horses up, saw the blood streaming from Volpax's neck, and without word — the night behind them loud with the cries of men and the blowing of horns — he hoisted Volpax to the back of one horse and swung himself on the other and they rode hard into the darkness. When they were well clear of the camp they pulled their mounts up and Arturo, ripping lengths of cloth from his cloak, tied them about Volpax's neck to stop the bleeding from the wound.

Choking over his words, Volpax said, ''Tis nothing. A glancing blow that will leave but a ragged scar and — '

He swayed and Arturo held him on his feet. From the way the blood had run and spurted from the wound he knew that it was far from nothing. The life was pumping fast from his friend.

He said, 'Save your words to spare your breathing.'

Suddenly Volpax's eyes closed and he fell

heavily against Arturo and, before he could be held, collapsed to the ground. After a moment as Arturo tried to staunch the blood flow Volpax opened his eyes. They shone dully in the starlight and Arturo knew with a heavy heart that the death look was on the face of his friend.

With his next words Volpax showed that he knew it, too. He raised a hand and held Arturo's, gripping it tightly, and said, fighting for breath, 'There is an end to every road. Mine stops here, Arto. *Aie* . . . ' A weak smile touched his lips, ' . . . and I go without the comfort of a wineskin. May the gods be kind and greet me with one . . . ' He coughed and swallowed violently as the blood gorged his throat. Then, in a moment of ease, he went on, 'Leave me. Take the horses — they are yours now . . . all of them. A parting gift from Volpax. In return say a prayer for me when you ride to Ambrosius to make your promise good . . . ' Then, with the faintest of sighs, his head dropped and he lay still in Arturo's arms, his dead eyes staring up to the frost-bright stars. As though in salute to his passing, from the depth of the forest about them a dog fox barked three times sharply.

★   ★   ★

Because of the comradeship which had been between them Arturo wrapped the body of Volpax in his cloak and bound him crossways on the back of the second horse. He had no means of burying him and would have thought it scant respect to have left him to be picked clean by scavenging birds and beasts. He rode the rest of that night leading the spare horse on its halter. The dun-coloured and the other pony they had abandoned near the camp in their flight. There was nothing in him now but sorrow for the loss of his friend. Horses he might have now in plenty, but for the first time he knew the measure of the loss of a friend. If the gods granted him his wishes he knew that the time would come when he would mourn other friends, but none, no matter how dear, would cloud his mind with the blackness of the sorrow he felt for Volpax.

At daybreak he stopped by a small forest pond to rest and water the horses and to eat the hard bread and cold meat which he carried in his pouch. The night had brought a thick hoar frost which now, as the sun strengthened, dripped from the bare tree boughs. A moorhen foraged among the sere tangle of dead rushes on the far side of the pool and a robin came timidly to pick at a crust of bread he threw it. Winter was fresh on the land and iron fast in his heart. The gods had given him horses . . . and now, as though to mock him in his need for men, they took from him Volpax.

Deep in his own misery, sitting with his elbows on his knees staring at the black surface of the pond, he was taken by surprise when from behind him a voice said, 'Reach not for your dagger. I come in friendship.'

Arturo swung round and half rose. His hand went for the knife in his belt, gripped it, and then was stayed from drawing it by the sight of a young man who stood on the fringe of the trees. He was on foot, a sword hanging from his belt, his hands held wide and free from any weapon. He was bare-headed, his hair, the rich colour of a polished chestnut and fired with sharp red glints from the rising sun, ran down the sides of his cheeks to a small, bushy beard. He wore a close-fitting surcoat and tightly gartered trews while about his neck was tied a blue Sabrina Wing cavalry scarf. He smiled as Arturo now stood slowly upright.

Arturo said, 'Why should one of the Sabrina Wing offer me friendship?'

The man came forward a few steps, his eyes going from Arturo to the two calvary horses standing by and then to the cloaked body of Volpax on the ground. He said slowly, 'Because if you are, as I truly think you to be, that Arturo of the famous promise, and also that same one who has set Corinium and all cavalry men talking about your message written on the basilica pillar, then I am no longer of the Sabrina Wing.' He raised a hand to the knot of the blue scarf, tugged it free and threw the cloth from him to rest pinned on the thorns of a leafless briar.

'I am that Arturo.' As he spoke Arturo's eyes went from the man to the thickness of the trees and scrub behind him. Soft words and friendship's appearance could be the forerunners of treachery.

As though he had read his mind the young man said, 'There is none behind me. I come alone, riding your dun pony and leading the other. 'Twas my comrade's spear that sent your friend to the Shades — the gods celebrate his coming. I followed on foot and found your ponies which you dared not stop to untether. *Aie* ... and then there was another trail plain to follow ... wet and shining on grass and leaf under the stars. And when that went the gods gave a quick night frost to bear your marks. The gods have grieved you with one loss, and now — if it is your will and you are truly the man I seek

— offer you the gain of myself and others like me. If I talk overmuch be not surprised. My father was a bard in Lavobrinta in the country of the Ordovices and I would have become one but that I loved horses more. My name is Gelliga.'

'You would offer me service and bring others of the same mind?'

Gelliga shrugged his shoulders. 'Why not? Three weeks past you stole my mount, a grey mare. We were both tired of empty drills and empty words. I come to join her. And there are others like me.'

For a moment or two Arturo said nothing, but there was in him now, growing fast, a rising exultation. The gods took and the gods gave. But in loss or in gain a man should never cease to honour and trust them. Volpax was gone. But was it not true that the very life blood he had shed on grass and leaf had brought one to stand in his place and he, a man from whom trust shone without flaw, one who should bring others.

He said, 'I am Arturo, and the gods have been kind. Go back to your friends. Tell them of this place and be here with them at the next full moon. I shall come to greet you and lead you to those who have already sworn service.'

'You will come alone?'

Arturo smiled 'Why should I not? The gods have marked me, and now they have marked you. I give you and your comrades my trust. To do other would shame me before the gods.'

Comrades of the White Horse

Arturo found Durstan waiting for him at the horse-keeper's steading. Between them they led ten of the horses back to the villa of the three nymphs through two days of wind and rain. On hearing of the death of Volpax and the promise which Arturo had made to go back and meet Gelliga and such men as would follow him, Durstan tried to argue Arturo out of such foolishness. But after a while, when he saw that Arturo was adamant, he shrugged his shoulders and said, 'So be it. May the gods protect you.'

Arturo, heavily cowled against the driving rain as they rode side by side, said, 'The gods have willed it through the death of Volpax. While I am gone there is work for you to do. Ride eastwards down the river. Talk to the farmers and the headmen of the villages. Take a good horse, dress well and carry a sword, and tell them Arturo sends his greetings, and that soon he will be riding with his comrades to clear the banks, the swamps and the woods of the upriver lands of all Saxon bands.'

Durstan's eyes widened in surprise. 'In mid-winter?'

'Aye, in mid-winter. Is it not then that Saxons find their bellies empty and begin to raid our people to rob them of their corn and root stores? I shall have a company which has long itched for true action, already drilled and sharp-set for fighting. Within three days' ride of the villa there is fighting and enough to pleasure them. Tell our river people that we come to protect them and to clear the headwater valleys of the Saxons.'

Despite himself Durstan smiled, recognizing the note of exultation in his friend's voice. Arturo was flighting again on god-given wings of daring, and he knew that it would be useless to say that the Saxon riff-raff — criminals and outcasts mostly from the lands of King Hengist — would withdraw to their swamps and riverside thickets where no horse could follow them. He said, 'And in return you will take tribute for your protection?'

'That would be to do as the Saxons do. I take nothing, but accept whatever is offered freely for the service and protection we give.'

Durstan made no reply. The river settlers lived a hard life. Since they seldom if ever found any willing to help them the habit of gratitude was almost lost to them. With the extra horses and men Arturo would bring the winter fodder and supplies at the villa would soon be gone. To point this out to Arturo, he knew, would only bring the reply that the gods would provide.

Twelve days later Arturo rode down the forest path under a full moon to the pool where he had first met Gelliga. He had dressed himself as proudly as he could from the meagre possessions of himself and his friends at the villa. He wore a woollen cloak caught at the throat with a bronze brooch donated by Timo, long trews crossgartered with deerskin hide thongs, his own tunic and belt from which hung his sword, sharply honed by Marcos, and on his head a leather cap with a stiff plume of white and red goose quills — the red quills so dyed by Durstan in the dark blood of a winter hare which had been trapped for the pot. He rode a chestnut stallion, the best of the stolen horses, and carried for lance a seasoned length of ash, the tip fire-hardened and capped with a sharp iron point fashioned by Marcos from a piece of scrap metal scavenged in the villa's ruins.

The moon threw ebony tree and branch shadows across his path, the stallion's breath plumed in the frost-sharp air and the ground rang iron hard under its hooves. Arturo came openly, armed and alert, but fearing no mischief for this night, this meeting, he knew had been long ordained, and the knowledge

— whose provenance he never questioned nor thought to prove — was in him with a noble certitude and filled him with a controlled but commanding arrogance. Openly he rode down to the hollow and came out of the cover of the winter-stark trees and brought the stallion to a halt at the side of the white rimed reeds of the black, star-mirroring waters of the pool. He sat and waited, curbing the horse firmly as it fidgeted. An owl called from the trees far up the valley side and the star reflections on the water were shattered into a maze of shifting silver as a water rat swam across its breadth. He sat there facing across the clearing, his eyes on the path by which Gelliga had first come to surprise him.

The owl called again and the waters of the pool grew calm, holding the reflections of the stars firmly fixed in its dark mirror.

A voice from behind him said quietly, 'Greetings to Captain Arturo.'

Arturo wheeled his steed about to find Gelliga standing at the foot of the pathway which had brought him into the clearing. Touched with a moment's irritation at the conceit of the man's manoeuvre, Arturo said, 'Greetings, good Gelliga. You come alone — and without horse?'

Gelliga shook his head. 'No, my captain. There are six others with me and we bring four horses. There is a high wind of suspicion blowing through the camp now. Guards have been doubled and a curfew keeps all men in barracks after nightfall. There were those who would have come but could find no way. But they will with time.' Then with a slow movement he drew aside his long cloak, pulled his sword from its scabbard and thrust it upright into the hard ground before him, saying, 'Here is my sword which I, Gelliga of Lavobrinta in the country of the Ordovices, pledge to you in true comradeship.'

He stepped back a few paces from his sword. As he did so another man moved out of the trees to his right. Heavily cloaked, tall and with a deeply wrinkled face, he too drew his sword and fisted it into the ground and said in a voice which was like the low growl of a bear, 'My captain, I, too, Garwain from Moridunum on the banks of the river Tuvius in the country of the Demetae, pledge myself to you.'

After him, and before Arturo could stir or say a word, another man stepped out from further along the ring of the trees and stabbed his sword into the ground. Short, lean and bow-legged he said in a high voice, 'Lacto of Calcaria in the country of the Parisi, my captain, gives his sword to you.' Then, clear in the moonlight, his face broke into a broad grin as he went on, 'My horse you have already for you sit upon it now.'

Arturo answered, 'It is yours again when we reach the villa of the three nymphs.'

Then from beyond Lacto another man moved into the moonlit circle and announcing himself gave his sword and pledge to be followed by four others so that Arturo sat the stallion within a crescent of swords. After Lacto came Bovio from Deva, fresh-faced and big-handed, Tarius from Olicana of the Brigantes, lean, hardbitten of face and older than all the rest, and then Netio of the Catuvellauni with a hawkish, hook-nosed face marked to one side by an old sword scar; and last of all the youngest of them all, Lancelo, short, broad-shouldered and with a round moon of a face set with smiling eyes who came from Corinium.

Arturo sat his horse and let his eyes swing from one to another and slowly there rose in him the beginning of a deep pride. Great oaks, he thought, from little acorns grew ... *Aie*, but the coming of such greatness would cover the life span of many men. But here was the seed which would grow fast to bring him a great company of men, a *comitatus*, a firm brotherhood which in a few years could become an army. Truly now he was poised on the brink of a god-marked destiny, and he saw now that the drama staged for his benefit by Gelliga must surely have been put into the man's mind by the gods. Seven men to pledge their seven swords. There was magic in the number, and magic in this moment which he must meet appropriately. Brothers they might be truly, but captain and commander he must remain to create an army from what otherwise might become a rabble.

He dropped his horse's reins, holding it firm and controlled by the clamping pressure of his knees alone, and he drew his sword with one hand, holding it upright before his face, and raised his lance with the other hand and began to speak without thought because he knew the gods would put the right words into his mouth.

His face tight drawn from the fervour which stirred in him, he said boldly, 'With this lance I give you welcome and will be with you as straight and true in comradeship, in valour and in faith.' Then drawing his up-pointed sword to his lips he kissed the broad, cold blade, and went on, 'On this blade I make the oath-kiss and swear that I shall never ask of you that which I would not dare myself. I shall be your true captain and you my beloved brothers. Neither in distress nor want, nor in courage nor in victory shall there ever be shadow or stain on the love and duty which I hold dear towards you. Swear then to accept but one destiny, to rid this island of all those who do now and would further oppress us, to bring back the glory and the peace which once were lodged with our fathers and their fathers. Swear this by the god or gods who rule your hearts!' He kissed his sword again and raised it high.

Before him in one movement seven swords were drawn from the ground, flashing in the bright moonlight; seven swords were raised as one to take on their cold blades the oath-kisses, and as though in one voice the seven cried, 'We swear! We swear!'

★ ★ ★

Then began, in the raw and savage days of mid-winter, the first of Arturo's true time as a captain of men. Durstan had returned to say that while he had been received with friendship by their own people none of them would move to help them or freely provision them. They had been left alone so long without help that the poverty and hardships of their life and the sudden attacks of raiding Saxons formed a pattern of their days which they met now with a practical stoicism. They hid in storage pits, cliff caves and woodland dells most of their harvest corn and lodged their lean cattle in secret pastures. When the Saxons came they withdrew to the woods and hills and the raiders took what they would from their poor huts and when they were gone the homesteaders came back to repair the damage and to mourn wife or child or the aged who had been butchered by the Saxons. They lived in fear on the knife-edge of want and prayed only for the coming of spring when they could open their furrows and sow what seed corn was left and look to the farrowing and calving of what swine and kine they still held. Spring and summer were the easeful seasons for the barbaric Saxon robbers had enough sense to leave them undisturbed to their cropping and folding against the fat time of autumn harvests and full cattle pens.

For a few days while his new comrades settled into the villa, and Durstan and Gelliga saw them mounted and in mock battle drills they learned to move and know one another, Arturo sat for long periods in his room planning his first move against the Saxons. More men would soon come to him, of this he was sure. But to hold a company of any size together he knew that he needed not only the friendship of the settlers, but a supply of stores and services from them. What the

Saxons needed they took by force. That way could never be his. He had to find some shift by which, swiftly and surely. he could bring the settlers to his side and gain from them a confidence which would turn them to him in true gratitude. For the first time, although his band of brothers was small, he found himself with the beginnings of the weight of true command. Slowly he came to a decision, but once reaching it he threw all doubts from his mind and moved to action.

Leaving Durstan and Lancelo with Timo and Marcos to guard the villa, he took the rest of his men and they rode out, scantily provisioned, on a morning of heavy, cold rain. They rode down the left bank of the river, skirting the swamps and the low-lying, winter flooded pastures and when darkness came they turned their horses into the marshes and swam them across the river. For the rest of the night they moved down the right bank of the river. When dawn came they made camp in the shelter of a tree-covered knoll. That evening as early dark fell they left the knoll, each man knowing now the moves to be made.

The river Saxons, unlike those in the settled lands who preferred to build their huts apart in widely scattered communities, lived in small groups by the water side where they moored their boats for upriver raiding. At midnight, circling around such a Saxon village, Arturo's men took it by surprise from the east. Arturo rode at their head and with a great cry of 'Arturo comes! Arturo comes!' he lowered his lance as they swept by the rough log-built and reed-thatched huts and speared from the heart of the watch fire a burning brand and lodged it in the roof of a hut. Behind him came Gelliga and his iron lance tip caught the throat of the startled, bemused Saxon on watch as he rose from sleep beside the fire. Behind Gelliga came the other comrades, spearing brands to fire the thatched hovels of the Saxons and then to wheel, following their captain, and with drawn swords cut down the Saxon men as they came tumbling, hands groping for seax and fighting axe, from their sleep into the flame-lit circle of huts. The victory was swift and bloody. No fighting man was spared. Most of them stood and fought, back to back, and died from lance point or sword's edge almost before the sleep which fogged their minds had time to clear. Spared only — and this long ordered by Arturo — were the women and children and the young boys whose chins had yet to know the roughness of a growing beard. These survivors were marshalled to the river bank where the

255

raiding boats were drawn up. There were seven boats and four were put to the flames. Into the others were hustled the women and children and two old men. Before these were pushed out on to the dark bosom of the racing stream Arturo spoke to one of the old men who, like many of them, understood his tongue and said, 'Know well that I am Arturo and hold my words firm in your memory. This night has begun the cleansing of the valleys of all your kind. Go down the great Tamesis and to all your race give warning that, under the gods, I, Arturo, begin now the purging of the upper river lands . . . '

Listening, watching the fire-lit faces of the people in the boats, Gelliga smiled quietly to himself. He was content — for, this night, he and his comrades had tasted action which had long been denied them, and this night, too, Arturo had begun to make good his promise. But there was this about Arturo which all his comrades now understood and were content to accept — in all things Arturo saw the hands and the will of the gods and believed without any shadow of doubt that he had been chosen to foster their work and their dreams for this country. At times he could be stiff and pompous in his role, but at no time could any man watching and listening to him fail to mark the sincerity of his conviction. Such men, Gelliga knew, were the stuff of great commanders, and those who followed them, as he and his comrades followed Arturo, knew well that behind the high words lay the iron will which took men into battle ready to give their lives for him and his god-touched passion. He looked across at Netio, his hawk-face wet with sweat, the blaze from the burning huts shadowing the great scar on his cheek, his blooded sword resting across his knees and there was no surprise in him as the warrior gave him the winking flick of an eyelid and his tongue ran slowly along the underside of his top lip. Aye, he thought, they had found a man who would give them all the battle and bloodshed so long denied them by Count Ambrosius. One thing was certain now, there were many men who would, if this were a true beginning, come eagerly to Arturo. This night, gods or no gods, Arturo had committed himself to a dream which would either bring him to quick death or to lasting life in the memory of all men; and despite himself the bard in Gelliga jostled aside the warrior and he knew that before they reached the villa a song would have been born in him, polished and repolished like a sword blade, and be sung without reproof from Arturo around the camp fires of his comrades . . .

They watched the three boats move downstream and slide from the light of the leaping flames into the murky curtain of night. Then they searched the houses and grain pits for all they could bundle and carry. They took plunder of bronze and silver armbands, and brooches and torques. They stripped the dead of their weapons but touched none of their clothes for the Saxon men with no love of cleanliness stank like polecats. Then in darkness they made their way up river. They swam their steeds across it at dawn, laden like pedlars and baggage men.

At midday they rode up the slope of a wide valley through which ran a narrow tributary of the Tamesis. Just below the crest a poor stockade of thorns and loosely piled turves enclosed a group of huts. Seeing them coming the villagers ran to the ridge crest and there halted to watch them.

Arturo, his men following, rode into the stockade and there unloaded the stores and plunder which they had taken from the Saxons. As they did so an old man came limping from one of the huts and approached Arturo. He was dressed in patched skins and loose woollen trews.

Greeting him Arturo said, 'You come without fear, unlike the rest of your kind. Look at us, do we seem like Saxon robbers to you?'

The man shook his head. 'No, my lord. But know that had I the full use of my old legs I would have run too. It is not only by the Saxon kind that we are plundered and robbed and killed. In these parts there are men of our own race who do the same.'

'The times are changing. Know now, that all the valleys of the river from here to the high wolds are the domain of Captain Arturo who now speaks to you. These last days we have taken war to the Saxons and this is our booty — ' he nodded at the corn sacks and baskets and the piled Saxon plunder and weapons, ' — which we now give to you and your people. In return we ask for nothing which you cannot find a willingness in your hearts to give. We are to be found at the villa of the three nymphs.'

Without waiting for the old man to reply. Arturo wheeled his horse and led his companions from the village. Riding at his side Gelliga said, 'No forced levies, no pressed labour — they will think us witless, my captain. We should at least have taken a pannier of seed corn.'

Arturo shook his head. 'No. We are not as Saxon robbers, or some thieving band of cut-throats who have forgotten their own race. The gods will touch their hearts with the finger of faith to rouse them to new hope and true generosity.'

259

Whether indeed the gods did this or, more likely, the villagers acted from a policy of caution scantily endowed with good will, the upshot was that four days later a pony-drawn cart on wooden runners came up the snow-covered valley to the villa attended by two youths whose curiosity showed clearly through their fears. In the cart were two earthenware pots full of flour, a basket of flat bread cakes, two skins of beer and half a deer carcass.

After Arturo had thanked them the two youths stood awkwardly by the cart without making move to leave the villa yard. Seeing their hesitation to go, Arturo said, 'You would eat and drink before you go?'

One of the youths shook his head and then answered hesitantly, 'No, my lord . . . We are to say that pony and cart are yours and . . . and, we go with it. To stay here and serve you.'

For a moment Arturo said nothing but he knew that in the most wretched of men there was always one heart spot which the gods could touch. For slaves he had no use since forced labour was the seeding ground of treachery. But a willing man was without price. Now, smiling at the two, he said, 'You look alike.'

'We are brothers, my lord. We will stay and

work for you . . . and . . . ' the taller of the two who was speaking, hesitated and then smiled, 'and perhaps one day you will arm and horse us to fight against the sea people.'

'For which we are impatient, my lord,' said the other with a sudden grimness, 'for the Saxons killed our father and carried away our sister.'

His face forced to severity to hide the sudden joy in him, Arturo said commandingly, 'So be it. Work hard and drill hard and the day will come soon.'

From then on through the slowly lengthening days until the first primroses began to push pale buds from their green leaf rosettes and the rooks in the leafless trees began to bicker and fight over their winter-ruined nesting sites and the trout rested thin with spawning in the valley stream, Arturo and his companions carried war against the river Saxons.

They struck in short fierce raids mostly by night. When they attacked a Saxon village by day it was always just as the light was going and the men were settling to their eating and drinking and the cooking fires flamed high and made the flinging of fire brands on to the hut roofs easy. Old men and women and children they spared but all able-bodied men were killed; and it must be said of them that the Saxons, once they knew there was no escape, stood and fought, facing the companions, ready to go to Woden's hall without the coward scar of a sword or lance thrust in the back.

Of his own men Arturo lost two. Lacto of Calcaria in the country of the Parisi was killed by the thrust of a scramaseax into his groin, and Tarius of the Brigantes, the oldest of his companions, had his horse ham-stringed, to be stabbed to death as earthbound he tried to fight off his enemy. But against these losses there came fresh cavalry men to join them for innocent-looking, moon-faced Lancelo returned secretly to his family home in Corinium and there recruited willing men from the Sabrina Wing and brought them through the high wolds and forests to the villa.

Since the death of a comrade was to Arturo like the death of a brother, he sought all ways to protect them. He took from the Saxon war booty their small round shields which were easier to handle than the large, cumbersome shields that Ambrosius's men were drilled to use. The Saxons facing mounted men came in fast and ducked the lance to make a great stabbing thrust at the rider's groin; but the small buckler could be quickly dropped to turn away the upward jab and leave the comrade free to ride the man down. Later, too, the lances were discarded. In a set battle charge they would have their use, but in quick night-raiding they were more dangerous nuisance than they were worth. Sword and small round shield were enough. Fortunately, too, the Saxons made no attempt to combine their scattered forces. The men of one village or marsh settlement gave no trust to the men from other communities. They lived in suspicion towards one another and, because of this, never once assembled in force to meet Arturo and his men.

In two months Arturo had cleared five miles of the upper river valley and the closely adjoining lands. Tribute came now willingly from the British villages and farms that knew a peace and safety long absent. In far Glevum Count Ambrosius had heard of Arturo's exploits and for a while had considered sending two troops of cavalry against him but had discarded the idea since he feared the men might desert from him and join Arturo and their comrades who had already gone to his side. At the moment Arturo was no more to him than the bite of a flea in his sleeping blanket. When the fine weather returned he promised himself that he would move against him. Now was not the moment to risk the ridicule of an open desertion of a troop of cavalry to the outlawed son of the chief of the tribe of the Enduring Crow. Already enough of his men had gone over to Arturo to make him quick with anger when his name was mentioned.

So it was that as spring broke over the land, Arturo could look with pride at the force he commanded at the villa of the three nymphs. He had enough men for a full troop of horse and, beyond fighting men, there were another dozen who worked and serviced the villa and the warriors. The villa itself was fast being repaired and warmed again to human life. The stables had been extended for the horses and a smithy set up for the repair of tools and arms, worked by a friend of Marcos from Cunetio who had sought him out. A wandering Christian monk, too, called Pasco — who would give no details of his life, though he spoke their tongue with the heavy brogue of a Scottus — had settled with them unasked and finally welcomed because of his skill with wounds and ills and his reluctance to preach or proselytize.

Among the comrades there were occasional small quarrels and jealousies but none so troubling that they went beyond the usual barrack life jealousies and mead or beer stirred sudden resentments at imagined slights. One bond held them all firmly together, their love and admiration for

Arturo. Though this was not so reverent that it stopped the quick wink or sly grin when their captain, in the exultation following a successful raid, or some felicitous turn of events which brought them food or services when sorely needed, spoke pompously of the great shield of the gods which covered them in battle and the all-seeing eyes of the deities which watched over them zealously each day. Smile though they might, and joke amongst themselves at their captain, there was none who would deny that Arturo's sure knowledge of being god-touched and god-directed was not as real to him as the sword he carried and the horse he rode. Unmarked by them, legend was slowly growing about him and the full truth behind his own words escaped even Gelliga when at night in the long eating hall, full of food and flushed with drink, he would sing:

> The knife has gone into the meat
> And the good wine fills the horn
> In Arturo's hall . . .
> Here is food for your hound
> And corn for your horse
> In Arturo's hall . . .
> But none there shall enter unless he be
> Swift with a sword and comrade to all

But with the passing of the evening and the drink Gelliga's and the other comrades' moods would change and then he sung of the yearning that not even battle and the chance of death waiting at the opening door of each day could smother.

Take my true greeting to the girl of thick
    tresses
The sweetheart I lay with in the glen of
    green willows . . .

It was of this sentiment that Pasco, the priest, spoke to Arturo one morning when the land lay iron-bound in hard frost and the horses were stayed from exercise by the iciness of the ground.

He said, 'You dream a dream, my son, for this country which I, too, hold dear in my heart. But that dream must be made real by men of human clay. Your comrades are cloistered here without the full and fulfilling submission to God's love alone which men of my kind know. Already now when the people around send tribute there are women who find reason to walk with the carts. As fox fight over vixens in the spring and the gentle doves grow fierce in courtship so stirs the same passion in the hearts of men.' He smiled, rubbed the tip of his nose, his eyes quizzical, and went on, 'The gods you worship may have made you in a different mould from your comrades — though I doubt it. You order things well here. Now you must order this, not as Count Ambrosius does with loose camp followers at Corinium, nor as your own Prince Gerontius with the stews of Isca. You are the captain of a brotherhood — but not a brotherhood of monks.'

Acknowledging the wisdom of Pasco's words Arturo talked the matter over with Durstan and Gelliga. Each week now two or three men filtered through the valleys and woods to the villa from Ambrosius's forces. Some brought horse and weapons, and some came on foot with nought but a dagger in their belts. But with these reinforcements, all of them well-trained, there were now more men than mounts. So, since for the time being the immediate river lands had been almost rid of Saxon bands, and Arturo was now nourishing a dream of action which would carry his name far beyond the domains of Gerontius and Count Ambrosius, he announced to his comrades that some of those who came from far lands could return to their people to visit sweethearts and wives. They would be chosen by the drawing of lots so that the main force of the brotherhood was not depleted beyond the number of horses they owned. For those whose homes lay around the westward side of the Sabrina basin permission was given for their womenfolk to visit the villa for limited periods. Quarters would be set up in the west wing of the villa, but at the first sign of discord or quarrelling then all the women would be banished.

Over all these concessions Arturo laid one adamant condition. All men would be back by the feast of Beltine, which was the first day of the month of Damara, the goddess of fertility and growth. At the end of this month — though Arturo kept this secret between himself and his two closest comrades, Durstan and Gelliga — he meant to move from the villa for this was a time when he guessed that Count Ambrosius might be tempted to strike at him. But more to his concern it was also the time when he meant to make his own move which would send his name echoing widely over the country and bring even more men to his side.

Among those who were unlucky in the first drawing of lots was Lancelo. But one of the comrades, who had neither wife nor sweetheart, nor immediate wish for either, had set his lot up for bid and Lancelo had gained it in exchange for a pair of old but serviceable bronze grieves taken as plunder in a Saxon raid.

Seven days later Lancelo rode out of the forest and into the courtyard of the villa. There were only two men in the courtyard at that moment for the rest were either at their work or exercising and drilling their mounts in the lower valley pasture. One of the men was Arturo who sat in the sunlight on the edge of the fountain of the nymphs with old, grey-muzzled Anga at his feet.

Lancelo rode up to him and dismounted. He saluted Arturo and said, his face grave, 'I bring no sweetheart or wife, my captain. Sweetheart I had, but on my second night in Corinium she betrayed me to Count Ambrosius's men. But one of the Sabrina men, an old friend, sent me warning in time so that we were able to escape.'

'We?'

'My family, my captain. Had I left them they would have been butchered by the troopers in their anger at my escape. I ask your permission for them to stay here until such time as they can move on to a fresh place of safety.'

'Where are they now?'

'They wait in the wood for a signal from me.'

'Then make it, good Lancelo.'

Lancelo's face beamed with pleasure. He put two fingers to his mouth and blew a piercing whistle. A few moments later an elderly man rode out of the wood on a small pony. He was small, bare-headed, and almost bald and wrapped in a great square cloak of sewn furs. Across the withers of his mount hung two bulky, awkward packs of stained and patched cloth At his side on another pony rode a woman wearing a cloak and cowl of red wool and her mount carried two slung panniers of plaited withy branches.

They rode up to Arturo and as they halted the woman pushed the folds of her cowl free of her face and a pair of clear blue eyes regarded Arturo solemnly. In that instant Arturo knew with a certainty that this moment was god-touched. At three different times in his life he had looked into those eyes, and now, this time, he knew that here was no capricious play of time and chance but the deliberate hands of the gods as they moved their pieces on the playing board of his destiny. For reasons he gave not a straw since all would be revealed to him in full time by the gods. Although he would have returned the smile he kept his face calm and turned to the man.

Smiling now, he said, 'I did not know that the father of Lancelo was Ansold the armourer and smith for here we ask nothing of a man's past or family so long as he brings loyalty and a ready sword. But you, good

Ansold, are more than welcome. *Aie* . . . and would be even without your hammers and tongs.' He nodded to one of the packs from which protruded the handle of a long pair of forging grips.

Ansold blinked happily and rubbed a worn, charcoal-grained hand across his chin, saying, 'Your welcome warms my heart, Captain Arturo, for the truth is that, although the lying will be harder here than at Corinium, I would rather serve you than Count Ambrosius who pays poor for good work and that only after long waiting.'

Pushing the cloak cowl free of her dark hair, Daria, straight-faced except for a slight curl at the corners of her berry-red lips, said, 'And what welcome does my lord Arturo give me?'

Arturo, smiling, speaking without thought as though the words flowed from elsewhere through him to her, said, 'You have no need of welcome for my heart has given it before to you. Once on the rain-cloaked moors when you would have taken a dagger to me. Again with the fleeting flash of your eyes in the Corinium market place and then lastly bowered with a scolding frown at my rashness in showing my tribal mark in old Paulus's workshed. And now — although you speak teasingly — I know there is a true kindness to

271

me in your heart since the faces of your father and Lancelo tell me that they have never known until this moment that we had met before. Though I count that caution not needed.'

Daria laughed and shook her head. 'Then you count wrong. Give my good father too much mead and in some moments his tongue grows too loose. As for Lancelo I wanted for him no more favour than rested in his own body and skills. Nor now do any of us ask for undue favours. So long as we are here we are at your commands, knowing that they will always be just.'

Before Arturo could reply, Ansold said gruffly, 'She is right about the mead loosening my tongue. But smithying is hot work and hard and a man's throat gets parched.'

When Lancelo led them away to find quarters for them, Arturo went back to the fountain and sat, one hand teasing at Anga's ears. The gods had sent him a master swordmaker . . . a man who could wander the breadth and length of the land and always find a welcome in any camp. And the gods had sent him Daria. In so doing there was no doubt in him that they moved him and the dark-haired, blue-eyed young woman in some pattern of destiny not given yet to the eyes or mind of man to know.

A Gift from the Gods

The winter, which had been hard, spent its strength at last and spring began swiftly to spread its coloured mantle over the land. The woods grew green and primroses and white and purple violets studded the mossy alder thickets along the valley stream and the gold of daffodil blooms was spread like largesse over the meadow banks. Blackbirds and thrushes sat their early clutches in the thorn tangles and the tall tree tops were noisy with the clamour of rook colonies. Buzzard pairs moved as they climbed in lazy spirals on the rising warm air currents and, as the sun rose higher each day, adders and grass snakes stirred from their winter sluggishness and sought their basking places on the warm-faced rocks and ledges of the old quarry behind the villa. Man, beast and bird . . . all living things began to move to the rituals of spring, to the divine dance of courtship, mating and increase which each year the gods decreed.

Although the affairs and the ordering of his small but growing command filled much of his days, there were times when Arturo, quick with the restlessness of the season, found himself turning away from the ordering of men and horses, from drills and cavalry exercises, to forsake the villa and walk by himself in the surrounding woods. Here, he found his mind full with two things. The first was the pattern of his own destiny which he was convinced now was god-ordained and to be of great moment — though that only if he himself could through his own skills, courage and imagination prove always worthy of the gods' favour. Sitting alone in a wood clearing he would become lost in a dream of the campaign which he meant to start as soon as the first days of summer came. Ill-provided and rash he knew it had to be, but there was no doubt in him that the gods would approve his daring. With a handful of men he would do what Gerontius with all his forces had talked long of doing but still had not found the will to effect. Active though his mind was with this dream, there were the times when its place was usurped by his second passion. From thoughts of coming renown and glory, he found himself slipping into thoughts of Daria.

Again and again the gods had put her in his path. He was in love with her and knew that she, for all her challenging and teasing spirit, looked with more than ordinary kindness on him. Yet one doubt tangled his thinking about her. Through her the gods might be tempting and testing him. Many men in history had been drawn from the path of greatness by their love for a woman; men who, as they stood poised on the edge of some great matter, as he did now, had by passion allowed themselves to be drawn away from the divine love of country to lose their favour with the gods who so tempted them to prove their worth. Brooding over this he knew himself to be poised on the blade edge of choice, to be left alone in his dilemma to read the mind of the gods, and to read it rightly or suffer. Because of this uncertainty in him he had more and more in the past weeks avoided the company of Daria.

Sitting late one afternoon in a small glade above the villa, idly stripping the young bark from a hazel wand with his thumbnail and frowning to himself as he teased his mind with the dilemma which Daria posed for him, he saw her come out of the trees on the far side of the glade and walk towards him. She sat down close to him. He gave her no greeting and kept his eyes from her.

Smiling, Daria said, 'There was a time when you had no lack of words boastful or bard-like to greet me. *Aie* . . . even in my first weeks here. Does the beginning of greatness which all your men claim for you begin to move you away from ordinary courtesies?'

Throwing the hazel wand from him, Arturo said, 'You are right to chide me. But do not think because I lack words that there is no greeting in my heart. You know what is in my heart as I know what is in yours. The gods have brought us together, and for purpose.'

'But you cannot read that purpose, is that it?'

'Can you?'

'I do not try.'

'But I must.'

'Why?' She leaned forward and cradled her brown arms around her knees and her dark hair fell about her cheeks.

'That I cannot tell you.'

'Then I can give you no help. But when the feast of Beltine is over and the women go from here I shall go with them. There is one who has offered me a place with her people.'

'Your father goes with you?'

'I cannot speak for him. Nor he for himself until the moment comes. I think that you, too, are much like him. You do not know what you will do until the moment comes. But when it does you find good reason for your actions. It is clear to me that you do not know your mind or your body's actions until you stand on the edge of unalterable circumstances. Like a hare disturbed from its form you bound away and even when you are moving you do not know why you have taken your line.'

Despite himself Arturo smiled, and said, 'What need to know till then — since the gods will have put it in my mind?'

'The gods control us, true. But not every moment of the day. There are times when they are too full of their own affairs.'

'For most men, yes. But not for me.'

To his surprise Daria threw back her head and laughed. 'Oh, Arturo . . . You have such faith in the gods. And true — there is that about you which speaks of greatness. Your men mark it and respect it. But the gods cannot be with any man for every minute of his life. Would you have them decide for you whether to eat fish or meat, to take this path or that, to sing one song or another?'

'The gods are always with me when the moment is of great importance. Since no man would talk to me as you do, then I will talk to you as no man would to a woman without shaming himself. I love you and would make you my wife — but this I cannot do unless I know it is in the will of the gods that it should happen.'

For a moment or two Daria was silent. Then in a low, angry voice she said, 'My lord Arturo, you forget one thing. Gods or no

277

gods, when a woman takes a man for husband it is a matter of her will, and hers alone.' Then standing up, her dark eyes narrowed, her cheeks flushed with emotion, she went on, her voice almost contemptuous, 'I am no woman to wait on the will of the gods for a husband. *Aie* . . . I would have been wife to you if you had asked me frankly out of your own true love for me. But now I am as far out of your reach to master and to cherish as is the wild white mare that roams these woods!'

She turned from him and walked away through the trees and Arturo, watching her go, was suddenly filled with a great elation and joy which almost made him call out to bring her back for he knew that through her the gods had spoken and given him the sign he needed.

For the next two weeks he spent much of his time away from the villa camp. He went on foot into the woods, by day and by night, and the only company he had was Anga. He searched the valleys and dales, the remote clearings made by long-dead charcoal burners, the places at streams and pools where deer, boar, fox and other forest animals came to drink. On the high meadows and swampy river pastures he marked the hoof marks and the cropped patches of sweet new grass that told of the passing of the white mare. He followed the trails which she used, found the resting places where she couched at night, and the bare sand patches among the wild heath lands where she rolled in the dust, and from fresh and stale dung droppings he began to have a clear picture of her movements about the country around the villa. Sometimes he heard the distant thud of her galloping as she scented him and Anga and hurried away. Once he saw her break free from a copse of young beech trees and canter away from him down a valley side, her long tail and full mane floating in the wind of her passage like silk, the sun turning her white coat to moving, polished ivory and her beauty made him catch his breath with its wonder. A joy rose in him at the sight of her which was known only to true horse-masters, to men like Master Ricat, himself, and most of his companions, such joy that there were those who would murder and rob without pause for thought in order to possess such a beast. She was a fit steed for a great commander and she was god-marked to be his. When the first days of summer came he would ride out on her at the head of his company. But before that he would come astride her, her master, into the villa courtyard and Daria seeing him would need no words to know his mind, and to know that he came to claim her as wife, the wife the gods had ordained for him.

Knowing now the ways of her coming and going to places of grazing and drinking he waited three nights running for the breaking of dawn when she would move from her couching place to find food or water. Above a narrow forest track he lay stretched out on a stout overhanging oak branch, a rope halter thrust inside his tunic, and Anga hidden at his command in a thicket a little way ahead of the oak at the track side. For two dawns the mare kept away from the track, but on the third as the sun lipped the eastern sky and the birds began to greet the morning with song, the mare came down the track, trotting gently and tossing her noble head so that her mane was wide flung like a floating web. When she was almost under his branch Arturo spoke his will silently to Anga with the art which belonged to all men of the tribe of the Enduring Crow.

Anga came out of the thicket and stood in the trackway. The mare shied a little and halted. Then seeing that she faced no bear or wolf she moved forward and stamped her right foreleg on the ground. At this moment Arturo rolled from his branch, twisted his body, and dropped squarely on to her back. As she began to rear with fear and surprise under him, he jerked the halter from his tunic, slipped it over her head and held its loop in either hand as he clamped his legs and thighs iron hard to her sides.

From that moment Arturo was translated into a world which held only himself and the wild movement of the white mare. There was no thought in him except to follow the will of the gods and make himself master of the white horse, and no art in him except the savage skill of muscled purpose which inhabited legs and knees and thighs and hands to make him one with the racing, plunging, rearing animal beneath him. Neighing with anger and panic the mare, blind to open track or glade, raced through the forest. Thorn and branch ripped at Arturo's hands and face and raked great swatches of cloth from his clothes, and the blood from his cuts and wounds dripped and ran from him to stain the white hide of the mare. Time and place lost their meaning. He lived in a world of savage motion as the mare sought to unseat him. She came out of the forest, bursting through a great bank of gorse thicket like a wind devil to set the new bloom scattered high in a golden drift. She thundered down a valley side and, as though with deliberate malice and intent, raced with long neck outstretched under the low branches of an old yew to sweep him from her back so that Arturo, laid low across her back, his face pressed close into the sweet horse smell of her wild mane, felt the slash of scaly branches rip and tear the cloth of his tunic's back. They went, man and horse like one beast, through copse and pasture, hooves throwing sand clouds high across wild heathland, and the mare's wild neighing filling the bright morning air. He knew the great gathering and surge of her muscles as she jumped brake and stream and when she reared and plunged and swung round on her hind legs the world spun before him in a mist of green and blue chaos. Then, as no sign came of let or stop to the mare's wild panic and anger, there slowly crept over Arturo the black humiliation of knowing that his strength could never outmatch hers. His body was bruised and battered and his hands and thighs grew weaker. He found fresh anger and determination to fight his growing weakness, but only for a while. Silently within himself he cried out to the gods to be with him, but all that rested with him as the mare raced plunging and kicking beneath him was now the certain knowledge that she would master him. The gods were with her and not with him.

The moment of defeat came when the

mare galloping wildly through a forest clearing which held a sedge-ringed pool suddenly from full pace, her hooves scoring great marks in the soft ground, pulled up to a violent halt such as Arturo had never known horse to make before. His body slid forward with its own momentum, but before he could fall the mare reared suddenly to full height and, as her forelegs pawed and threshed the air, twisted herself in violent pirouette and flung Arturo from her.

As he fell, and in the few moments before his head struck the ground to send him into oblivion, Arturo knew that the gods had truly deserted him. They had given him the sign and he had gone gladly to the task to prove himself — and he had failed.

He lay on the ground close to the pool's edge, face and hands bloodied and cut, his clothes ripped, and he was lost to the world. The old hound, Anga, long left behind, came loping into the clearing and sat near him, panting with exhaustion, his great tongue lapping free over his jaws, and whined when Arturo made no move. Time passed and the moorfowl which had taken cover in the new-sedge growth came out on to the waters of the pool. Chiff-chaffs sang in the tall trees. Distantly a cuckoo called from the forest depths, and a rust-red hare, moving into the clearing, saw Anga, leaped high and raced back into the trees. Anga moved closer to Arturo, sniffed at his face, and then settled beside him and snapped at a fly which teased his muzzle. The sun climbed higher, clearing the tree tops, and a shaft of light began to warm Arturo's face. He groaned and moved, came slowly back to his senses and knew only two things, a great aching in all his limbs and his mouth parched raw with thirst.

Slowly he sat up and, seeing the pool, crawled towards it on all fours and like a dog lowered his head and lapped at the water. With the easing of his thirst memory came back to him. He sat back on the grass and, resting his aching head in his hands, knew that he was truly forsaken of the gods. They had seen his pride and arrogance and had set him to a task which would break and humble him For a moment or two he was near to weeping but before his manliness could be breached a new pride suddenly flared in him. starting him to anger and the fire of bitter challenge. This country, his country, torn and parcelled by warring tribes and ravaging Picts and Scotti, knowing no true leader or destiny except the greed and self-seeking of petty princelings like Gerontius, Ambrosius and the discredited, ageing Vortigern, was at the mercy of the growing strength and arrogance of the Saxon Hengist. His own proud boast which had sustained him for so long that Count Ambrosius should one day sue for his help suddenly meant nothing to him. In the mire of his humiliation, a new and fuller cause was born in his heart. Gods or no gods, from this moment he was dedicated to the cause and the great matter of Britain and would follow it and master it and all his country's enemies so that as the name of the great warring Caesar could never die from men's minds nor should his. Forsake him the gods might, but there was that in him which forced him to scorn their desertion.

He pulled himself to his feet and turned away from the pool but, as he raised his eyes across the glade, he saw that which was a humble and a wild joy in him and a never to be forgotten sign. Henceforth he could pursue his dream held up always by the truth which a few moments before he had named in anger to be a lie. The gods had tried and tested him, humbled him in misery, but from that misery they had sparked a fire to kindle in him the life flame of his destiny. Never again would he deny them for clear against the bright green of new forest leaf stood their sign of favour. Cropping peacefully at the lush spring grass was the white mare, her briar and thorn-raked hide flecked with her own and his blood, the halter hanging slack from her lowered neck, and the long white tail switching across her quarters to break the tease and bite of worrying flies.

Sure of himself, Arturo walked slowly across to the horse and the mare stopped cropping, raised her head and looked at him from her dark-pooled eyes and showed no sign of fear or flight. He stood by her, put out a hand and stroked her muzzle, and she took his touch with a gentle blowing of breath through her nostrils. He spoke to her gently then and called her white one, called her queen of all horses, breathed and crooned the low love talk of a horse-master and ran his hand along the proud line of her neck and promised her cherishing and honour for all the days of her life.

He took her halter and led the white one back through the forest paths to the villa. He could have mounted and ridden her but would not on this day for he knew her pride was like his own. They came together down the slope to the villa of the three nymphs. And when his people and his comrades came running and hurrying to gather about him, the mare stood quietly and without fear and Arturo knew with an enduring and passionate truth that he and the white one were god-fingered.

He said to the crowd about him, 'She is the White One, the Shining One, and wherever we ride against the enemies of this country she shall be known and seen as the White Horse of Arto and all the shields that follow shall be marked with her emblem and all our scarf and helmet colours shall be the white of her shining hide and the crimson of her blood and mine which dapple it now.'

Then, from the crowd, he called a small boy who had come with one of the visiting families and he handed the loose halter end to him and said proudly, 'Lead her to the stables and remember always that after Arturo you were the first to have her gentle obedience.'

The boy led the White One away and she followed without let, stepping like a queen along the lane which the crowd fell back to make for her passage. As she went Arturo turned away from his people and walked across the yard to the ruined steps which led up to the colonnaded open way which ran across the face of the west wing of the villa where Daria stood, the morning breeze flicking free the tendrils of her dark hair and moulding the soft wool of her blue gown about her tall, full body.

He took her right hand and said humbly, 'You know what is in my heart, and I know what is in yours. Although I have mastered the White One, to you I say I would take you for wife and between us for all our days there shall only be cherishing.'

Daria was silent for a while. Then, raising a hand and brushing her dark hair from her face she said, smiling, 'You do me honour, my lord Arturo, in the asking. *Aie* . . I will gladly and lovingly be wife for you. But though we shall lie in the long grass and listen to the golden birds sing and drink the new wine, those times will be few and far spaced for I know that there will be often the loneliness of longing for you when the White One takes you away. And now — ' she smiled broadly, mocking and teasing him with her eyes, ' — you must do grace to my father and go ask him for leave to make me your bride. I doubt that he will refuse you, but should he then make him a gift of a jar of beer and ask again when he has drunk it.'

* * *

Inbar of the tribe of the Enduring Crow had been well drilled by the captain of the guard on how he should behave before Count Ambrosius. Stiffly drawn up to his full height he stood before the low wooden table at which the Count sat on a folding stool and waited for the man to raise his head to mark his awareness of his presence. All he could see at the moment was a bald head with fluffy wings of greying hair over the ears bowed low over a sheet of new parchment covered with writing. On a bed against the far wall of the room lay an old but well polished cuirass, a red cloak, and a horse-haired plumed bronze helmet as old as the cuirass. Count Ambrosius, all knew, kept to the old Roman ways and ordered his army so. The word from some was that he was a fool who lived in a dream, but there were many more who knew the real truth of the commander. It was that truth of the man which Inbar was hoping to use for his own advantage now. *Aie* . . . and many a long week it had taken him to get this audience.

After a while (and Inbar, whose judgement of men was shrewd, gauged the waiting imposed on him to be deliberate) the Count pushed the parchment to one side and raised his head. As their eyes met Inbar lifted his right hand in a military salute but said nothing, remembering the words of the guard officer who had been one of the last he had bribed to get this interview. A pair of shrewd, narrow-lidded, pale blue eyes fixed themselves steadily on him and a bare arm was raised to jerk the folds of a white toga to comfort about the thin shoulders. A small, hard man, thought Inbar, with no comfort in him for others and need for none himself . . . a shadow Roman, dreaming of the past, but a weasel of a man, swift and deadly. And on that he was placing his hopes.

'Name yourself and your business.' The voice was low but gritty like the rub of sandstone on sandstone.

Inbar said, 'I am Inbar of the tribe of the Enduring Crow, cousin to Baradoc its chief, and uncle to Arturo, the son of Baradoc.'

At the mention of Arturo's name Ambrosius's lips thinned and from his hands which he held locked together as his elbows rested on the table came the crack of his knuckles as his fingers tightened. He said, 'I have heard of you from Prince Gerontius and know you to be a dead man for shaming the wife of Baradoc.'

'Shame there was none, my lord, for the woman would have been willing and I would have made her my wife. Dead I should be, but am not for the gods were on my side when I took the long run and the death drop. Out of their bounty I hit the water cleanly feet first, sank deep and then swam underwater to the cover of the cliff foot where that night my wife came — '

'Yes, yes, the gods were with you, but spare

me the rest and come quickly to your matter with me.'

'Arturo has taken men and horses from you, my lord, and his company grows.'

'You tell me what I already know, man. Come to your point.'

'I would kill Arturo for you.'

Ambrosius raised his head and the cold blue eyes widened in surprise. With an impatient wave of his hand he said, 'What need to come to me and waste my time? Any man is free to kill Arturo for he is outlawed and then the blood-price will be paid.'

'So it would seem, my lord. But beyond the seeming is now the truth that there is not a man in this land who would kill Arturo for a blood-price that he could not live long to enjoy. The blood-price must be claimed openly before you or the noble Prince Gerontius and proof given of the deed. Such openness would mark a man for life, but that life would be short for there are those among his companions who would make it so.'

Count Ambrosius was silent for a while, the thin fingers of one hand fidgeting with the neck yoke of his toga. Then quietly he said, 'It is true that must be the manner of the paying of the blood-price. It is true, too, that I would have him dead. At the moment he is a gadfly but others begin to gather with him. So, what is in the mind of Inbar of the Enduring Crow?'

'Much, my lord, which I would wish to rest secretly between us. Alone, unmarked, and unknown to any, I will kill Arturo for you. As return I ask little. First I would have a small command in your army for I am tired of wandering like a lone wolf. After that, and I can be patient over the years, I ask that when his father Baradoc dies you should through your friendship with Prince Gerontius have me named as Chief of the tribe of the Enduring Crow.'

'Baradoc's death would not clear the road for you. He has another son by the Roman woman Gratia he married, and could have others.'

'No, my lord. From my own wife who still lives with the tribe I know that the woman Tia is now barren since the birth of a fourth child, a girl-child.'

Ambrosius gave a thin smile. 'And it is to your wife — since you are forbidden to go west of Isca — that you would look for the end of the second son . . . a wasting disease, a destroying fever? So, so, and if needs be — for barrenness is no more a certainty in a woman than her affections — she would see that no future man-child lived long?'

'Yes, my lord.'

Count Ambrosius lowered his head on one hand and with the other fingered the edges of the parchment on the table. Arturo and his companions were an annoyance to him. He was a young man of spirit and wild dreams and loud boasts with thirty or forty men at the most (but *his* men and *his* horses). For a moment or two he was on the point of dismissing Inbar. He had greater worries on his mind than Arturo. Vortigern, sunk in senile debauchery in Demetae, had sent no levies this spring and Prince Gerontius, growing in power and ambition, but unwilling yet to move, had cut his levy heavily. The great sickness over the eastern lands was passing, though slowly; and wily Hengist, who had once fought as a Roman auxiliary, was fast drawing fresh men from across the northern sea and would soon begin to move, for no Saxon warrior sat content in camp for long. Warfare and plunder was their only contentment. Feasting, fighting and looting was barbarian joy. Against all this, while he sat there, lacking men still to make his move, waiting on promises, Arturo surely was a single gadfly. He was at the point of dismissing Inbar when the thought quickened in him that even the great Caesars and conquerors were ever at the mercy of time and chance. The sting of a single gadfly could make a mount rear or stumble and a noble captain fall to his death.

Raising his head he said curtly. 'Let it be as you promise, and it shall be as you wish.'

'I thank you, my lord.'

As Inbar went out through the ante-room the captain of the guard said, 'How was the old lizard?'

Inbar smiled and said, 'In the mood for taking flies.' He reached into his belt pouch and handed the man a worn and clipped silver piece of the reign of the Emperor Gratian which had been in the baggage of a trader whose throat he had cut for loot on the Salinae-Glevum road coming south. So, too, would he cut the throat of young Arturo, striking suddenly and without warning.

★ ★ ★

During the handful of days which led up to the feast of Beltine which was on the first day of the month dedicated by the Romans to Maia, the goddess of growth and fertility, Arturo lived in two worlds. There was the world of his love for Daria and hers for him, and the world of the passion in him to set out on his first campaign — though he knew in his heart that with the forces at his command it must needs be more a demonstration of audacity to make his name widely known and bring more men to his side than one of military worth.

In the world of men and horses he passed most of his time, and this without chiding from Daria for she knew the temper of the man she was marrying and secretly approved it. The companions now numbered nearly fifty, all of them mounted. With them were the retainers and craftsmen and workers at the villa who attended the crops, the stores, the cattle, the repair and making of weapons and the care and fashioning of all the horse gear. At first Arturo was here, there and everywhere, attending and supervising to all he could, but as time went by he gave way to the common-sense of leaving many things in the hands of his two chief companions, Durstan and red-bearded Gelliga. He learnt fast that the art of command was to have eyes and ears for everything and everyone, but to turn from wearying himself and worrying his troop leaders by his unnecessary presence and concern at activities and with matters which they could handle as well as himself.

The other world was the one into which he rode most afternoons with Daria on a hide saddle before him and old Anga trotting at the heels of the White One. They went to a withy bower on the far fringe of the water meadow below the forest which the companions had made for them. There they lay in the long grass, and drank, not new wine, but the fresh stream water, yet they listened truly to the golden birds sing, for the hawthorn thickets on the forest edge were full of yellow-hammers in full song. It was there that they talked and caressed one another and between the long sweetness of kisses learned those things of one another which makes the sturdy frame and sheltering roof to house the heart and strength of true love.

One afternoon Pasco the priest came to them and, sitting down on an old grass-covered anthill, spoke to them of marriage.

He said to Arturo, 'The lady Daria has told you that she is of the Christian faith?'

Arturo nodded. 'Yes, but not long since.'

Daria said, 'Why should I talk of something which, in good time, Pasco could talk of far better than me?'

Pasco said, 'It is logic — of a womanly kind. Which means, contrary to most people's thinking, that it is wise. So, my lord Arturo, you know that I cannot marry a follower and worshipper of Christos to one who worships all the heathen gods?'

Arturo nodded, unconcerned. 'Yes, I know that, but it seems to me that you threaten to close a gate against a young ram when he is already within the pen. I worship my country's gods and those of my race. Are not your Christos and his great father gods like other gods?'

'They are indeed, and more so than any other gods.'

'That is no uncommon thing among gods. Some are greater than others. So I am happy to worship your Christos and his father for they are gods and I worship all gods. How else can a man live in grace and under heavenly protection unless he gives homage to all gods? From my mother and my teachers I learned long ago that all the gods the Romans worshipped were but our gods with a different name. Great Bellenus was their Apollo. Our great Credne, who made the silver hand for the god Nodens, was their Vulcan, and so with all of them to the highest. Our all-powerful Dis was their Jove. A name is nothing. There must be as many names for the gods as there are races on this earth with different languages. Have no worry, good Pasco. You can marry me to the lady Daria with a clear mind since I will happily worship this Christos and his great father.'

Pasco rubbed his chin and sighed. He had much admiration for Arturo and knew the goodness and driving passion in him, though there was much about him which gave him doubt. To argue with him further was to invite a spreading of confusion and trouble. In truth he had some sympathy with Arturo's attitude for his own Christian beliefs were touched with paradox and schism which had brought his departure from his own land. The lady Daria would have Arturo for husband for she loved him. For that, if need arose — since her faith was not well-tempered — she would unhesitatingly declare herself no longer a Christian. It was better he gauged to keep the lamb in the fold than lose it forever to a young ram from a strange flock. And was it not true that Christos often chose to bring the heathen by strange paths to grace?

Seeing Daria's eyes attentive on him and her hand holding Arturo's in a union which his common-sense told him, since the season was spring and young blood was young blood, must soon be celebrated, he said. 'Then I will marry you. But there is one small rite of the Christian god you must make.'

Arturo smiled. '*Aie* . . . I know of that, too. You would have me stand in the fountain of the three nymphs and duck me under in baptism? So be it. Cold the water may be, but what could be colder than a heart denied of its love? And know, too, good Pasco, that I shall take pride in being a follower of your Christos. Many of my men are such. Was it not the great Christian Bishop Germanus who gave our people the miraculous Alleluia Victory over the Saxon and Pictish forces of the young Hengist when he first came to these shores?'

So it was that, in a courtyard crowded with all his followers, Arturo — stripped to a loin cloth — was baptized in the great stone bowl of the fountain of the three nymphs. The water which he had expected to be ice-cold seemed warm to him and he gave thanks, as Pasco spoke his ritual words over him, to the goddess Coventina for her favour.

They were married and feasted and then taken in procession by torchlight to the bower in the water meadow, and all that night the forest and stream edges of the meadow were guarded by his companions to watch over their safety, and as the first slip of a late rising moon paled the sky the nightingales began to sing from the hazel beds. The next morning, when the two came out from the bower to face a morning lively with a fresh breeze from the south, Arturo was greeted by the sight of a tall lance fixed firmly in the turf. From it, its folds curling and uncurling in the wind, flew a red war banner which had emblazoned on its centre the device of a rearing white horse, mane and tail flaring as though the breeze itself were giving the animal life.

Daria said, 'This night you have had my bride's gift. This morning I give you my first gift as your wife. May the gods protect you whenever you go into battle with it.'

Arturo, putting his arm around her, his eyes fast on the waving banner said, 'If ever I bring dishonour to it or to you may all the gods desert me.'

★　★　★

Three days later in the early afternoon came the high warning call of the horn of the watchguard on duty at the southwestern edge of the camp lands. The call was three high-pitched blasts which told of the approach of strangers. As the guard men of the day came running from their quarters and the companions working and training about the villa grounds began to muster to arms the horn called again. But this time it was the long high sustained note which told that the strangers came in peace.

Shortly afterwards a small party rode into the villa courtyard where Arturo and his men stood waiting to greet them. Arturo's face lit up as he watched them approach. At their head rode his father, Baradoc, with his mother, Tia, at his side. Behind came three of Prince Gerontius's men as bodyguards followed by two youths leading heavily laden baggage ponies. They greeted each other affectionately and Arturo presented Daria to them as his wife and saw the quick gleam of pleasure and approval in his mother's eyes. Tia, now in her fortieth year, had grown matronly. Time had not flawed her beauty, but the years had given her the noble bearing of a queenly woman. Her hair was still corn gold and her eyes quick and all-embracing as she looked around her. His father, though little older than his mother he knew, looked much older and there were iron grey streaks in his russet hair. His sword arm which had been injured in his fight with Inbar had grown stiffer and when he embraced Arturo it was only with a clasp of his left arm around his shoulders. His face was stern but more, Arturo guessed, now from habit than mirroring any immediate emotion. But his directness of manner was still the same. Daria led Tia away to the women's quarters, and the guard of the day took charge of the comfort of their mounted guard and baggage men. Baradoc, left alone with Arturo, walked to the edge of the fountain basin and sat down. He accepted the cup of wine which one of the camp women brought to him, touched his lips to it and handed it back. When the woman had gone, he said to Arturo evenly, 'We stay not the night for we are in Count Ambrosius's country and that would be a discourtesy to him.'

Arturo, smiling, answered, 'This is my country — but I take no issue with you, father. That you are here, and my mother, too, is a joy to me. But I would be foolish to think that you come simply as father to greet his son.'

Baradoc nodded. 'That is the truth. I would it were otherwise.' Then looking around him, he went on, 'You have things well-ordered here. Your horses in the pastures are a delight to the eye. The crops show fair, and your men walk and hold themselves with dignity and pride. You and your time here are wasted, though. You live in a dream of defiance.

'I live to make a dream come true. And the gods are with me.'

Baradoc smiled and, rubbing his stiff right shoulder, said wryly, 'You are as ever, I see, a familiar of the gods and enjoy their favour. Well, I will not argue with you about that. I come from Prince Gerontius on other business. He has entrusted to me a task of great importance — I go now, in fact, to persuade Count Ambrosius of this. For this task I would have one at my side whom I can trust. Someone to take the place of this . . . '

he half-raised his stiff right arm.

For a moment or two Arturo said nothing. From the companions who had come to him recently he had heard of the great fortress which Prince Gerontius planned to raise in the country of the Durotriges, west of Lindinis, an armed camp to be a bastion against any future westward move of the Saxons. Then seeing his father's eyes shrewdly watching him, he said, 'I have heard something of this work. But to me . . . ' He shrugged his shoulders. 'Well, my father, it is one thing for a hedgehog to roll itself into a ball of spikes until the fox walks away, but Hengist and his Saxon kind are not to be so easily baulked. They will sit themselves down around your hedgehog and wait for it to starve to death.'

Baradoc shook his head. 'There is more to it than that. I would have you know it and work for it with me. That is why I am here. Prince Gerontius will withdraw the warrant of outlawry on you. When I have seen Count Ambrosius he will do the same — for in return he will get a levy of troops he thinks not to have. The Prince expects no humbling of yourself before him. You give him your allegiance truly. In return, you are free, and you can come with me to help in this great work and you bring your men and horses and all your people as your command.'

Arturo, tight-lipped, shook his head. 'In a fashion he sues for my help. But now the wind blows from another quarter. I have men here who have only one thought in mind — and that is not to sit them down and protect the building of this great fort which you would raise in the country of the Durotriges. Nor have I such thought. Within a month I would have no men. They are hungry for war and defiance — and so am I. We begin small, true, my father. But after the flowering of one blood-red poppy who can count the seeds that burst from the pod? To turn aside now would shame me before my men, and — greater evil — be a betrayal of the bounty which the gods have given to our company. With the gods we can dare all. But sitting on our backsides about a great fort would invite their mockery.'

Baradoc shook his head and sighed. 'You think too much of the gods — but, remember this, there are those they touch with madness in order to destroy them. Still I make no further argument with you about this matter. Your answer is what I expected. Nor, in truth, would I have pursued it this far were it not for the urging of your mother.'

Before the little party left Tia walked alone with Arturo along the terraced plots below the villa where now the young bean shoots grew high and the spring cabbage fattened to say her farewell to her son. Another son she had and two daughters, but this one was the marked one. For him, not long after his birth, the water in the silver chalice had fired to crimson and she had known then and still knew that his destiny was his own to make and — no matter the wish in her heart which had brought her here — she had never had any true hope of turning him from the perilous path which he so strongly believed the gods had set before him. He was Baradoc's son, but where the fire of steady purpose burned evenly in Baradoc, the blaze of destiny in Arturo was like the wild, wind-swept flaming of a heath fire. Her sole joy was to have seen him again and to know an increase in that joy in learning that he was married to Daria to whom her heart had warmed so immediately that, putting aside any thought of a last plea that he should join his father, she said to him now, 'The woman you have taken to wife pleases me. I know that she shares the dream you have. But remember this, Arturo, for I speak to you as a man, not my son, the constancy of a woman's heart-troth for her man is no polished jewel to be untouched by time and absence. It is a living plant which can wither under the killing frosts of long absence while her lover dedicates himself to an all-consuming love of his country — or selfish glory. If you love her truly then find at times the strength to turn aside from your dreams. The gods were never truly jealous of any man's hearth with wife and children round it.'

Arturo took her hand fondly and said with a present honesty and passion, 'I shall never cease from cherishing Daria, nor ever give her true cause to turn away from me. Do I not remember how it was with you during the years my father was away? Your virtue was a sword which went before you.'

Tia made no answer for she knew that he spoke as he would want things to be and, knowing only the strength of his young manhood, had yet to learn how weak and barren the spirit and body of a woman could be who lived in loneliness. Later, as she rode away in the party with Baradoc, the memory came back sharply to her that Daria might not ever have even the comfort of children for Merlin had long ago written of Arturo before his birth on the grey rock of a Caer Sibli cliff face —

Name him for all men and all time
His glory an everlasting flower
He throws no seed

Under the Banner of the White Horse

After the feast of Beltine all sweethearts, wives and children left the villa, except for Daria and Ansold who were to go to the nearest forest settlement when Arturo and his men left. Of all the men who had gone away to visit their homelands and their families only two never returned and it was known much later that of these one had been killed in a drunken quarrel and the other had died of the slow sickness in his home town of Ariconium west of the Sabrina river. This sickness had been spreading now for over two years from the north. It came slowly and unevenly. It left great areas of the country untouched, worked up some main river valleys but left the tributaries untouched, broke out in one village and left its neighbour unplagued, and turned one town into a desert while another a few miles away went unscathed. Against it there was no defence. It began as a mild heating of the body that sent a man gently sweating and gave him a thirst which slowly grew with the passing of the days until within a few weeks his body was a furnace and his strength burned away until the day came when he died, his body unmarked by any blemish. It was no new thing. The oldest of men could remember it in their boyhood and held the memory of their fathers' memories of it. It was accepted as the seasons were accepted, and this year it was being said that it was as bad as any could remember and was the cause of Hengist and his fellow chieftains showing no signs yet of moving their warbands westwards across its direct path.

Arturo gave it little importance. Disease was the lot of man and beast. A beast was at the mercy of the good keeping and feeding of his master, but a man was his own master. He should drink clean water, eat good meat and bread, and — in his camp — keep the privies clean and, except in the coldest of seasons, wash the body thoroughly every two weeks. So far there had been no sickness in his camp, nor any sign of it in the neighbouring country.

The slow sickness held no part in his thoughts for they were full of the move which he was poised to make with his companions. Each day now was filled with preparations for the march eastwards, and although he knew that it would be no great army he led he was fired with the thought that from the exploits and daring of his handful of men an army would grow and, with its growth, the renown of his name. From its victories must come the approval and favour still further of the gods.

On the night before the morning of his leaving the camp with his company of comrades he lay awake on the bed in their chamber at the villa with Daria. The wall sconces were alight still, the wickering flames giving life to the birds, beasts and flowers of the shabby, peeling wall paintings. Holding Daria's hand, he leaned over her and kissed her and then said, 'I say my farewell to you now. Tomorrow morning will be too full of affairs. While I am gone, pray to your God for me, and know that everywhere I go I carry you in my heart. I shall sleep with my shield at my shoulder and my sword at my side, but in my dreams I shall walk with you beneath the sweet yellow apple tree by the stream and there shall be no sadness in the voice of the storm thrush, nor melancholy in the call of the blackbird from the bower of the white blossomed thorn tree. I shall see your bright cheeks, red lips, eyebrows as black as a chafer and your teeth pure as the noble colour of snow . . . '

Daria made no answer, though she smiled at his words, knowing that with the comrades in his hall he had feasted and drunk the last of the over-winter mead. But her heart was full with her love for him and she needed no words to show it. She drew him down to her and held him in her arms. When he slept she lay awake and kept him harboured within her embrace all night.

They rode out the next morning to leave the villa of the three nymphs to the foxes and the birds, to the basking lizards and snakes, and their growing crops to the care and mercy of the surrounding settlements. At their head rode Arturo on the White One, wearing a leather war cap from which the red and white horse plumes swayed in the morning breeze. About his neck was knotted a red and white scarf and tight around his leather tunic a studded belt which carried sword and knife, his trews cross-gartered with braided deer-hide thongs, his legs guarded by a pair of old bronze greaves. Over his shoulder he carried, as did all the companions, a small round buckler painted red with the device of the rearing white horse on it, and he held himself proudly, his head high so that the low sun set dull fire flecks amongst the growth of the campaigning beard he had grown. At his side rode Daria's brother Lancelo, red and white plumed and scarfed, armed with shield and sword, and carrying high the war banner of the White One.

Behind them came the companions, all plumed and scarfed and armed and buck-lered, but clothed for war variously. Some wore the clothes of the Sabrina Wing from which they had come. Some were cuirassed fore and back with padded leather plates, and a few proudly bore old bronze cuirasses which had seen service nearly a hundred years before in the days of Stilicho and Constantine, the sad days when the Second Legion had been withdrawn from Isca and the Twentieth from Deva to strengthen the defences of the great Shore Fort at Rutupiae as the Western Empire crumbled and the lights of law and order and prosperity guttered low in Britain.

They mustered near sixty horses, and Arturo had divided his force into two troops of twenty-four horse each. The first troop was commanded by his closest friend Durstan with Garwain of Moridunum on the river Tuvius as his second-in-command. The second troop was led by the bearded, sweet-singing Gelliga from Lavobrinta in the country of the Ordovices who had for his deputy the young fresh-faced giant-handed Borio from Calcaria in the land of the Parisi. Behind them came the remount section of six horses, ridden by two other companions, the brothers dumb Timo and Marcos and the two young men — Barma and Felos — who had first come to the villa bringing tribute from the surrounding Britons. Behind them came a string of pack ponies, led and ridden by the priest Pasco and other workers who had attached themselves to the community of the companions over the months.

It was a small force but a brave one, well trained and disciplined, and now fully aware of what was in Arturo's mind. The only man who travelled unarmed was Pasco, and as the column rode out of the courtyard he intoned in a loud voice a prayer — to which for Arturo's sake he added a few unorthodox touches —

O chaste Christ well-beloved, and all
the native gods of this great country, to
whom every verdict is clear, may the
grace of the Sevenfold Spirit come to
keep and protect these Thy servants.

Let neither sword nor spear restrain
them, nor the enemy slip from their
grasp like an eel's tail, so that under Thy
banner neither barbarian, bond, fortress
or bare waste can stop their course.

O powerful Creator, and Protectors,
rule our hearts, that Thou mayest be
our love, and that we may do Thy will.

And so they went down the hill slope to the pasture and into the water meadows to follow the streamside which would take them by midday to the valley of the young Tamesis river. Here, they would turn eastward until they came to the ford which carried the Corinium road that ran to Spinis and Calleva and beyond into the heart of the waste lands waiting yet to be fully claimed and held by Briton or barbarian. As they moved along the stream the feeding mallards rose in flight and their young broods scattered to hiding in the reeds and sedges and the kingfishers fled before them like moving tongues of flame.

High up the valley side, on their right flank and hidden in the woods, Inbar watched them move, sitting his horse which switched its tail lazily against the summer flies. He wore a long brown woollen cloak which hid the sword he carried from his belt. Across his back was slung a hunting bow and a plaited-straw sheath of arrows, and lashed behind him was a roll of baggage to serve him in the slow hunt which was now beginning. Only the gods could number its days, but he knew that it would be long. Of patience he had no lack, but he prayed, his thick lips twisting wryly at the irony, that the gods would protect Arturo from Saxon sword or spear so that his death should come at his

313

hands, that he could cut the young head from its broad shoulders and carry it secretly to Count Ambrosius to claim his due.

★　★　★

Two days later Arturo and his company rode into Calleva of the Atrebates. In their progress, riding along the old road, its ditches ruined, its surface broken and long despoiled in places, they had met no travellers. In the crop fields their fellow countrymen watched them from a safe distance, offering them no friendship, and the cattle-minders seeing the cloud of dust that rose about them drove their beasts fast to distant safety. They trotted in over the old earthworks, the setting sun rose-tinting the ruined walls, and through the west gate opening, bare now of the great portals which had once swung close to protect the town at night.

Except for a few old people, spinning out their handful of days, left in misery and hunger, the town was a place of the dead. There was nothing of value left. Here no man pursued his craft, no merchant his barter, no housewife her marketing. No children played and even the sparrows and kites had deserted the place. Between the Saxons of the East and the Britons of the West and North the country was a nomansland where safety lay in forest and river marsh or the openness of the high downs. If a town were visited by the people scattered in the surrounding country it was done in strength and then only for the pillage of masonry and wood or metal water pipes.

They slept that night in the old, almost ruined *mansio* close to the south gate. The horses were quartered in the inner courtyard and the company slept either in the surrounding lodging rooms of this old official inn of Roman days, or lay rolled in their blankets under the balmy night sky. A courtyard well held good water still for men and horses. Doing his rounds that night to the sentries he had posted, Arturo, his footsteps echoing through the ruins, could imagine the days when travellers and staging Roman officers and officials had made the place a hive of warmth and talk as they passed through on their way to new postings in distant legions or to seek fresh markets and trade as far north as the Antonine Wall. His lips tightened as he thought of those ordered, prosperous days and of his country now. A country which was being torn apart by so many forces and made a ruin and a desert to offend the eyes of man and the hearts of the gods. That night he swore that his companions should never be quartered again in any town so long as this campaign lasted. *Aie* . . . he thought, grinning ruefully, if campaign it could be called with none it seemed ready to stay the way of his handful of companions.

Yet despite this moment of self-doubt, the next morning he had his men round up all the miserable people who still stayed in the town, bringing them limping and halting into the old Forum through the ruins of its monumental east entrance to be greeted by his companions, mounted on parade and drawn up in line along the front of the shell which had once been the basilica.

Riding out from the centre of his companions, the White One curvetting and restless beneath him, and with Lancelo holding the red banner of the white horse behind him, he spoke first in his own tongue and then in the tongue of his mother to them. Listening, Pasco smiled to himself for it amused him to recognize that in the warrior a great preacher had been lost. The smile went as he wondered why it was that war and bloodshed could silver a man's tongue so readily where love of God and one's neighbour so often left him dumb.

Arturo spoke as though he were addressing a crowd of ablebodied, just-minded citizens and seeking recruits and support to his cause which he called the Great Matter of Britain and for which, he proclaimed with sincerity, the gods of his country had fingered him as the chosen one to achieve. To his side must come the warring and jealous princes and kings and warriors of his own country, all men of good intent, to revive the greatness of the past, to restore peace and prosperity, and to order justice and free passage for all. But to this end there could be only one beginning — the barbarian Saxons of the East must be swept away, driven to the sea to seek their ships and the safety of their own countries.

Although his companions had heard it all before when he had told them of his dream of this great progress which would give them fighting enough and also carry his message abroad, and had mostly latched their minds to the prospect of battle, there was something in his manner this morning, as he spoke to the miserable handful of old crones and broken men before him, that kindled a new fire in their spirits. A horse and a sword, the dust and sweat and blood of war had been promised and would be given them. But now they began to see the shape of a greater glory than their passion for battle had ever promised. They saw themselves now, each according to his faith, the picked of the gods or God. From that moment, though none showed it openly, there was a new dignity of the heart and a bolder, nobler edge to their allegiance to Arturo which they would take with them into battle counting the loss of their life for a comrade's safety no loss but a gain to be rewarded in Heaven or the Shades.

As they rode out of Calleva, Arturo, loosening his neck scarf against the morning's growing heat, turned to Pasco, who had come trotting up to give him company on his right side, and said, 'And what does the good Pasco think of my preaching in the Forum?'

Pasco smiled, wetting his lips with his tongue, and said, 'The preaching was good. But the congregation was poor. What gain will you have for your cause in such few and wretched hearts? There was not a man among them with strength to raise a sword nor any woman with her mind on aught but the hope of good pickings to fill her supper pot.'

Arturo nodded his head. '*Aie* . . . that is true. But they have that which I need. Each mouth has a tongue and when they go into the countryside to steal or beg amongst the scattered country people they will talk of the strange company in Calleva this day. And since country people are hungry for news and gossip they will listen, and the story will pass and pass until it begins to blaze like a summer fire through dry glasslands. Though I have sworn to quarter no more in towns, for their ruin and misery sickens my heart, there is none we shall pass without a herding of its wretched people to hear my words.' He paused for a moment and then added slyly, 'Does it not say in your religion that in the beginning was the Word?'

Pasco, surprised, raised an eyebrow and asked, 'How do you know the disciple John so well?'

Arturo laughed. 'From a Druid priest who taught me well when he was sober enough to sit his stool without falling.'

'Do not forget that since you have been baptized it is your religion as well.'

'Nor shall I. A man cannot have too many gods to watch over him.'

Pulling up his horse sharply Lancelo said, 'Then let us hope they are all with us now.'

From the top of the gentle hill which they had just crested he pointed ahead down the slope. At the bottom of the broad valley where the road crossed a small stream a body of about thirty men on foot barred the way in three ragged ranks.

Arturo, reining in, said, 'They would have done better to have chosen this hilltop than the valley bottom. Sound the horn for Gelliga's troop.'

From inside his cloak Lancelo pulled his bull horn and blew the four sharp battle notes and then a long fifth which was the call for

Gelliga's command.

Without looking back Arturo sat the White One and watched the men at the valley bottom. Many a time the manoeuvre which must come now had been made in mock attack from the forest hill down to the stream at the villa of the three nymphs. Many a time this situation and others had been drilled and redrilled into men and horses. But now across his path stood his first real enemy, and on this bright morning there awaited him his first real attack. His breath quickened a little with pleasure. The moment had come sooner than he had thought, but it was more welcome for that. He looked back and saw Gelliga leading his men at a gentle trot away from the road and up the hill slope to the left to stop just short of the skyline. Keeping to the road came Durstan's troop to ride openly on to the crest and halt in four ranks of six behind Arturo. Farther back the remounts and baggage horses were being taken well away to the right flank.

Durstan rode to Arturo's side and said, 'They cannot know our strength or they would not stand so bunched and ready for plucking.'

'There are many things they will learn and those that live will tell. Now let us see what days and nights of aching backsides and sore thighs have done for us.'

Pasco, steadying his restless, sturdy hill pony, sat and watched. The men were Saxons and were a rabble, though well armed. They were, he guessed, the war party of a scattered community of outcasts or adventurers who had moved away or been banished from the settled lands of the Saxon shore. There were many such pockets along the line of the valley of the river Tamesis and those communities often lived in uneasy peace with the native British of the district. The rumour of Arturo's coming must have spread ahead of him. They stood now to dispute his way unless he chose to make a detour around their lands — which he well knew was not in the character of Arturo whom he had come to love well, to regard highly and — from a religious point of view — to indulge gently for he knew well that Christ chose His servants with a wisdom and understanding beyond the minds of men.

The skirmish was brief and to be repeated with variations dictated by ground and chance many times to come in their advance eastwards. Lancelo's horn sounded the long, high, wickering call to advance. Durstan's troop put their horses to the gallop and charged down the slope towards the Saxons who awaited their coming with heavy, sharp-pointed, single-edged scramaseax swords drawn and their small round shields raised, not for defence so much as for striking at the face of their enemy once he was brought to ground to fight foot to foot. Arturo and Lancelo stayed on the hilltop.

Seeing him restraining the impatient White One, Pasco smiled to himself. He knew well what was in his mind. This was no full battle that needed him at the head of his force. Both Durstan and Gelliga knew his mind, and he would take away no part of their pride of command. Also, too, Pasco guessed, more than the pleasuring blood-surge of moving into action, he would be drawing a greater pleasure from seeing the long hours of cavalry attack drills at the villa now pass into reality itself where a ham-stringed horse could send a man to the ground to meet the swinging scramaseax, the face-smashing shield and — if the gods were unkind — have a ready seax dagger sharp-slit his throat.

The dust clouds rose behind Durstan's troop as it swept down on the Saxons, and the unruly barbarians, eager for fight, broke ranks and ran to meet it. But the moment that the troop was within a spear's length of the foremost Saxons every horse swung to the right and raced across the front of the enemy as though their riders had suddenly lost heart. A great shout of triumph went up from the Saxons as they turned and chased them, calling taunts and bellowing their derision.

It was then that Gelliga's troop came over the hill top and charged at full gallop down the slope to take the Saxons in the rear. Hooves thundering, tails and manes flying, the morning sunlight bright on drawn swords and helmet crests and streaming crimson and white scarves, the troop, with Gelliga and the great-handed Borio leading its centre, the companions' line spread out into a horned crescent and scythed its way into the rear of the Saxons. Some turned to meet their foe and died with wound in throat or chest, but most were killed from behind and went to their end not knowing they carried the death mark of those who die with their backs to the enemy to be banished forever from Woden's hall.

In a short while the attack was over and the few Saxons who had survived were running away from the road and along the stream and over the marshy ground where they were left free from pursuit. Amongst the companions there were few injuries. One had taken a spear thrust in the shoulder, another a slash from a seax which had cut through the hide cross-gartering of his leg and scored his calf with a long, though shallow wound, and others had cuts and bruises of no importance.

But one horse had had its windpipe and neck artery slashed with a sword and died as Gelliga's troop reformed. It was left for the crows and kites and foxes and rats to pick clean. None said a word to the companion who had ridden it, for there are no words that can pass with any comfort to a man who has lost a loved mount. He sat by it, stone-faced, until the party moved on and then took his remount and cantered to his place in his troop column. Behind the troop came the baggage party its cart and pony packs loaded with the pick of sword and knife and axe and the meagre plunder taken from the bodies of the dead Saxons.

From that day they moved no longer directly to the east. Staying south of the Tamesis, which hereabouts took a great loop northwards, they travelled in zigzag fashion, meeting little opposition, but when they did having scant trouble with it for the Saxons, hating village or town life, lived separately in single huts in the woods and hills, and had no firm leader or trust in their own kind to band together often to oppose them. Wherever he could find a British village or settlement, no matter if it only contained a handful of people, Arturo would stop and, with his companions on full parade behind him, make his declamation as he had done at Calleva, so that the news of his presence and progress ran before him. To his delight now and again men of worth who had long deserted Count Ambrosius and Vortigern to return to their homes came to join him. Welcome they were when they came mounted and armed, but those who carried only the clothes they stood in and the itch for action were mounted and supplied with arms and such war gear as Arturo's force took from the Saxons in their path.

By the time that Arturo reached the town of Pontes and the now south-curving Tamesis he had almost the makings of a third troop of horse under his command. He stayed three days in camp on the banks of the river outside the town and was pleased to see small groups of local people come close to the camp to watch and — he knew full well — to go back to their settlements and homes to talk about him and his men.

Sitting that evening on the river bank by the side of the ford which they would cross the next morning, for the old wooden bridges had long been wrecked and pillaged for the sake of their timbers, he knew that far and near now the name of Arturo and his companions was working in the minds of more and more of his countrymen like a ferment in the honey and water of new mead.

On this progress he commanded no force large enough to fight great battles, but he would have blazed his name and intent across the country to catch the eyes and ears of every man who longed for true leadership and an end to his present misery, and so bring many of them to his side. With that for this year he would be content.

As he sat there a thin summer drizzle began to fall and suddenly from the smooth surface of the rolling Tamesis a great salmon, running the river to the spawning beds of the headwaters, leaped like a great bow of silver into the air. Seeing the fish he remembered the story of the goddess Latis who wept and brought the rains to fill the rivers to bring back her warrior lover who deserted her each year to go to the sea as a salmon. Remembering this, he thought suddenly of Daria who sat now and waited for him, Daria who grew more and more absent from his mind if not from his heart.

He had then a black sense of shame that he, whose eyes watched always for signs from the gods who controlled his destiny, saw now a sign from the peaceful, gentle Latis which should not have been necessary.

He rose and with the Latis rain dewing his face went into the camp and found the youth Felos.

Arturo, the shame still clouding him, said, 'Go to Marcos. Tell him to give you a horse, weapons and food. Ride back to the lady Daria and give her all the count of our days and progress. Then, returning, bring with you all her news.'

'Yes, my lord.'

'Say that I am well and bear her always in my thoughts and heart.'

'Yes, my lord. And where will I find you, my lord?'

Sharply, Arturo said, 'Only the gods can say. But . . . ' he smiled, to ease his tartness, ' . . . find me and from that day you and your brother Barma shall ride as companions.'

Felos, beaming, raised his hand in salute and was gone at a smart trot to find Marcos.

★ ★ ★

Three weeks later they rode out from the great elms which crested the high ground to the north-west of Londinium. They were now a company of two troops of thirty-two horse, each still commanded by Gelliga and Durstan, and a reserve troop of fifteen horse commanded by one of the new companions, Cuneda, from Lactodorum in the country of the Catuvellauni, a man of forty, built like an ox, black-bearded but without a hair on his head.

Their camp servants had increased and they now had two carts, the second taken from a burnt-out farmstead which they had repaired and fitted with runners to carry their food supplies and grain for their horses — though the grass being abundant and sweet at this time of the year their mounts needed no more than a few handfuls of corn a day. Five of the companions bore wounds which, under Pasco's care, were fast healing, and two companions had been killed the day after leaving Pontes when riding ahead of the column as scouts they had been ambushed by a band of robbers and cut-throats who stripped them of clothes and weapons and disappeared into the thickness of the surrounding forest where none could follow them. They were buried where they lay and, as Pasco finished his prayers for them, Arturo turned aside and rode alone with his grief, knowing it to be the beginning of a burden of the soul which he must from now on learn to endure as the never-ceasing lot of a commander of men.

Below them now the silver loops of the Tamesis snaked away eastwards to the sun-blazed spread of its estuary, and at their feet lay the once great city of Londinium. Only a few wisps of smoke rose from its houses. It was a dead city for these days, without true commerce or trade, there was no gain or security to be found in it. People in these times drew away from towns and settled where a living was to be found, in their hovels and sparse communities close to their poorly cropping fields and cattle grounds.

Arturo sent two of the companions to ride down to the city gate close to the ruined fort at the north-west corner of the walls to bring him back news of the place. When they returned they reported that the two western gates, though unmanned, were open and in good repair, that the fort was empty and that the great wooden bridge over the river was broken and gapped in many places and would give no crossing. There were people in the half-ruined city still, but they were a miserable set of wretches who lived by pillage which they bartered to the surrounding country folk, and there was scarce an able-bodied man or woman amongst them. Where there had been greatness and the noisy bustle of commerce and trade, and the ring of horses' hooves and the clank of armour as well-furbished and well-ordered troops had garrisoned the great fort and the walls, there was heard now only the scavenging cries of the kites and the carrion birds and the barking of dog packs that roamed the alleyways and deserted houses. And that they were there was due to one thing. The slow sickness had swept through the city since the beginning of summer and, although it was now almost abated, the streets and houses still held the corpses of the dead, lying as they had fallen to make a feasting for all the city's carrion.

Hearing this Arturo was for a while in two minds whether he should risk his company in such a place, but then the conviction came strongly to him that since the gods had led him thus far under their favour, that favour would still run only if he entered the place and raised the white horse banner for all to see so that the report of his coming would spread like a great ripple across the country. This was Londinium Augusta, once sacked and burnt by the great Queen Boudicca, greater than Camulodunum or any other city, the capital of the great Roman province of Britain. Through him, he knew with unquestionable conviction, this capital and his country would one day become great again.

He left the reserve troop of horse to guard the baggage train and with the rest of his companions. Lancelo carrying the white horse banner before them, he rode down to the city and entered it through the most southerly of the two western gates. Men, women and children, dull-eyed from the slow sickness, lay in the gutters and doorways and gave them no greeting as they waited for death. Hooves

330

clattering on the broken paving and rubble of the streets, the crows and kites rising in wild flight from the bodies that here and there littered their way, the dog packs retreating from them, snarling and barking, they moved along the Tamesis side, past the ruined warehouses and collapsed river stockades, the gulls and river birds, disturbed from their low tide feeding, flighting from the beaches. Past the broken and burnt and pillaged Londinium bridge and the ruin of the great river palace they went, and then swung north to breast the rising ground and finally rode in proud formation into the old Forum and drew up in a long line of horse across the face of the ruined and derelict basilica. With them came a growing drift of miserable human flotsam and jetsam, men and women with nothing to lose but their lives which for most would be a happy release, ragged, half-starving and moving like famine-weary cattle.

Arturo rode forward a little and to these, as though they were proud, well-set citizens, he made his declamation. When he had finished there was for a while a low muttering among them and then it died as the sound of a slow flurry of passing rain dies before the wind. Arturo and his men rode away and the crowd stayed where they were, no strength or curiosity in them to fire their wasted limbs and weak spirits. Helmet plumes tossing, the white horse banner before them, the companions passed from the city, splashing over the summer-low river which flowed down through the heart of the city, past the ruined Baths, past the shells of once noble buildings with their broken statues and defaced and cracked tablets of dedication, and out into the clean air and the green grass of the hill slopes where the rest of the company awaited them.

At Arturo's side Lancelo said, 'Can such a city ever live again?'

Arturo, stiff-faced, moved by all he had seen, said with curt emotion, 'Under the gods, some day, it must and will.'

The next day, at low tide, they forded the river well above the city and the column turned south to begin a great sweep which should bring them westwards to move along the fringes of the great forests that rolled northwards from the shore line of the country of the Regnenses, from the sea towns of Anderida and Noviomagus.

★   ★   ★

Twelve days later they fought their first and only battle of the progress. In the early hours of the morning as they were camped below the crest of a steep scarp of the hills it started

332

to rain heavily. Since they lay in the open, rolled in their blankets without cover, Arturo gave the order to break camp and move. Every campaigner amongst them knew that the misery of rain soaking through blankets and clothes is abated if it can be met marching rather than lying on wet ground.

The companions formed into their two troops and moved off while the baggage train followed them more slowly with the half troop of reserve horse in their rear to prevent surprise attack from behind. But as the morning wore on the ground became soaked and soft and slowed up the movement of the two baggage carts and the rearguard screen of cavalry. Little by little the leading troops gradually drew out ahead. Two troopers rode wide on each flank of the column as scouts, their cloak hoods drawn close about their heads against the still driving rain. At mid-morning as they rode along the crest of a broad upland sheep run, the turf studded with gorse and broom bushes and clumps of wild hawthorn and bramble thickets, the two leading troops dropped down into a great dip in the land and disappeared from the sight of the reserve troop and baggage column following.

At this moment, from the bushes well to the left flank, there arose a party of fifty or sixty Saxons which came running hard, howling and shouting and brandishing their weapons, to drive a wedge between the head of the baggage train and the forward two troops of horse now lost to sight. Then, too, from the right flank more Saxons ran from their hiding places and raced to the rear of the train to form a barrier between it and the following guard troopers.

Long before Cuneda, the rear guard commander, could reach for his horn and call the alarm the two parties of Saxons had swept round and among the baggage carts, killing all those who had not escaped at the sight of their coming. As the first notes of Cuneda's horn wailed the alarm the Saxons formed a circle about the carts and stood firm in three ranks to defend their position and their plunder.

That morning as Arturo, the alarm horn sounding in his ears, forced the White One hard back up the slope to the down top and saw the Saxon force surrounding his baggage carts, he learnt a lesson he was never to forget. Hard rain makes a man seek what comfort, even on the move, that he can. His scouts had ridden with their cloaks cowling their heads, their eyes part blinkered, their minds on their discomfort rather than on the country around them. But, more important, and this came from instinct rather than deliberate thinking, he knew that any hesitation now would only feed the wild temper of the Saxons who ringed the baggage carts while others of their comrades were already pillaging them. The situation before him now was none that had ever been faced in mock attack at the villa of the three nymphs. He acted from impulse and instinct without time even for a prayer to the gods to be with him, for anger and humiliation at being so surprised possessed him completely.

He shouted a command to Lancelo at his side and as his horn began to sound, he drove the White One forward into a gallop with the troops of Gelliga and Durstan following him in a combined wedge-shaped formation.

Pasco, who had been riding his pony with the leading troops, came back up the slope on to the level ground in time to see the tight wedge of flying horses, great scuds of turf flung up behind them by their pounding hooves, burst into the ring of massed Saxons, the swords of the companions swinging and flashing in the rain.

But the Saxons, shouting insults, held their ranks as the cavalry swirled round them on either side, the horses neighing with excitement and others squealing with pain as they were cut down or ham-stringed, leaving their riders to fight on foot. Around the baggage carts men and horses circled like a great whirlpool. The air was full of the shouts of the Saxons who stood their ground; and the bright and bloody flash of sword and axe and swinging scramaseax. Watching, Pasco realized — for he had travelled far and seen much in his time — that these were no cut-throat, outcast, plunder-hungry men such as harried the valley of the Tamesis. They stood and fought like warriors and there was one among them, towering head and shoulders above the rest, who wore an iron-banded leather helmet and a short white sheepskin cloak that fell to his waist and was caught there by a sword belt with a silver clasp, who was clearly the leader. These men were Hengist's men from the settled Saxon lands to the east, seasoned men who would stand their ground so long as the faintest flicker of victory burned for them.

Lancelo's horn blew and the two troops drew back and reformed, and then the horn blew again to send in the rearguard troop under Cuneda and then Durstan's. Arturo watched Cuneda's attack break against the Saxon ring, swirl about it and pass by, and then, his anger passing and his brain clearing, he realized that cavalry could only do so much against men who stood and fought and kept their ranks.

Durstan's troop followed Cuneda's to the attack. As it went in Arturo dismounted followed by Gelliga, Borio and all their men to attack on foot. The cavalry swung left and right of the Saxon ring to harry its flanks and the dismounted companions flung themselves against its front. Leading them was Arturo, sword swinging, his buckler held low to prevent the swift Saxon thrust to the groin, cutting and hacking his way into the ring of men, forcing his way towards their leader in the sheepskin cloak. The Saxon chief, seeing him come, recognizing he must be the leader of the companions, pressed forward through his men to meet him. They met with a great clash of sword and scramaseax, Arturo silent while the Saxon shouted taunts and insults at him. In the few moments before the lust of battle claimed him Arturo called silently to the gods to be with him, and then all thought deserted him as he became one with the flash and hiss of his sweeping, jabbing sword.

Pasco, watching them fighting face to face in the confused and bloody throng of men, saw the swing and thrust of cavalry sword and scramaseax flash above the sea of heads and straining bodies, lost them, saw them again while the air rang with the fierce shouting of men and the screams of those who fell. Then suddenly, the white-fleeced cloak was gone. A great shout went up from the companions and, like the concerted movement of a raiding flock of crows taking wing in alarm from a field of young corn, the Saxons broke and ran. Pasco, who had seen battle against the Saxons many times, knew their mind and their temper. With hope of victory they would fight and stand and die, but when hope or strong leadership went, they would turn and run. Only if they were hopelessly surrounded would they bunch and face their enemy and fight to the end, taking their wounds from the front and going gladly to their death to claim a warrior's welcome from Woden.

As the Saxons ran, the cavalry reformed and harried them along the down top until Lancelo's horn blew the recall. Pasco, riding up on his pony into the carnage and destruction that surrounded the baggage train, found Arturo standing over the dying Saxon chief.

Blood running over his white fleece cloak from a great sword thrust into his chest, he lay with his eyes closed. But after a few moments he slowly opened his eyes, looked up at Arturo and said something in his own language. Then his head dropped to one side as life passed from him.

Arturo, leaning on his sword, said to Pasco, 'You know their tongue?'

Pasco nodded. 'Yes, my son. He said that

now in Hengist's hall the name of Arturo of the White Horse will no longer make men laugh in scorn.'

Arturo, after a moment's pause, said solemnly, 'May his gods honour him, as this day we humbly honour ours for the victory they have given us.'

That evening they camped beside a muddy, slow-flowing stream and Arturo, after eating, sat by himself on the bankside in a brooding mood which kept his companions from him.

The day which was passing had taught him many things and among them those which he knew he should have long marked from his own understanding. Ten of his troopers had been killed, and six of the baggage train, among them Timo the dumb one. Six wounded horses had had to be destroyed. If his name were not now to be held in scorn in Hengist's hall there was much about his own conceit of himself which gave him self-scorn. The gods, though they had kept his side, had given him lessons which he would never forget. Chief among these was that cavalry by itself was useless against men who would bravely stand and fight on foot. He had to have such men, men who would march and fight afoot, to come behind the cavalry and hold the ground or pour through the breaches made by his horse. He knew now that he had fed too long on his dreams. From this day the hard work began. He had made his progress and the name of Arturo had spread and was spreading. Behind the Word now he had to work and build and shape the reality of a great command.

Then, looking up into the evening sky, pearl-streaked and as lustrous as the inside of a mussel shell, he saw a peregrine stoop from its high pitch and heard the hiss of the scarred air as it came down to take a teal duck which was planing down to the river for its evening feeding. But the teal, seeing the peregrine coming, swung aside in alarm and dropped like a stone into the safety of the streamside flags to leave the peregrine to fly down the river calling angrily, and he knew that it was a sign from the gods to him. Swift and deadly might be the cavalry, but when the prey went to ground there must be means to flush it from its place.

Dawn Meeting

For more than a month Arturo and his company moved westwards and wherever there was town, hamlet, settlement or village to be found they would stop and Arturo would draw up his companions and address the people. The news of the manner and purpose of his coming running ahead of him, there was now no fear of him so that on the high downs when they rested for a night the cattle and sheep minders would come from their runs to see and hear him, and in the wooded valleys he drew the lonely charcoal burners and swineherders wonderingly from the trees into the clearings. Now, when he called for men to join him, there were those few who stayed after their fellows had left. He went south down the river valley to the outskirts of Venta which, although a shadow of its former self, was more prosperous and inhabited than most towns, and although the gates were closed against him there were those who came over the walls secretly by night to hear and see him. He moved like a man in a dream and spoke like one possessed and there were many of his companions who were hard

341

pressed to keep patience and face with him. But others, like Durstan, Gelliga, Lancelo, Garwain and Borio, who knew his mind and purpose and read them right, knew, too, that he had long forsaken his old vow that he would only return to the banners of Prince Gerontius and Count Ambrosius when they should sue him for his help. That fire was dead ash now. Arturo meant to raise his own army and own no master but himself. When the day came to league himself with Gerontius and Ambrosius it would be as equal and with his own troops. Pasco, firm though he was to his own religion, had times when he could not but believe that the old gods lived still and, from first touching Arturo with their fire, now claimed and possessed him wholly.

From Venta they turned north-west and at the end of that day's march Felos rode into camp. He found Arturo grooming the White One after feeding and watering her for he would let no one serve her but himself.

Arturo said, 'Greetings, good Felos. You have been so long gone that I had thought never to see you again, that some danger had taken you.'

Felos, smiling, shook his head. 'I would have been with you sooner, my captain. But your lady Daria kept me many weeks at her side.'

'She is well?'

'She is, my lord, and full of deep content.'

'Then why should she keep you so long and deny me the happiness of this news?'

Felos grinned. 'Because she would be certain that I might bring you the happiest news you could have.'

Arturo, stroking the neck of the White One with his hand, knowing that for days on end his mind had held no place for Felos or Daria, said, 'What news could I have greater than to know she is well?'

'That of which she would be doubly certain before my return. She bids me tell you that she carries your child and all is well with her.'

Arturo's hand dropped from the White One's neck and his face stiffened with the quick spasm of his inner joy and pride. Then, with an impulsive movement, he reached into the pouch of his sword belt and drew from it the silver buckle which he had taken from his first true Saxon foe and gave it to Felos, saying, 'Such a great gift as you give me with your news deserves a return. Take this in token of my joy. And now go attend to your horse first and then yourself.'

Felos moved off happily, and smiled to himself at his master's last words ... *your horse first and then yourself.*

When he was gone Arturo stood alone in thought for some time, and there was a mixture of emotion in him which tinged his joy with shame. His love for Daria was deep and true, but it was of a different nature from his love of his country and his desire to see it become great again. This love the gods had given him to nourish and it could never be absent from him since it burnt in him constantly like a flame. But now Daria carried his child . . . *Aie*, more than that, his son it must be if the gods were truly with him; and as though they were and would have him know it there came to him the bright conviction that without delay he must ride to their place and give them his thanks; and more than that, to show no disrespect to the god of Pasco, in whose name he had been baptized, he would take from the place of the gods a gift for the child from this other god to bear home with him.

Impatient now, he called for Durstan and said, 'I saddle and ride this night to the Circle of the Gods for there is a thing I must do to set my mind at peace.'

'Alone?'

'Alone, yes. Our company moves that way tomorrow and I shall be waiting for you. Give me no talk against it for my mind is set. Felos will give you the news he brought me and from that you shall, since our thoughts keep pace together, know my reasoning.'

For a moment or two Durstan hesitated, but the look on Arturo's face told him there would be no shifting him. He said, 'There is a moon tonight and you ride through peaceful country. Go, and the gods watch over you.'

'They will — for I go to give them all thanks.'

Losing no time Arturo saddled the White One, armed himself, and rode out of camp. The night was still and balmy and the full moon was passing to its last quarter. He rode north away from Venta to the high ground and then swung westwards. Fox and fowl marked his passage. The hares on the grassland held their place as he passed while above him the hawking bats called thinly as they hunted the high-summer moths. But well behind him, trailing on his left flank, another marked and followed him, a man on a dark horse, heavily draped in a cloak which had grown ragged and torn and hid the sword he carried. Behind him was slung a bow and a sheaf of arrows hung at his side. The man's face, under its unkempt growth of beard, was drawn and haggard, but there was a dark gleam in his eyes which seen close would have told his joy. Many a time had Inbar in the past been on the point of turning from his hunt, but now he was joyful that hunger and thirst and hard lying and the perils of following the companions had not drawn him from his quest. Why Arturo should leave camp and ride into the night alone he did not know nor care. One desire only burned in him and he waited now only for the meeting of time and place to give him the reward and the reformation which his manhood demanded.

Towards dawn with a light ground mist rising knee high over the land Arturo came from a belt of trees out on to open ground and saw ahead of him on the sheep-bitten slopes of the down the great circle of henge-stones silhouetted blackly against the westward dying moon. As he had ridden through the night his thoughts had been full of Daria and the coming child, and of Daria and his days with her. Sparse though they had been, each one now seemed like a wondrous jewel inlaid with precious stones and enamelled with flaming colours. He saw her riding up to him as a girl on the rain-swept moors, Daria of the blue eyes, brighter than the periwinkle flower, smiling at him across the market place, and Daria lying in his arms in the meadow bower while the larks sang and the scent of fresh-cut hay filled the air with perfume and her heart beat under the palm of his hand so that the joy in her moved like a slow fire into the depths of his being. The gods had marked him for greatness to serve his country and he would make her by the grace of the gods a queen for all men as she was now queen for him.

He rode into the great circle of stones and, slipping from the White One's back, took his knife from his belt and walked towards the fallen slab where long before he had hidden for safe-keeping the silver chalice which had once held the blood of Pasco's god. As he moved away the White One lowered her head and began to graze on the sweet downland grass and herbs.

Kneeling, Arturo dug into the turf and quickly unearthed the chalice. He brushed it free of soil with his hands and the moonlight touched it so that it gleamed dully. At this moment Inbar, on foot, his horse left tethered to a thorn bush out of sight, stepped noiselessly from behind one of the tall stones. In his hands he held the drawn bow and the goose-feather flighted arrow, armed with its sharp iron tip. There would be no honour in this killing, and he needed none since honour had been long lost to him. To his right the White One raised her head from cropping and looked at him. The sun, yet to show itself over the edge of the eastern land, already paled the sky with light and touched the underbellies of the low morning clouds with red and gold wash. The kneeling figure of

Arturo was clear against the growing light, and already overhead a lone lark sang and the meadow pipits looped their way in morning flight across the juniper-tufted downland.

As Arturo slowly began to rise to his feet, the White One whinnied gently and uneasily. Arturo, knowing her moods and manners, swung round, suddenly alive with an instinct of coming danger. The arrow, meant to take him below the left shoulder blade, sped true across the stone-encircled grass, the hiss of its feathered flight one long, low note against the morning quiet, and the deadly point sank deep into his body below his right ribs. He cried aloud with the sudden shock of pain and staggered backwards, the silver chalice dropping from his hands. He would have fallen but the great stone behind him held him up and through the mist of pain which briefly dimmed his eyes he saw Inbar racing towards him with his sword drawn.

They fought then, without shield or buckler, sword-armed, and no words passing between them while the blood ran dark over the linen shirt under Arturo's open tunic. The sparks leapt blue and gold from the clash of their swords and the White One, disturbed and frightened, raced round the great inner circle and whinnied high. In a moment of withdrawal Arturo reached down with his left hand to the hampering shaft of the arrow lodged in his side and snapped it short. His hand came back, dark as ebony with the spurt of his own blood, and he prayed to the gods, if it were his destiny to die, to give him life blood enough and strength to kill Inbar before he fell himself.

And the gods were good to him and gave him this boon. He fought with the blood-veil fast clouding his eyes and fighting he remembered how his father had faced and fought this man, and of the dishonour which had been planned for his mother. From memory of time long-passed but now sharply recalled, he drew the last of fighting strength from within himself. They fought without words in the growing light of the burgeoning morning. The grass about them was trampled and scarred and bloodstained and, when the moment came that his sword slashed across the neck of his foe and Inbar fell with his death cry bubbling from his blood-filled throat like the wailing cry of an upland curlew, all reality passed from him. He fell to the ground and passed from violence into the calm of a dream of fair days and love's delights. He walked with Daria in the river pasture and plucked for her the scent-heavy meadowsweet plumes. He rode the forest paths with her lodged between his arms, riding before him on the White One, her dark hair in the wind making a moving lattice before his eyes and the sweet warmth of her woman body filling his nostrils with a headier perfume than any that could come from the flowering summer blooms. With time out of joint, he walked with her through the villa courtyard to the fountain of the nymphs and she held in her arms the man-child which was his, and the child, seeing the splashing waters fling a veil of drifting, jewelled spray to trap the sunlight in rainbow colours, stretched out his hands to take them and crowed with delight; and with the sound of his son's voice in his ears and the sight of Daria's red lips parted to touch the child's warm cheek with a kiss, lips redder than the breast of any spring-fired robin's, he drifted further into the dark shades of oblivion.

★ ★ ★

A long-haired, shaggy moorland pony grazed close to the White One within the circle of great standing stones. The pack which had been on its back lay open on the ground beside the body of Arturo which was half-propped against a fallen lintel, his head cushioned by his own blood-stained cloak and tunic, and his body naked above his trews except for the tight binding of torn strips of cloth that circled his body below his ribs and held, tight pressed, a great moss wad which blocked and staunched the flow of blood from his wound.

At his side sat the man Merlin whom he had last seen on the high scarp above the Sabrina river, the dark-haired, stocky, brown-robed man known as the ageless, the wandering one. On the ground lay a half-empty water skin and a piece of old cheese resting on a great dock leaf. The man ate and, from watching Arturo's face, he turned now and then to look at the body of Inbar lying a little way off, the flies and bluebottles crowding the wound in his neck, the eyes upturned and open, staring sightlessly at the mid-morning sky.

A pair of grey-polled jackdaws, scavenging and eyeing the cheese below, sat atop one of the great stones and called noisily. At the sound Arturo slowly opened his eyes. He lay without moving for a while and there was a weakness in him that made him feel without body or contact with the turf and stone which supported him. But that he lived he knew. For slowly there grew in him a raging thirst which fired his throat and brought him to an awareness of his own flesh and blood. Seeing the man, his mind clearing, he said weakly, 'I live.'

Merlin smiled. 'And will for it is the wish of

the gods. Why else would they have set my steps this way? Once by happen-chance we met. But now they stir themselves and begin to meddle with my affairs and give me dreams to plague my path. Yes, you will live. While you rested in limbo I cut the broken arrow head from you.'

'You have my thanks.'

'The years ahead may turn them to reproaches.'

'You talk in riddles. Thanks I give you, and more thanks would for a drink. My . . . my throat is like a smithy's furnace and my body burns.'

Merlin reached for the water skin and then took from the ground at Arturo's side the silver chalice. He filled it and, with an arm around Arturo's shoulders, lifted him a little so that he could drink in comfort.

Arturo took the chalice in his weak, trembling hands and drank. The water went into him with a coldness that suddenly made his body shake. He half-lowered the chalice and coughed, holding it in his cupped hands against his breast, and closing his eyes against the shock. When the spasm passed he opened his eyes, felt strength stirring in him and moved to raise the chalice to drink again, but slowly stayed his hands. Within the silver bowl cradled between his palms the clear water was slowly flushing with a crimson hue that deepened and, as the water stilled, took the morning light and glowed with a high brilliance to show his own bearded, fight-sweated face mirrored in it.

He raised his eyes in wonder at the sight and saw that Merlin, too, had seen the colouring. They looked at each other without words and then Merlin smiled gently. Above them the jackdaws suddenly screeched and took to wing, and the White One, raising her head, whinnied high and fiercely and cantered across the marjoram and thyme-laced turf.

From the dip in the land to the east there rose then the sharp, echoing call of a horn. Over the crest of the land came the leading troop of Arturo's companions with Lancelo at its head, the white horse banner streaming in the rising morning breeze, and behind him cloaked and scarfed and helmeted moved the ranks of the companions with scarlet and white plumes tossing and swaying.

Merlin, speaking almost as though to himself, said, 'Your people come and there is no more need of me. But there will come a day when I shall be with you in an hour of your own choosing when the war horns shall blow neither for victory nor defeat, but to set echoes rolling for evermore over this land to give your name everlasting life while you take the long sleep which the gods have decreed for you.'

But as he spoke, and scarcely hearing him, a great weariness and weakness seized Arturo and the chalice fell from his hands as he passed into the first sleep which would stage him well on the road to full force and proud intent again.

We do hope that you have enjoyed reading this large print book.

Did you know that all of our titles are available for purchase?

We publish a wide range of high quality large print books including:
**Romances, Mysteries, Classics
General Fiction
Non Fiction and Westerns**

Special interest titles available in large print are:
**The Little Oxford Dictionary
Music Book
Song Book
Hymn Book
Service Book**

Also available from us courtesy of Oxford University Press:
**Young Readers' Dictionary
(large print edition)
Young Readers' Thesaurus
(large print edition)**

For further information or a free brochure, please contact us at:
**Ulverscroft Large Print Books Ltd.,
The Green, Bradgate Road, Anstey,
Leicester, LE7 7FU, England.
Tel:** (00 44) 0116 236 4325
Fax: (00 44) 0116 234 0205

Other titles published by
The House of Ulverscroft:

BIRDS OF A FEATHER

Victor Canning

A fortunate man, Sir Anthony Swale is married to a loyal wife; he lives in a grand house in Somerset and leads a very privileged life. He devotes most of his time to collecting rare art treasures, particularly from behind the Iron Curtain. And he will pay any price for the right piece — including treason. But then his treachery is discovered — and agents working for the Government decide it is time to take discreet action . . .

THE BOY ON PLATFORM ONE

Victor Canning

Cheerful Peter Courtney, a fourteen-year-old, is an unusual boy. Exceptionally gifted, he's able to repeat, fully, any text which is read to him once — even in French. When his widowed father's business fails, he takes Peter around London's social clubs to perform professionally. Because of his skills he finds himself involved with the Secret Service. He is required to use his gift to receive important information regarding traitors to the British and French Governments — but this places Peter and his father in danger. Now they must escape and leave everything behind . . . in hiding from an assassin who is thorough and systematic.

TALES OF MYSTERY AND HORROR: VOL.III

Edgar Allan Poe

These *Tales of Mystery and Horror* include the story of Bedloe, a wealthy young invalid, who has a strange tale to tell his physician, after he experiences a form of time travel, in *A Tale of the Ragged Mountains* . . . And *The Conversation of Eiros and Charmion* is a very strange tale of a comet approaching earth, causing it to contain pure oxygen. The result of this has a devastating effect on people . . .